2018

Raylene,

You are my blessing. Thank you Girl Friend

♡ hugs xo
Carmen Thomas

What people are saying

Carmen sews this book's story and characters with the golden thread of faith. The history of a family unfolds, each member of that family a relative part of a fluid and moving foundation, all leading to an undeniable conclusion.

—Robert R. Hines
Captain of Dove II

The story is amazing. I love the characters. It has a lot of twists, which kept me on the edge of my seat. A great read and an inspiration to all women that they can rewrite the chapter of their lives.

—Lana Neeb
Women Against Violence Advocate

Undeniable is the story of a young woman's journey through grief, secrecy, and prostitution. Discover how faith intertwines in her life despite her best efforts to keep it out. Throughout the story, the reader is challenged to consider: does life play out merely through coincidences or are there other forces at work? The novel is a wonderful read with an ending that will capture your heart.

—Dr. Bernadette Gallagher
Author of *Seven Sisters Dancing*

A first novel... a moving and powerful story of redeeming love.

—Donna Yuke
Classroom Teacher

This book is so encouraging. Once you start reading, you will not want to put it down. I encourage everyone to read this book! The author is a wonderful lady!

—Pastor Sam Haag

Undeniable

Carmen Marie Thomas

UNDENIABLE
Copyright © 2018 by Carmen Marie Thomas

All rights reserved. Neither this publication nor any part of this publication may be reproduced or transmitted in any form or by any means, electronic or mechanical, including photocopying, recording or any information storage and retrieval system, without permission in writing from the author.

This is a work of fiction. Names, characters, places and incidents either are the product of the author's imagination or are used fictitiously, and any resemblance to actual persons, living or dead, businesses, companies, events, or locales is entirely coincidental.

Scripture quotations marked (NIV) are taken from the Holy Bible, New International Version®, NIV®. Copyright © 1973, 1978, 1984, 2011 by Biblica, Inc.™ Used by permission of Zondervan. All rights reserved worldwide. www.zondervan.com The "NIV" and "New International Version" are trademarks registered in the United States Patent and Trademark Office by Biblica, Inc.™ Scriptures marked (KJV) taken from the Holy Bible, King James Version, which is in the public domain.

ISBN: 978-1-4866-1640-4

Word Alive Press
119 De Baets Street, Winnipeg, MB R2J 3R9
www.wordalivepress.ca

WORD ALIVE
—PRESS—

Cataloguing in Publication may be obtained through Library and Archives Canada

This book is dedicated to all those who have struggled with their faith or surrendered to the uncomplicated ways of God. In memory of dear friends, Carole and Gloria. I can still see your smiles shining down, even on the cloudiest of days.

"Good night, Mattie."

Acknowledgements

First of all, I thank God for lining up his plan for my life and placing within me seeds of inspiration. Although at times I've no doubt given you a run for my attention, I realize that I've never been exempt from your work in progress. I reflect each day on my blessings, regardless of their size. Thank you for your grace, for placing faith in my heart, and for surrounding me with the following people who continually support and help fuel my spirit. I am forever in awe of your goodness. Thank you, Lord.

To my husband, for his unconditional support and for believing in this book from its very start. Your encouragement has been second to none. XO, always.

To my children and their families, for just being there. Those early morning phone calls and young voices shouting "Morning, Grandma!" let me know that it's another blessed day. Thank you! Also, to my mother for her support and passing down a trickle of the storytelling gene. Thanks, Mom!

To Susan. Thanks for your encouragement and crazy conversations throughout this process.

To Ruth, whose encouragement has been precious throughout this project. I extend a grateful heart.

I feel very blessed for the enlightened support of Patty, Gloria, Dawn, and the girls of the 12th. Always, with gratitude.

To Jim Phillips for patiently making his way through an early manuscript. I wasn't sure at first if you could understand my "folksy" vocabulary. Being from two different worlds, I'm sure you weren't sure either. You are a courageous soul. Thank you!

To John and Carol Ann, I am eternally appreciative for your ongoing support. I am so grateful God has placed you in my life for many seasons. Thanks for sharing your faith. You are simply the best.

Carmen Thomas

To Roger and Barb, you exude a kindness that could only come from our creator. Thank you for your support and prayers. They mean more to me than words can say.

To Mr. Ray and Ginny, just one more sunbeam in my heart. Thank you for sharing your knowledge. You're an amazing duo!

To Brenda and Carl and the Eastwood Gang, thank you for welcoming me with open arms into your wild world of small furry bundles. It made the grieving for my beloved dog Mattie just a little easier. Hugs, always.

Definitely not least, to Pastor Dave and Heather and Pastor Sam and Debra. Thank you for walking the walk, and your encouragement. I'm grateful to all of you.

Thank you to those who were so kind to provide written endorsements from my working manuscript. I don't know who was braver—me for giving it to you, or you for reading it? Regardless, thanks for believing in it!

Lastly, to Raylene and Red for "loaning" me your perfected computer skills. I still can't get it! You both are patient, exceptional, and appreciated.

For all those I inadvertently missed, you know who you are. I extend my apologies and sincere thanks. You have all contributed to the completion of this book in some way. I am so fortunate to call you my friends. Blessings, everyone!

Prelude

You could hear snickers around the room as Pastor Matthew held the book in midair.

Matthew knew he might as well just wait for the tears to fill his eyes. It always seemed harder to fight it. Through the years, he had learned that every tear shed while telling this story represented God's love for him—for all people. Welcoming the wetness, the tears slid down his face.

"For those of you who want to hear a story that has never been sugarcoated, this is about as real as it gets." He lowered the Bible onto the podium. "Get comfortable and sit back. I'm starting the engine!"

Chapter One

The rumor mill in Shelbytown, Indiana had it that Olive Harring wouldn't succumb to an evil demise. That fate was said to be reserved for the next generation of the family.

Dr. Flocker told Olive she would never bear children—and when she became pregnant the first time, he said it was luck. The second time, he proclaimed it to be the work of God's own hand.

Apparently Olive had had so much love to give that each time she'd learned she was going to be a mother, she was overtaken by excitement and ended up passing out on her storied sofa. The red velvet piece of furniture had been the only investment she and her husband Clifton made during the Depression. Prior to their purchase it had been used as a fainting sofa for the Too Tight Corset Syndrome. Trying to help out a less fortunate family, they had traded six laying hens for it. The owner had glanced down at Olive's oversized paunch, and offered to throw in a used corset.

"Well, it's a little easier than giving up all the pastries!" the woman had said.

Olive had grunted as she snatched the corset from her hand. Remembering Almeda's frosted sugar loaves, she grinned and quietly thanked the woman and made her way to the door.

With only two children, Olive felt that the pregnancies were blessings, even as she grew older. She never complained, no matter how much of a handful the children could be at times—especially their youngest, Jane.

Julie and Jane were the pride of Olive and Clifton's world. They'd had the two little girls back to back, seemingly as refreshing as a field of wild sunflowers, even more so since they were born near the end of the Depression. The girls had been perfect... at first.

Julie had been slightly older, and most of the time Olive had thought one day she could become the next Greta Garbo. Displaying a quiet grace, Julie had been content with whatever happened around her.

Jane, on the other hand, had been full of vigor, mischief, and questions. With one look from her Bette Davis eyes, she could hold the toughest of hearts hostage. Jane had also demonstrated a knack for overriding every peaceful moment in the Harring house. At first, Olive and Clifton had thought they babied her too much. After all, she had been the youngest. But even a good paddle to her behind didn't seem to affect Jane's wild outbursts. Jane tested her mother and father's patience at every opportunity.

Eventually, stressed beyond their ability to cope, Olive and Clifton had late-night discussions about putting Jane up for adoption. Her screaming fits had increased, and the more time that passed, the worse things got.

The doctor had fumbled for answers, then changed his previous assumption about Jane being heaven-sent. But he'd wanted to help, and Jane met all the criteria for a new behavior modification treatment called shock therapy. He had said that it might be the answer for the Harring family, and that the state would pay for the treatments. All Olive and Clifton had to do was agree.

However, both parents had read stories about the lasting effects of the treatment. Zombie behavior was not an option, so they decided against it.

After months of grueling bedtime discussions, they finally figured out how to get Jane the help she so desperately needed.

Chapter Two

"Yes, Missy!" Olive insisted. "You ARE going to get into that car! That's all there is to it! You need a vacation, and Mother and Father need one too!"

Jane stomped her feet hard. "Well, what about Julie? Is she coming too?"

"Yes, she's coming too."

"Well, how come she doesn't have to take all her clothes?"

"Because, Jane, you have all her hand-me-downs. That's why!" Olive huffed as she passed the huge black suitcase to Clifton.

"Well, who's going feed the cows? And what about Chomps? Can he come with us?"

"Not this time," Olive said. "It's too long a ride for the dog. He'll be just fine here with the farmhand. Besides, we won't be long." Olive tied Jane's shiny dark hair into a ponytail, then reached for the hairclips and snapped them shut on each side of the girl's long bangs. "That's better. Just like your sister. Now we can see those big eyes of yours again."

As Olive walked away, two hairclips suddenly flew through the air, followed by a black band.

"I'm not wearing these stupid things," Jane screamed, shaking her head violently. "Not even to Aunt Almeda's!"

The car rattled slowly along narrow gravel roads through the beautiful autumn countryside around Shelbytown.

"I want to stay and play with my friends!" Jane yelled, pushing her feet hard into the back of the front seat.

Julie had become accustomed to Jane's outbursts, ignoring them as she looked out the window.

Jane kicked the seat harder. "I don't want to go to Aunt Almeda's, ever! And Mommy, you and Daddy can't make me! I want out right now!"

Clifton and Olive glared at each other, not saying a word. This trip was becoming impossible.

After one final kick to the back of his seat, Clifton pulled to the side of the road, jolting the brakes. Dust filled the cool air as he patiently got out. He tipped the front seat forward, grabbed Jane, and pulled her out of the car.

"So you want out, do you, Jane? Okay, you're gonna have it your way then." With his arm tight around her, he marched her to the back of the car and opened the trunk. "Olive, will you come get these suitcases and put 'em in the back seat beside Julie?" He turned back to Jane and yanked her up off the ground. "In, now! You can yell all you want in here. Let's see if you can kick hard enough to get yourself out."

He closed the trunk and tied it loosely with a rope.

Rubbing his calloused hands together, he heard his wife's voice on the cool Indiana breeze: "Make sure she gets one of these, Clifton. We still have a long way to go."

Looking up, he saw one of Olive's sandwich bags slicing through the air, coming straight toward him. He reached up just in time to catch it.

The rest of the trip was peaceful. Julie only heard low muffles and felt intermittent soft knocks hitting the back seat. It had always been the same with Jane, no matter how hard Julie had tried to keep out of trouble. She felt guilty that she couldn't seem to help her sister, being the older of the two. At any rate, hearing the thumps meant Jane was still alive.

They had last seen their aunt two years ago when she was supposed to come for a short visit. She'd ended up staying for the summer.

Olive and Almeda had been the closest of the ten children in their family, although the furthest apart in age. Olive figured that the love they had for each made up for the absence of their mother. After their mother's disappearance, Almeda had been scooped up by distant relatives who owned a bakery. Both remembered that day clearly. They had both assumed after their goodbyes on that distant morning that neither would have any tears left to cry in their lifetimes.

That had been true, until Jane came along.

From the inside of the car's trunk, Jane heard the pings from the gravel slowly stop. Seconds later, the trunk lifted. Sunshine stung Jane's eyes as she brushed the hair from her face.

"Now, that wasn't so bad, was it, Jane?" Clifton asked calmly. "And look, at least there's still some daylight left."

He tried helping her up.

"I can do it myself!" Jane yelled, jumping out.

What Jane saw before her was a white two-story house situated behind a large maple tree on a corner lot. The black window frames seemed to have a personality of their own, neat but slightly crooked as they hugged the distorted glass panes. A huge wooden veranda encircled most of the dwelling and a small shed sat quietly off to the back.

The shed, shining with black paint, looked dilapidated and appeared only large enough to hold one person at a time. Jane thought it was the smallest shack she had ever seen. She walked away from her parents and apprehensively approached the shed's door, recalling something her mother had once said about Aunt Almeda's outside restroom. Apparently it was mostly used for emergencies. Jane thought no emergency could be that serious. She swore to herself that she would never set foot in that shed.

She rejoined her parents and sister, walking alongside Julie toward the veranda. Almeda, wearing an apron and brown duster, darted from the house. She looked almost the same as she had on her last visit, except her hair was different. Instead of the tight greyish ball that used to be stuck to the side of her head, her hair was longer and dark.

"I've missed you so much!" Almeda bellowed, putting her arms around Olive. "And Clifton, my favorite brother-in-law! Why, you are still as handsome as ever. That farming business must really agree with you." She laughed, squeezing his thick forearm. "And Julie, my pretty little Julie! My goodness, you are even prettier than you were than the last time I saw you!" She embraced Julie, and then turned to Jane, smiling. "Come here, girl, and give your aunt a big hug."

She squeezed Jane gently and brushed the hair out of the girl's eyes.

"You know, dear, you really should do something with those bangs, so people can see your big beautiful eyes."

As Almeda gave Jane a final squeeze, Jane felt something hard underneath her aunt's apron. She looked down and saw a wooden handle.

"Now come in and make yourselves at home," Almeda said as she led the way inside. "You must be hungry. I made two lovely rhubarb pies and there are also two pots of freshly brewed tea sitting over there in the pantry. Help yourselves!" She pointed to a glass jug on the counter. "Oh, and girls, I just finished squeezing the lemons. I remembered it's your favorite!"

Sparsely decorated, the furniture appeared to be strategically placed. Two sofas faced each other, neatly covered by plain white blankets. A long wooden table occupied the center of the kitchen with a stack of books set evenly upon it.

Hands shoved deeply into her pockets, Jane squinted as she took a closer look at those books. Although just entering the sixth grade, reading was her best subject. The big bold letters on the top book read *Turn Your House into a Home with the Magic of Paint.* Jane picked up the instruction manual, noting that the book underneath was a Bible.

On the wall, she saw various pictures of old people. Strangers.

"Eeeew, that's creepy," Jane whispered just loud enough for her sister to hear.

"You better not touch anything, Jane. Aunt Almeda will know if you do."

"Okay then. Hey, let's go up there." She pointed to a wooden staircase and immediately lunged up it. She found herself in a hallway, as neat as everything had been downstairs. She tiptoed down the hall, then stopped as a gust of wind slammed a door shut behind her.

"Oh!" Jane screamed.

Even Julie jumped in midair. "What was that, Jane?"

"Don't know!"

"Well then, maybe we should leave."

Jane walked back to the door that had slammed shut. "First let's see what's in here."

"Well, I'm not opening it."

"Oh, you are the biggest chicken ever. I'll look then." She turned the doorknob and the door creaked open.

Inside, a music box sat on a dressing table off to the side, a small wooden cross on a gold chain in front of it. Beside these items was a silver chain configured with an image of an unusual-looking butterfly. One of its wings was stretched straight out, appearing much larger than the other.

Looking up, Jane gasped, her eyes taken in by the huge black corner posts of a bed. Two of the posts looked like they were growing hair; they seemed to resemble the legs of a monster bug, the kind one might see on Halloween. On her toes, she inched closer, Julie following.

"What are those things?" Jane whispered, stretching her neck to get a better look, and at the same time trying to keep her distance.

"Looks like hair!"

"Why does Aunt Almeda have someone else's hair?"

"I'm pretty sure those things are called wiglets, or something like that," Julie said. "Think I heard about girls wearing them over their hair, especially where the movie stars live."

Getting closer, Jane reached out and touched one. "Ah! It *is* hair, Julie! It's real hair!"

"Ew. Let's get out of here."

"Girls! Everything all right here?" a voice echoed from behind them.

Turning quickly, they found themselves almost face to face with Aunt Almeda.

"Admiring my new hair?" Almeda grinned, walking up to the nearest bedpost. She smiled, petting the hair. "This is actually my favorite one. Your Uncle Arthur bought this for my last birthday. He worked in the factory every minute they needed him just so he could get it."

It looked like a big, furry grey hairball to Jane. With swirls of shiny black streaks, it was the ugliest thing she had ever seen.

Both girls backed slowly towards the door.

"Girls, I think it's time you went down and got some of that special lemonade," Almeda said. "I think my pie should still be warm too."

Almeda breathed deeply, savoring a whiff of freshly baked rhubarb pie.

"Sure you can't stay long, Olive?" Almeda asked, adjusting her hairpiece. "You know, Arthur and I don't get much company. It would be our pleasure to have you stay longer. Well, anyway, suit yourselves. I turned your beds down. And oh, before I forget, Arthur has such daw gone trouble sleeping, he can't have any light on. So it may be easier if we all just use the restroom before bed. Oh, and remember the one outside too, girls! Arthur just took out the latest newsprint. I'm sure Jane will get used to it."

Jane and Julie tried to look inconspicuous as they exchanged glances. Julie shrugged.

Jane wasn't sure what her aunt had meant about getting used to the outdoor bathroom. It seemed odd that her parents had rushed to Almeda's only to rush off again.

Taking a gulp of lemonade, Jane's stomach turned. She looked at her mother, and then her mother turned to her father. Almeda just smiled at Jane.

Her stomach rolled again. Something was wrong. Very wrong.

Saying goodbye was always hard for Olive and Almeda, though neither would admit it.

"Make sure you phone or send us a letter," Almeda called through the fresh morning air.

Julie had already grasped what was going on, although she wouldn't breathe a word. The last thing everyone needed was for Jane to lose her temper again. She knew that having her sister stay with Aunt Almeda and Arthur was the best thing, at least for now. Besides, she could tell how much Aunt Almeda loved Olive. She would do anything to help her.

While packing the car, Almeda sent home so many of her specialties—pound cakes, apple twirl, bread, and pastry—that it seemed almost as if they had been visiting for months. There was no end to it. No one could bake quite like Aunt Almeda. She always made sure of that. Sneakily, she always left out one ingredient when people asked for her recipes.

Everyone hovered around the car, except Jane, who was nowhere to be seen. They all said their final farewells, then piled into the car, waving goodbye.

At that instant, Jane came sprinting out of the house. The tips of her dark hair flopped in the breeze, a mound of curls perched sloppily on her head and a wooden spoon in her hand. She charged at Almeda and Almeda ran in terror.

That was the last that Olive, Clifton, and Julie saw of Almeda and Jane for a long time.

Chapter Three

IF ANYONE IN THE STATE OF KENTUCKY COULD GET THE JOB DONE, IT WAS ALMEDA Thorne. She and Arthur had never wanted to put in the time and energy that having children demanded. But she and Arthur had never had a problem filling their time without a family. For example, Almeda loved to plan and help at charity events, especially if she could bake for them.

Shortly after they had married, Arthur lost his hand in a piece of machinery at the old Fitten factory. Eventually he'd had it replaced by a metal hook.

"Come an' give Uncle Arthur a hug," he would say, motioning to Jane with his hook swinging in the air.

Arthur tolerated children, but now Jane had turned his quiet home with Almeda into chaos. Still, he took her out to the creaky old wooden chair that sat in front of the cedar hedge. With the autumn wind howling, he spoke in low tones, gently swaying his hook back and forth. He loved telling her ghost stories. Arthur thought if he could scare Jane enough, it may deter the devil inside her. He imagined that one day the devil would just up and vanish, leaving Jane to be the pleasant child God had intended her to be. It seemed worth a try—until Arthur realized he was only fooling himself. He gave up when Jane turned the table one night by pouring a dozen raw eggs down the back of his neck.

That's when he realized he needed his old life back.

The morning's new sun welcomed him as it beat down on the old wooden porch. Uncle Arthur wrapped his hook around Jane's thin waist.

"You know, Jane, Your aunt and I've been thinkin'. You have been with us, well, almost two years now. You know, we do see you settlin' some with your new medication. Remember, the doctor told you that you'll probably always need it to help with those moods of yours."

"Yeah, I remember, Uncle Arthur."

He smiled. "Well, Aunt Almeda and I were wonderin' if you would like to start attendin' church with us." He tapped her lightly with his hook. "God's been watching you and he sees you have been makin' some big improvements. So now we think it would be in your best interest to attend his church."

"Uh... church, Uncle Arthur?" Jane looked at him, puzzled.

"That's correct, Jane."

"Uh, well... I thought only really good people can go to church."

"In a way that's true. But as long as you can behave yourself there, I don't think God would have a problem with it. Besides, Jane, God's wooden spoon is a lot bigger than your aunt's." Arthur gave Jane's hair a tussle.

"Yeah, I think it's time the good Lord put a touch on you. It sure ain't going to hurt anything. We know it's probably far from a finishing touch, but I'd say now is a good time to start. So, Jane, do you want him to help watch over you or not? What do you say?"

"Do I have to?"

Arthur chose his next words carefully. "Well, only if you want to get back home sooner. I'm sure Julie and your friends can't wait."

"Yeah, I guess. I kinda miss my friends. But I really miss Chomps!"

"Okay then." He smiled at her again. "It's a deal. Church it is."

Interlude

Patting his Bible, Pastor Matthew looked out across the congregation. "Yes, we serve a mighty big God. No matter how high the mountain, how low the valley, God is always there. Can I get an amen?"

"Amen," the crowd shouted.

"Well, how do you know God is always there, pastor?" a voice asked.

Pastor Matthew laughed. "He was finally sending the girl home, wasn't he?"

"But I'm having trouble finding God in your story so far. So where is he, Pastor?" another voice asked.

And another: "Yeah, we want to know more."

"All right, settle down. I'm getting on with the story." Pastor Matthew looked around the room. "Keep in mind, God is good all the time. And by the way, who do you think had Arthur and Almeda's back during that trying time?"

"The devil in little sheep's clothing!" a frail voice called out. "That's who!"

"Well, if only good people were allowed in church, I guess most churches would be empty, now wouldn't they, Pastor?" said another voice, this one confident. "And why did that Arthur guy want to put the fear of God into that young girl, anyway? Shame on him. He's gonna have her even more scared before she reaches the church doors!"

Pastor Matthew smiled. "Hold on. Like I was saying, Jane started to attend church with her aunt and uncle. Believe me, Arthur just wanted some peace back in his life. Almeda had been putting her heart and soul into the young girl, and Arthur knew it wouldn't be long before Jane could return home. He wasn't about to jeopardize that. It was just a matter of time, and he was counting every day. Yes, God's always turning his kaleidoscope. Hallelulia! Can I get an Amen?"

"Amen."

"So people, listen up, because there's a lot more to this story. You see, Arthur just got a new set of wheels..."

Chapter Four

Although Almeda and Arthur lived modestly, Arthur sometimes liked to flaunt his earnings. That spring, he carefully picked out the color yellow for his latest Ford, even though Almeda reminded him that he didn't like yellow. She also said that his new cars were a way of showing people how hard he worked at the factory, especially given the fact he only had one hand. He was a proud man.

But those who knew Arthur could tell that Jane was taking a toll on him. The rumor mill at work said he'd bought the new car because there was no way he would take the chance of only getting Jane halfway home.

Besides, someone at the factory had told Arthur that yellow was an appropriate color for celebration.

The rain tapered to a trickle as the wipers slapped together in the heavy spring air. A dark outline of rolling hills seeped through a white blanket of haze. The Depression had ended a decade ago, but memories of its toll lingered. Even the larger farms appeared dull and rundown.

Jane sat squished between boxes of baked goods and her belongings as the sweet smell of banana and cinnamon swirled through the car. Before they had left to go back to Indiana, Almeda and Arthur had devised a plan to make everything fit in the yellow Ford. Almeda had been assigned a spot inside the vehicle, then Arthur had lined the trunk with two sheets of thick plastic and placed six paint cans, six brushes, and several rolls of tape and glue on top. He liked giving away items from his workplace. Almeda said it permitted Arthur to talk to the recipient for hours about his knowledge of the old factory, although it often ended with the other person snoring.

"You took all your pills before we left this morning?" Almeda asked, turning from the front seat.

"Yep. I sure did, Aunt Almeda," Jane replied as she watched the grey scenery fly past. Her heart pounded in anticipation of seeing her family again.

The car had barely stopped when Olive and Clifton came barreling out of the house.

"Mommy and Daddy missed you, Jane!" Olive cried as her daughter approached. They embraced. "And look at those pretty pigtails. You look all grown up!"

Jane then ran for Clifton, who swooped her up in his arms. "So how's my girl? I heard you're almost all better, and you've even learned how to bake."

"Sort of, Dad." Jane turned just as Julie and Chomps came flying at her, Julie running as fast as she could.

"Jane! You're back. Look how tall you are!"

"Look how tall you got, too, Julie."

The sisters locked hands, jumping up and down. Chomps wasn't about to be left out. Lunging, he knocked Jane to the ground, his tail swinging violently as he ran his tongue across her face.

Olive and Almeda exchanged hugs again, and Arthur and Clifton shook hands.

"Well, at least I've got lots of help to unpack the car," Arthur said. "You know, Clifton, we've got a bakery, a hardware store, and I'm sure we have a girl's store all packed to the roof in my latest Ford. Yeah, the beauty is sitting right out there in your driveway. And I think we got a drug store in there too."

Arthur threw his hook over Clifton's shoulder, roaring with laughter. So far, this was the best day he had experienced in a long while. His gut fluttered with excitement, but he bit his tongue. He knew from past experiences with Jane that it could turn sour quickly.

"Did I tell you we're making a new kind of paint at the Fitten place?" Arther asked Clifton. "It's a good sign. Things are picking up, and they've got me in charge of almost the whole darn load now. I don't know where the daylight hours go..."

"One more thing, Olive," Almeda said later, getting into the car. "Make sure she takes those pills every day, you hear? The doctor thinks she has one of those things called split personality disorder. Do you hear, Olive?"

"Yes, Almeda. I hear you."

"And before I forget, he also said the only way you'll know if the pills are working is if she keeps minding herself while she's on them. So far it looks promising. I think they may be right, so keep an eye she keeps taking them, for heaven's sakes. Oh, one more thing. I packed her a Bible, just to help with her spirits. Believe me, you and Clifton have more help with that girl than you realize. Jane knows the good Lord is watching over her too."

The car door slammed and Olive waved goodbye. "Thanks, Almeda!"

Honking, the car became a yellow blur as it disappeared into a cloud of dust.

Chapter Five

THE EARLY FIFTIES WAS A TIME FOR REBUILDING A DEPLETED ECONOMY. HOPE FILLED the air, and most people felt a desire to get ahead; past uncertainty propelled them toward hope and assurance through faith. Most were in search of some kind of normalcy after the Second World War, whether by latching onto old family beliefs or finding new ones. America and its people were getting back on their feet.

People also attended church, opening their hearts to something much bigger than them. Randy Moonie was no exception; he had his own place in the middle of the new American dream. Any high school girl would have agreed. Even Jenny Hall, Jane's best friend, who had only crossed paths with Randy once, swore he was the first wonder of the world, though she knew there were already seven others. It wasn't even his looks. It was everything else, all those indefinable qualities that were crystal clear to girls. Smart and from a middle-class family, Randy seemed to be the student most likely to succeed. And his denim jeans, white T-shirts, and black leather jacket didn't lessen his magnetism. Maybe the attraction was that he was so unassuming. He never preened himself or strutted about.

Julie and Jane were both fond of Randy, too. Julie knew from the first time she saw him, at a sock hop, that he was the only guy she would ever need. As they danced that evening, she thought they made a perfect couple, she in a red poodle skirt and Randy in pressed navy slacks and matching tie, his red jacket spinning freely with every twirl. Julie hoped they would soon be going steady.

The problem was Jane felt the same way. Because she was more outgoing than her sister, the contest for his affection proved to be no match at all.

One bit of gossip at the time had Jane storming into Julie's closet and gouging the tail out of her meticulously embroidered brown poodle skirt. That's when the sisters' relationship started to go downhill. Things never returned to normal between them.

Not long afterward, Jane and Randy were seen walking out of Dr. Flocker's office with a baby book—and soon after that they were engaged.

Their autumn wedding day was intended to be the first perfect day of the rest of their lives. There was crispness in the air and Jane's lace dress fit her like a glove. Beneath the pearled veil, her lipstick matched the crimson leaves swaying on the majestic maples. At the end of the ceremony, Jane flung her bouquet in the air. It headed straight for Julie, but she didn't reach for it; Jenny caught it instead.

As time passed, Julie realized there was a plan for her life, and it was different from what she had expected—different from what any young girl would ever want.

Meanwhile, Jane's mood swings appeared to get worse again with each child she birthed. The doctor recommended the couple be content with the two girls they had. Since Randy worked out of town, and most of the child-rearing was done by Jane, Dr. Flocker's advice made sense.

Julie still had a heart bigger than the whole outdoors when it came to her sister, but Jane had stolen her first and only love. Julie knew she would never find a man who could measure up to Randy. She felt the next best thing was to help out with his children, Abigail and Francine. That way she could be loyal to her sister and still hold on to the pieces of her broken dream. After all, second place was better than the alternative—no place at all.

Chapter Six

Francine stood on the small wooden stool, a reminder that she wasn't quite as tall as her older sister, Abigail, who stood at the kitchen counter stirring a pitcher of Kool-Aid.

"It's my turn to stir!" Francine wailed.

"Well, it's my Kool-Aid stand," Abigail said sternly. "Besides, you must remember that I'm a lot older than you, Francy. That means I'm the boss until Mother gets up."

Francine reached into the drawer and grabbed a second wooden spoon. She dipped it into the plastic jug and slapped the spoon back and forth.

"No, Francy. Shh! If you wake Mother up, she won't like it! Stop it, Francy, I mean it!"

Pushing their spoons around the purple sea of liquid, the war was on. Francine plowed her spoon through the water with all her might. Then, with one last thud to the jug's side, it suddenly lifted and fell, tumbling onto its side and bounced on the counter. The girls looked at each other helplessly as it hit the floor.

Francine jumped from the stool as both girls ran for towels. They tried to soak up the sticky purple mess. Rubbing the large cloths across the floor made their small hands look even smaller.

"This wouldn't have happened if you had listened to me, you know," Abigail said. "If Mother didn't hear, don't say anything, Francy. Pinky swears!"

They wrapped their baby fingers together and whispered, "Pinky swears."

"Abigail!" yelled the voice from their Mother's bedroom. "I need my pills! The yellow bottle, and grab my smokes!"

Abigail scurried to the clutter of bottles and pulled out a yellow one. Then she swooped up the red and white package while Francine poured a glass of water. Cautiously, they made their way to the bedroom.

"It's five cents for the red one and ten cents for the purple one," Abigail told the customer.

"Dear, could you tell me why the purple Kool-Aid is twice as much?" the woman asked.

"Uh, because we have two times as much of that one," Abigail said, pointing to the red jug.

The lady smirked. "Well, all right. I guess that does make sense, dear." She handed her a dime, smiling. "In that case, I'll have a glass of your lovely, rare purple Kool-Aid."

Francine passed a glass to her. The lady took a gulp and made a sour face.

"Um, I don't know if you girls know this, but I think perhaps you may have forgotten the sugar."

Abigail glared at Francine.

"Tell you what. Because you seem like nice young ladies, I'll give you an extra fifty cents if I can try the red one as well?"

Abigail smiled as she poured the red Kool-Aid and handed it to over.

Taking another sip, the customer made another face. "Sweet, but very interesting. Have a wonderful day, girls."

While contemplating what went wrong, the girls heard their mother's commanding voice calling from the house. "It's time to pack it up! Looks like rain! Hurry up, and don't forget your jackets. We have errands to run."

The girls scrambled as they loaded the wagon and made their way up the walkway.

"Girls, let's go! And don't forget the stand you left out there!" Jane bellowed out the window, pointing toward the street.

Like lightning bolts, they sped back to get it. Francine trailed behind, her spindly legs moving as fast as they could.

"Wait for me, Abby!"

She had almost caught up when she misjudged her awkward strides. Her lanky body flew up in the air and crashed to the ground. Abigail darted to her and assessed her sister's condition.

"You know what Daddy would say, Francy?" She brushed her sister's hair back. "'It's a long way from your heart, groovy girl. So don't cry.' That's what he'd say."

Dusting herself off, Francine noticed her gold chain broken into pieces on the sidewalk. Just past the small strands lay the small wooden cross that went with it.

"It was just a stupid necklace anyway," she muttered to Abigail, picking up the pieces. She studied them briefly, then shoved the ball of gold strands into her pocket.

"Grab that end, Francy. Mother wants us back now."

They picked up the stand and huffed their way back to the house.

The drive to town seemed longer this day. Jane wore her hair in a bouffant style, her lips hot pink. The girls knew their mother usually dressed according to her mood. Even at their young age, it didn't take long to realize that this served as a type of warning. Jane's lip color was always the giveaway. Thick red lipstick meant a shorter drive, and look out. Pink meant everything was still good, but don't cross me. No lipstick only happened on rare occasions, but when it did it meant a quiet trip and usually their mother just needed to go back to bed.

Main Street looked quiet for a Saturday. Most visitors probably saw it as cute and quaint, but if you were a local kid, chances are you saw it as boring. Rainclouds hovered low. With the heaviness in the air, you really couldn't blame a kid for feeling that way.

The car pulled up to the boutique. "Now, no sass out of you two, understand? First umbrellas, then shoes. Okay, girls?" Jane reached for her handbag. "Abigail, did you bring the change you made? We're going to get you the best pair of running shoes we can find."

Abigail rattled the small pocket of change. "Yes, Mother."

The girls scurried into the store.

"I like this one!" Abigail said, jumping up and down in front of an umbrella. It wasn't hard to tell which one suited her best. Images of Barbie adorned the pink plastic canopy while small yellow boots lined the green metal handle.

"Abigail, settle down," her mother demanded as she examined them.

Abigail stood on her tiptoes and shuffled through the sparse rack. "How about this one, Francy? I think this one looks pretty too."

Francine turned up her bottom lip. "I like the Barbie one better."

"Okay, girls," Jane said, kneeling between them and whispering. "We can settle this rather quickly. Listen. Mommy doesn't need any bickering between you two, especially when we're out in public. Where are your big-girl manners, huh, Abby? And Francine, what did I tell you about chewing gum in stores? Do you always want to look like one of Grandpapa's old cows chewing its cud? People are going to think I haven't taught you a thing!"

"Sorry. I forgot, Mommy."

Jane pulled a Kleenex from her leopard handbag and Francine spit the yellow ball of gum into it. The girls knew they shouldn't have to be reminded about manners, especially when out with their mother. Jane always made that clear.

But today they knew there was a little leeway with their mother. The pink lips said so.

"Girls, this is what I'm going to do. Francine, I know how much you'd like the pink one, but you still haven't been acting as well as you should. Especially this week, young lady, so the Barbie umbrella will be your sister's."

Abigail clapped. "Oh, thank you, Mother!" Trying hard to contain her happiness, she glanced at Francine.

Jane lifted the umbrella off the rack and handed it to Abigail. "There you are, Abigail. Now, go with Mrs. Tasker and she'll find you the best pair of running shoes she has."

The saleslady, Mrs. Tasker, nodded to Jane. Abigail turned quickly, leaping over to the lady with her pocket jingling.

"Slow down, Miss Abigail!" Jane warned, then turned to Francine. "Now young lady, which one would you like?"

Looking the umbrella rack up and down, Francine crossed her arms. "I don't want none of them. They're all ugly."

"Well, if that's the way you feel, I'll pick one for you." Jane scoured the rack. With little to choose from, she noticed a black umbrella with mauve flowers. "This one will be yours, Francine, whether you like it or not."

She grabbed Francine's arm and marched her to the counter.

"Thank you for my shoes, Mother," Abigail screeched as she ran back toward them.

"You're welcome. But you do understand that all Mommy needs in return is another first place ribbon, right?"

"Yes, Mother. That won't be hard. Not with these new shoes!"

"These two girls always look like little showstoppers," Mrs. Tasker said from behind the counter. "It's quite obvious you're doing something right, Mrs. Moonie."

Jane gave a small laugh. "Lord knows I try, but they always seem to need endless reminders that they're young ladies. Especially little Francine here."

Abigail reached into her pocket and proudly handed her mother the change.

"Is this all you made this morning? I guess it'll have to do." Adding the money to hers, Jane handed it to Mrs. Tasker. "Thank you. I'm sure the girls will appreciate these. Now come on, girls. We have things to do."

They piled back into the green Chevelle and Jane lit a cigarette as she drove away. She took a long drag and let it out slowly. Grey smoke swirled towards the windshield.

The girls didn't say a word. They just hoped their mother wouldn't pull the red lipstick tube from her bag. Even today, Jane's pink lips silently let them know it was in their best interest to head straight home.

With their umbrellas between them, Abigail whispered across the seat. "Francy, when I'm not using mine, you can use it. Okay?"

Francine sat with her arms crossed as her feet swung impatiently back and forth. She tried to think of a way to lose her new umbrella when she got home. Looking out the window, she knew it wouldn't be long.

"I'll race you to the house, Francine," Abigail shouted as her new white running shoes hit the grass. Carrying her new umbrella, she charged toward the house.

Although Francine was used to losing, she sped off with her umbrella swinging beside her.

"Francine, Abigail! Slow down!" Jane's voice echoed through the still air. "Do you hear me, girls?"

Bolting down the walkway, Francine tripped, flying headfirst into the shrubs. Her body flopped like a ragdoll, her legs stretched out behind her.

Jane marched up behind her and helped her back onto her feet. She passed the unscathed umbrella back to Francine, then brushed off a black skiff from her freshly pressed blouse. "Just how old is Mommy's little girl? Two or three perhaps? Francine, I need you to pull up your socks and start acting your age. Right this minute, young lady!"

Francine looked down at her stained white knee-highs. "But, Mommy, they *are* up!"

"That's just a figure of speech, young lady. Oh, please just start acting your age, child. It sure would be nice if you were a little more like your sister. You know, Francine, your father will be home soon, and just like every Sunday, you know where we'll be going."

Giving her a tap, Francine walked away slowly.

"Young lady, if you think I'm not watching you, you know Mommy always has a backup," Jane sneered, looking towards the sky. "You understand that, don't you?"

Francine glared back, picking up her pace. "Yes, Mommy."

She tried to catch up with Abigail, only pulling even as they darted into their bedroom. Francine threw the umbrella onto the floor.

Abigail twirled around on the tips of her new running shoes with her Barbie umbrella stretched overhead.

Francine plunked herself on her bed and pulled out the broken necklace. "Abby, do you miss Aunt Julie?"

"Yeah," Abby answered, twirling away. "Do you miss her, Francy?"

"Yeah, I guess," she said, hugging her pillow as her brown sandals waved back and forth through the air. "But I still hate this stupid cross she left me. Hey, Abby, can I trade it for your butterfly necklace?"

"I don't think Aunt Julie would like that." Abby hesitated. "But I don't think Aunt Julie would mind if I let you keep my butterfly for me sometimes. But only sometimes. Would that be okay?"

"Sure." Scooping up the cross and broken gold strands, Francine slid a small music box out from under her bed. She set the necklace in the box. "But we can't ever tell Mommy, right?"

Abby held out her pinky. "Okay."

"Promise to the moon and back," the girls said in unison, locking fingers.

Sprawled on her bed, Francine watched her sister spin; the umbrella went around in circles. "Abby, what are you going be when you grow up?"

"Um, think I'll be a movie star. Yeah, a dancing movie star." Giggling, she spun around again. "Or maybe I'll just run across the whole of America!" She paused. "Uh, but not at night, cause I'm still a little afraid of the dark. Or maybe I can help big sisters with their little sisters." Abigail plunked onto her bed, out of breath. "What do you want to be, Francy?"

"Umm, maybe a candy striper. Or, umm, maybe have my very own candy store. I would have a hundred million bubble gum machines and... and Kool-Aid. Lots and lots of Kool-Aid! And I wouldn't take any people's money for it either." Francine bounced up from the bed. "I would make a hundred zillion different kinds and just give it all away!"

"Yep, you'd be good at that, Francy. But you know, you can't ever mix up the sugar again, right?"

Francine just smiled.

"Hey Francy, are you going to wear high heels and lipstick like Mother does?" Before Francine got a chance to answer, Abigail asked, "You're not going to smoke cigarettes, are you?"

Francy shrugged her shoulders.

"Well, you know, Francy, because I'm older, Mother will let me do everything first. But don't tell her." Abigail shook her head. "I'm not wearing those shoes, ever. I think they're ugly—and no red lipstick either! Well, aw, maybe a really light white would be okay. Yeah, light white lipstick." She smacked her lips. "But no fancy shoes. Yuck! Besides, I love my new running shoes, and I'm going to run right across America. I might even run across it two times! But what are you going wear when you grow up?"

"Don't know yet. Guess it depends on what boys like." Francine grinned.

Abigail glared at her. "What boys like? Why would you say a stupid thing like that? You're bad. Don't you know boys are dumb?"

"Well, Daddy isn't dumb. And he likes it when Mommy wears her big shoes. Remember the time he tried to dance around in her shoes and then fell down?"

Both girls started laughing. "Yeah, I remember. Mother was laughing too."

Francine's laugh had turned into a string of snorts. Finally she caught her breath. "When will Daddy be home?"

Abigail threw her umbrella on the bed. "Tonight! Okay, Francy, I'll race you to the kitchen."

The smell of dinner floated down the hall as Abigail and Francine made their way to the kitchen. Looking at the set table, the girls turned to each other with dancing eyes. They knew what four plates meant.

"One of you girls stir the pasta," their mother said. "Francine, hurry up and get the stool. For heaven's sake, you know you can't stir properly from down there. How many times do I have to tell you?" Placing her stained cigarette butt into the shiny ashtray, Jane pointed to the counter. "Abigail, you mix the salad. I needed you girls down here ages ago. Guess that will be another one for this week's confession, huh, girls?" Jane reached for her pills. "How's your list so far, Francine? Do you have enough paper? Maybe your sister can lend you some of hers."

Stirring the pasta, Francine peeked over her shoulder. She saw that something was different with her mother. Her lips had changed from pink to red.

Feeling her heart skip, Francine begged under her breath, "Come on, Daddy. You need to get home now."

Chapter Seven

The door slammed, but the girls didn't think twice. They dropped what they were doing and raced for the door.

"Daddy! Daddy, we missed you!" they said in sync, throwing their arms around their father.

Kneeling, it was hard for Randy to keep his balance. First his briefcase made a thud. Next it was him on the floor. Francine and Abigail wasted no time pouncing on him.

He roared with laughter. "Missed my girls too. Wow! I've only been gone four days and Daddy's little girls aren't acting so little anymore," he said as he peeled the girls off. "Could you please give this old man some time to get up and say hi to your mother?"

Backing off, the girls ran toward the kitchen.

"Francine, you burned the pasta. Now what are we going to do?" Jane said angrily, standing behind a cloud of smoke. "Honestly, what in the Lord's name am I going to do with you?"

Grabbing the hot pot, Jane heaved it toward the sink.

"Sorry, Mommy," Francine said. "But Daddy came home."

"What's all the commotion in here?" Randy asked as he made his way to Jane. Embracing her, he realized how much he had missed her.

"You know you have to stop babying her," Jane whispered in his ear. "As a matter of fact, Randy, they're both getting harder to handle. But Francine is taking the cake lately."

"Gotcha," he said softly, giving his wife another squeeze.

"A little bit of church will do that girl a whole lot of good," Jane said, placing a new pot on the stove.

It was clear to Randy, looking at the napkins flowing from the highball glasses, that Jane hadn't lost her knack for setting a nice table. No matter what kind of day she'd had, she always tried. And it showed.

"Francine, would you say grace tonight?" Jane asked, sitting down.

Bowing their heads, Francine started. "Bless us, oh Lord. And thank you for Abby's new shoes and her pretty pink umbrella, and for Daddy being home again. Amen." Francine crossed her chest.

Jane looked at Randy, then back to Francine. "Well, young lady, you're not always going to get away with saying grace any way you want. You know that's a slap for the good Lord. It sure is frightening to think you are probably going to learn everything the hard way. So what about your beautiful new umbrella?"

Francine shrugged.

"For the life of me, Francine, if I told you once I've told you a million times..." Jane pointed to Francine's mouth.

Spitting the grey wad of gum into her folded napkin, Francine slowly lowered her head. She tried to avoid eye contact with her mother. "Sorry, Mommy. Sometimes I do have some more to say to God, but I couldn't think of anything else for today."

"Well, Miss Too Big for Your Britches, hopefully you'll think of something by the time we get to church tomorrow."

"I'll try to, Mommy."

"It's good to be home, girls," Randy said enthusiastically.

Abigail stuck her hand out. "Daddy, can you pass the spaghetti please?"

Interlude

Looking around the room, Pastor Matthew paused for a moment. He watched his audience sitting intently as he wiped the dampness from his forehead.

"All right, ladies," he said, "I know how you like to get dressed up and all to meet with Jesus every Sunday, but I think now most of you have come to realize that God doesn't care how you show up. As long as you show up. Churches are changing. Yes, Lord. Still, one thing always remains the same: that's God's word. Can I get an amen?"

He cupped his ear.

"That's right." Grinning, he pointed to a young lady. "Don't get me wrong, ma'am. It doesn't mean you lovely ladies should stop wearing your big hats. No, they do the soul good too. Don't they, gentlemen?" He laughed. "Okay, now where was I heading? Oh yes..."

Chapter Eight

As Francine bent down in front of the pew, she especially hated her dress. And her black umbrella didn't help. On her knees, she glanced at her sister beside her. Francine felt some relief because Abigail's dress looked even worse. Still, she had the prettier umbrella. People probably wouldn't even notice her sister's dress because of that umbrella.

Peeking up, Francine saw how pretty her mother looked, even if she could barely see Jane's face under the huge brim of her hat. She could sort of tell why her father had married her. No matter where she was, Jane always fit in, and this morning she was the good, happy mommy wearing light pink lipstick. Francine was old enough to know that God only wanted nice mommies in church. She knew her mother was aware of this also.

Francine often wondered why God never left the church. She had asked Abigail, but her sister didn't know either. Francine had always thought it would be really nice if he'd just show up at their house sometime. For sure her mother would be a lot nicer if he visited.

The Sunday morning service always made Francine yawn. She could only remember one time when it hadn't. When she had been younger, she'd gotten excited about the big plate of money that was passed around. One time it arrived right in her hands, and that's when she finally got the chance to take out her share. Her mother had slapped her fingers. Hard.

Francine often thought that was when the boredom had started. Subsequently, her mother had told her that she knew two strategies to keep from yawning in God's house. The first involved opening the big book that sat on the small shelf in front of her and sounding out its letters, quietly. The other was to remember everything she was going to say to the man who hid behind the tiny window in the small room.

Although these things were supposed to keep her from falling asleep, Francine tried several times without success. If anything, they made her yawn more.

Feeling a yawn coming, she turned her head toward Abigail. Her mouth opened wide, and with heavy eyes Abigail yawned back.

As Francine drifted off, a loud voice filled the church. "Matthew 5:30. 'And if thy right hand offend thee, cut it off, and cast it from thee.'"[1]

Francine sneered at Abigail as she tucked her fingers under her legs.

The fresh air after church always felt welcoming.

"Good morning," Mr. Webster said looking toward the sky. One of their parents' friends. "It's going to be a grand day after this rain passes."

"Believe so," Randy replied. Jane gave him a passing smile.

"Good morning, Mr. and Mrs. Moonie. Good morning, girls," another familiar voice said. Turing around, Francine saw Abigail's homeroom teacher quickly walking past them. "Don't forget about gym day this week. It's going to be good. Keep practicing, Abigail! Heard you are doing good."

"Yep, got my new shoes!" Abigail told her, peeking out from under her umbrella. "And I'm already ready, Mrs. Wilson."

"That's great news! And I like your umbrella. Have a blessed day, everyone!"

"Okay, girls, what would you like to do for the rest of the day?" Randy asked as he opened the car door for Jane.

"Daddy, can we go to the Stop 'n Go for hot dogs?" Abigail asked.

"Yeah, Daddy! Can I get a big ice cream cone this time? Please, please." Francine placed her umbrella on the seat beside her.

Randy started the car, then stopped and looked at Jane. After all these years, nothing had really changed except they were getting older. Randy was still struck by Jane's poise and beauty.

"Hey honey," he said, reaching over and gently touching her hand. "What do you think? In the mood for an Oscar Myers and ice cream?"

Jane lifted her hat and slowly ran her polished nails through her hair. "I guess. But you know, Randy, you don't have to spoil these girls every time you come home. I think they're starting to expect it."

Smiling, Randy put the car in drive. "Hold on, girls!" he yelled as he wheeled around onto the main road. "Wheeeeee!"

---

[1] Matthew 5:30, KJV.

Francine and Abigail howled with laughter.

"Really, Randy! What in God's name are you doing?" Jane said.

"I like hearing our girls laugh. Can't you just get over it for one day?"

"What do you mean by that?" Jane snapped back.

Randy kept his eyes on the road as he tried to collect his thoughts. He knew from past experience that this was headed somewhere he dreaded. He hated being the bull in the china shop. He considered his words carefully, but his gut told him it was too late.

"If you didn't need all those drugs, I would be able to be home a lot more," Randy said, trying to stay calm. "Pretty much every night. And if that was the case, I wouldn't have to spoil my girls so much. You know I miss them. And, um, while we're on the subject, I might as well say it again: you can't keep going on and off your medication. You're making it hard on all of us. I don't want to hurt your feelings, but can't you see that?"

Jane was silent. Randy reached for her hand as she yanked it away.

"If anyone can tell me how many miles it is to Whipperton, to Whopperton, they get an extra scoop of ice cream!" Randy shouted, changing the subject.

The girls giggled, bouncing up and down.

"Daddy, I say it is, uh, ten miles!" Abigail exclaimed.

"You're wrong, Abby." Francine sprung up from the seat. "I think it's twenty-five miles!"

"Okay, girls. I hate to tell you, Abby, but your sister is way closer. It's twenty. Francine, you win the extra scoop!"

Abby reached over and sprayed Francine with a wet raspberry, followed by a light punch.

Jane didn't flinch.

"Another ten minutes, girls, and we'll be there." Glancing out the window, Randy watched as a sea of tombstones swallowed up the scenery. "Hey everyone, while we're out this way, does anyone want to stop and have a visit with Aunt Julie?" He looked over at Jane. "I bet she would love to hear from her favorite nieces today."

"Aunt Julie would like that," Abigail piped up. "I can show her my new umbrella. You can show her yours too, Francy."

Jane adjusted her hat as she lit a cigarette. "I guess, Randy, but can we make it short?"

The car stopped and the girls jumped out. The sun peeked out from behind a dark cloud. The smell of fresh-cut grass filled the air as the perfectly manicured landscape appeared before them.

Abigail held her umbrella tightly, bolting down the walkway onto the greenery and through the headstones. Francine skipped slowly, not even trying to keep up.

Randy and Jane trailed behind. One look at the lush grass and Jane knew her white heels were in trouble. She kicked them off and Randy caught them like small footballs.

"See, I still haven't lost my touch," he joked.

Jane flicked her cigarette.

Abigail weaved in and out of the headstones. "Right here! I found her!" she shouted, fumbling to open her umbrella. "See, Aunt Julie, isn't this pretty?"

She held it high, twirling it around and almost falling on the grave.

"Mother bought it for me, and she got one for Francy too! Didn't she, Francy?" She peered around the stone, glancing at Francine's empty hands. "Where's your umbrella? You know Aunt Julie would like to see yours too."

"Forgot it in the car," Francine answered, glancing at her mother.

"Aunt Julie, you would really like Francy's umbrella. Mother picked it out for her. It has flowers on it!"

Abigail stopped to notice the untouched arrangements surrounding the grave. In front of the glittery headstone, Francine's long dress swayed in the breeze.

Abigail rubbed her fingers across the inscription. "Mommy, I memorized this. See." She squeezed her eyes nearly shut. "Julie Francine Harring, January one thousand nine hundred and thirty-seven." She made a stroke in midair. "December one thousand nine hundred and sixty-nine." She opened her eyes and looked at her mother.

Wiping away a tear, Jane lowered her head.

"Honey, you know it's okay." Randy put his arm around her. "But don't you think it's time to get over it? Remember what the doctor told you? Look, neither of us could have prevented the road conditions that day, and besides, do you think Julie would want you to be sad?"

She didn't say a word.

"The more you come here, the easier it will get and the better you'll feel. Jane, you never have to stay long, just show up. Your sister would like that."

Randy gave her a squeeze, seeing that her eyes were red and empty. "And these girls like visiting their aunt. They need you here with them too, not just me."

He handed back Jane's shoes.

"Okay, everyone ready?" Randy asked. "Hot dogs and ice cream coming right up! But one more kiss for Aunt Julie before we go, girls."

Both girls raised one hand to their mouths and looked up to the sky. Each blew a kiss into the warm breeze.

Abigail went skipping across the grass. "Don't worry, Aunt Julie, we'll be back soon!"

Francine and Abigail were excited. They could taste the ice cream already.

"That was the best hot dog ever!" shrieked Abigail as she devoured the last sloppy bite.

"And how are you doing, double-scooper kid?" Randy asked, giving Francine's hair a toss. As soon as the words were out of his mouth, he watched Francine lose the battle to secure the fast-melting scoops with her tongue. The brown balls tumbled slowly from her lips, hitting the ground with a plunk.

Abigail giggled as she watched the last of the cone vanish. "See, Francy, I should have won the second scoop. I would have had it all licked up by now!"

"Okay, groovy girl," Randy said, glancing at Jane. "It's time to split this place. Don't you think, Momma Jane?"

Jane gave a slight nod.

"I'll race you to the car, Francy!" Abigail shouted.

"Last one there is the rotten wiener," Randy called as he flew past the girls.

"I'll be there soon," Jane muttered, her heels clicking across the pavement.

"See, Abigail," Randy huffed. "This is where you get your lightning speed from!"

Francine was out of breath. "But that's not fair, Daddy. You're not wearing a stupid granny dress."

Randy laughed.

They opened the car doors and jumped in.

"What does everyone have planned for this week?" Randy asked as they pulled onto the road.

"When are you leaving again, Daddy?" Francine pouted, watching the telephone lines pass by.

"In the morning," Randy said. "How about you, Abigail?"

"I'm gonna win the biggest trophy and all the red ribbons in the whole school this week. And then, someday, I'm gonna win them all in the whole of America!"

"You sound pretty confident, young lady."

"Yep, because I am."

"You know, that's a good attitude to have, Abigail," Randy said. "I used to have that outlook in school too. Mind you, there was the odd time I got my butt kicked, but it sure helped knowing I always tried my best. Besides, being the most handsome, smartest guy on the track team, I think all the girls wanted to chase me just so they could kiss me. Lucky for you, your mother was the only one who ran fast enough. Yeah, I pretty much had to fight them girls off!"

Randy grinned, glancing across the seat. Jane rolled her eyes.

"Oh Daddy," Abigail laughed.

"How about you, Miss Francine?" Randy asked. "What are your plans for the week?"

"Don't know, Daddy, but I might work on my Scouts badge. I have to plant seeds so I can watch them grow into beautiful flowers."

Randy adjusted the rearview mirror. "I bet your sister could help with that, Francine."

Francine looked at Abigail uncertainly.

"Tell you what, Francy," Abigail said. "If you get stuck, I'll help you. But the gardening badge is easy, you'll see."

With the car barely stopped in the driveway, the girls jumped out and disappeared up the walkway to the house.

"Where does the time go?" Randy asked Jane as he rolled into bed that night.

"I don't know, but when you aren't here it doesn't go by fast enough," Jane muttered. "At least not most days."

Randy watched her slide gracefully into bed. He still loved her. Though her battles of adversity were slowly taking their toll, her beauty remained. For now, the only thing he could do was pray that the worst was behind them, and that his girls would never have to face the same demons.

He snuggled close. "Honey, just because strange things happened in your family years ago doesn't mean Jane Moonie has to give in to the darkness. It doesn't matter now how your grandma Agnes disappeared. We know the story of the strange butterfly necklace that was left sprawled across the coach seat. Heck, Jane, we'll never know if she just plain went crazy or was snatched from the old coach trail." Randy grabbed her side. "Boo!" he shrieked. Jane screamed.

"Stop it, Randy! Who knows? Maybe she just got sick of ten children hanging off her." Jane sighed. "Lord knows we only have two and most days that's more than I can handle."

"Why do you have such a hard time counting your blessings?" Randy yawned. "We have Jesus on our side. Besides, they're coming up with new medication all the time. The market is full of happy pills these days. Thank you, Lord. And you want to know what else I think? Unfortunately, I believe this is exactly what Satan wants. He would like nothing better than for you to live a life of misery. He knows he's stealing your spirit. He keeps filling you up with darkness Jane and then in some twisted way you keep allowing it to happen. Then you have no room left for the good stuff, the stuff that really matters." Randy held her tighter. "He knows he already has a foothold with you. He knows it, and he's running with it. Don't you get that, Jane? Do you remember anything the priest said today?"

"Yeah, I guess. But it's easier said than done. Do *you* get that, Randy?" Jane rolled over, facing the wall.

"Sure I do, but you know God always has the upper hand. You just have to trust him. And honey, speaking of upper hands, you really need to get your groove back. Have you thought about getting back to one of those PTA meetings, or even helping out at a church bazaar? You know there was a time you even loved to conjure up some of your Aunt Almeda's recipes. You enjoyed those things. Look, it's been months since Julie passed, so how about taking back at least some of your joy, Jane? What's wrong with celebrating her life?" Randy ran his fingers through her soft hair. Looking into Jane's eyes, his heart sank. Silence filled the air. "Well then, how about a bingo night with Jenny? You two have been friends forever. Don't you think she misses you too? Your mom could watch the girls. Or, on second thought, we could always get my mother. She would like a month's holiday."

Sitting up, Jane grabbed her pillow and swung it at Randy. "Yeah right! And you want me to feel better, really?" She sighed, pushing her head back into her pillow. "I promise I'll get out sometime, Randy. But not right now."

Chapter Nine

"ABIGAIL! GET MY PILLS AND CIGARETTES! PILLS ARE ON THE COUNTER, YELLOW bottle! Marlboros are on the coffee table! And Abigail, you need to grab the blue bottle too!"

Abigail scooped up the empty bowls and tossed them into the sink. "Hurry up, Francy! The sooner we give these to Mother, the sooner we can go to school."

Francine filled a glass, then scurried over to Abigail and handed it to her.

"Francy, clean the table and get the lunches," Abigail said. "And don't mix them up this time. Yours is beside the milk."

This morning, like all others, Abigail knew it would be exactly eight minutes before her mother made her entrance.

Over in her bedroom, Jane swallowed her pills, smoked her cigarette, put her lipstick on, and topped everything with a usual fashion statement: the hat on her head. She always had to look presentable from a window view.

Getting herself even half-dressed was sometimes the most ambitious part of her day.

Abigail and Francine stood by the door with their matching lunch pails when Jane came out wearing a blue pillbox hat. She flung a sweater over her blue nightgown, smacking her red lips together.

"Come on, girls, I don't have all day!" Passing the sink of dishes, Jane glanced at her daughters. "Whose turn was it for these this morning?"

They looked at each other. Before Francine could get the words out, Abigail cut her off. "It was my turn, Mother."

"Well, being the oldest you should know better," Jane snapped as she butted out her cigarette.

The girls knew the ride to school was going to be fast. Still, they looked forward to getting in the car. Abigail leaned across the vinyl seat. "Don't ever tell Mother it was your turn, okay?"

Francine grinned. "Okay."

※

"Students, the final relay practice will be held on Field B. It will start in fifteen minutes. See you there, and good luck. Thank you."

Mr. Hackett, the gym teacher, was nice but no-nonsense. Everyone knew that when he spoke, you listened. At the beginning of each year, he'd made it clear that he would help any student if they asked for assistance. But they had to be serious. He didn't like to have his time wasted.

Abigail thought Mr. Hackett was cool. He always made time for her, and she knew she wouldn't have worked as hard in school without his attention. Tommy Hall had told her once that Mr. Hackett had been in the army. Judging by the way he walked, Abigail suspected he had probably been the boss.

Abigail sprinted to the distant field. She hoped to be the first person there, but Wendy was already waiting. Abigail took her position beside the other girl, who looked daggers at her.

As the remainder of Abigail's rivals straggled in, she glanced down at her new shoes.

"Good luck," she said to Wendy.

Wendy spat on the ground, then placed her hands on her hips.

Despite her intimidation tactics and longer legs, Wendy didn't scare Abigail. Besides, Abigail's father always told her that Jesse Owens better move over. He claimed that one day his girl would add a whole new meaning to the word *supergirl*, leaving everyone eating her dust.

Suddenly, Abigail thought she heard her name being called from a distance.

"Abby, Abby!"

She glanced at the crowd and spotted her sister's familiar wave, but Abigail needed to focus right now. She waited for the signal.

"On your mark, ready, set, go!"

Abigail launched like a rocket, beige powder shooting up around her white shoes. Her heart raced and her arms swung in rhythm to each step as they reached the track's halfway point. Out of the corner of her eye, she saw Wendy closing. Abigail worked to keep her own space, but it seemed the more she fought, the closer Wendy got.

While they were rubbing arms, Abigail looked for the finish line. It was close. People were waving and yelling.

Making an instant decision, Abigail tried to maneuver left. She struggled to breathe, but with only seconds to go her feet became entangled and she hit the ground hard. As she looked up, Wendy burst across the finish line, her rivals trailing behind like snails.

Abigail brushed herself off and wondered what had gone wrong. Then she looked down at her new shoes. One lace was dragging. She felt like crying but remembered what her father had told her about trying your best.

Head held high, she walked off the track.

"Good job, Abby!"

"You almost got her. Better luck next time!"

"Hey, Wendy cut you off!"

The cheers she had heard just minutes ago became distant chatter as she walked toward the school and analyzed the scrapes on her knees. They were nothing compared to the way she felt inside.

"Abby. Wait, wait!" Francine tried to catch up, breathing heavily. "Mr. Hackett wants to see you. You have to come, now!"

"What does he want?"

"Don't know, but you gotta come right now."

They headed back to the finish line side by side. Abigail heard clapping.

"Well, good for Wendy," she muttered to Francine. "I hope she had fun in my lane. And I hope she has fun tomorrow with all the ribbons she'll be getting."

Abigail approached Mr. Hackett with her head down, searching for the courage to speak. Her gut was knotted. She looked up just as Mr. Hackett brought the bullhorn to his mouth.

"The final practice race goes to Abigail Moonie!" Mr. Hackett smiled, lowering the horn. "Well, Abigail Moonie, you did it again! Good race. Get lots of rest tonight, because tomorrow looks very promising for you."

"But Mr. Hackett, Wendy won this one! I fell, remember?"

"You may have fallen, but that was clearly after Wendy cut you off."

Abigail felt overwhelmed. The cheers and shouts faded as she watched Francine jump up and down.

"Good one, Abby! I just knew you could beat her! Mommy is going to be so happy, and Daddy too!" Strolling towards the school, Francine put her arm around her sister. "All you need tomorrow is a good luck charm. Then you'll win for sure."

Abigail smiled. "Yep. And I think I know where to get one."

Undeniable

The lineup out the school door was long as Wendy tried to edge her way through. She threw Francine a look of disgust and gave her a nudge.

"Good luck tomorrow, Wendy! You're gonna need it!" Francine fired back, sticking her tongue out.

Francine reached for her sister's hand.

※

"Mommy! Abby won the race!" Francine screeched as they climbed into the Chevelle. "She came in first in the practice for the whole school and tomorrow she is going to win everything. Mr. Hackett said so, didn't he, Abby?"

Abigail plunked down beside her. "But Mother, it was so close."

"Yeah, it was close 'cause Wendy tried to cheat. Mr. Hackett caught her, and now she's really mad!" Both girls giggled, and Francine let out a huge snort. "Yep, it's gonna be good, Abby!"

Jane butted out her cigarette. "Okay, girls, settle down."

Francine couldn't contain her curiosity. She peered over the seat to see what shade her mother's lips were. Focusing on Jane's ruby-red head scarf, she suspected her lips were a similar color. Even more curious, she stretched her neck and leaned into the seat.

"Sit back, Francine," Jane snapped. "And quit chomping. You know, one day your jaw is going to fall off. Lord, I'll never understand you, young lady."

Francine sat back in her seat. A brief silence filled the air.

"Well, good for you, Abigail," Jane said. "Now make sure you remember to smile when you cross that finish line tomorrow. You know how important it is to always come in first? Second is never an option. Understand, Miss Abigail? Not in the Moonie house, right? You don't ever want to live with that regret, believe me. Mistakes like that will mess up your life. Right, Abigail? You do understand?"

"Uh, yes, Mother."

"And hard work always pays off," Jane ranted. "Right, Francine?"

Francine glared out the window. "Guess so."

Chapter Ten

The ride home was quick.

"Wanna practice, Abby?" Francine asked, darting from the car.

"No. Mr. Hackett said I should rest tonight."

They made their way into the house. Emptying their lunch pails, Abigail grinned at the empty sink. Then they scurried down the hall and flopped onto their beds.

"Tomorrow is gonna be really good, isn't it, Abby? Wendy is going to be sorry she cut you off!"

"Francy, you know that isn't very nice. But yep, I'm gonna leave her eating my dirt!" Abigail laughed.

Francine couldn't hold her laughter either. Charging at Abigail's bed, she pounced on it and let out a huge snort. "You're the best big sister ever, Abby. Don't ever change."

"Okay," Abigail smirked as she jumped up. She went to her dressing table, opened the drawer, and lifted out the necklace. Carefully, she passed it to Francine. "Francy, you have to wear this tomorrow. It will be good luck for me, but don't let Mother see."

"Abigail! Francine! I need you here!"

Francine shrugged. No matter how many crises the girls had been through with their mother, each one always felt like the first.

"Come on, Francy," Abigail tried to reassure her as they filed their way to the kitchen. "It won't be that bad."

"Is it leftovers or sandwiches for supper?" Jane asked them.

Abigail looked at Francine. Both knew having a choice was plain weird. Jane was abrupt. "Well, what will it be? I haven't got all night, girls."

"Uh, sandwiches," Francine reluctantly answered.

"Same for you, Abigail?"

Abigail glanced at Francine. "Uh, sure."

"Come on, girls. I said I don't have all night."

They took their places around the table.

Jane looked at them intently. "I'm going out tonight. I was going to call your grandma to come stay, but I think you're capable of looking after your sister, aren't you, Abigail? Besides, it's only for a few hours. You know your bedtime. And don't forget to brush your teeth and say your prayers. Hear me? If you give God any grief tonight, if you even so much as bend his ear, he'll have his own way of dealing with both of you. Right, girls?"

They nodded.

"Yes, Mother," Abigail chirped. "I'll take charge of Francine."

"By the way, did either of you see my bingo chips?" Both girls shook their heads. Jane looked puzzled. "Well, that's strange. At any rate, I do believe it's Miss Abigail's turn to lead us in grace. I think you have a lot to be grateful for today." She didn't take her eyes off her older daughter. "Could you please start?"

Bowing, Abigail prayed. "Bless us, oh Lord, in these thy gifts which we are about to receive from thy bounty, through Christ our Lord. Oh, and thank you for letting me win today and for my new shoes. And could you please remind me to double-knot the laces tomorrow? Amen." She crossed her chest.

Lifting their heads, Francine found it difficult to contain her curiosity. "What's a double knot, Abby?"

"I'll show you later, Francy."

"Mommy, can you pass the Spam please?"

Under their blankets that night, Abigail wondered aloud, "Francy, do you think Mother is getting better?"

"Why?"

"Well, she went out tonight, didn't she?"

"Yeah, but she still wears that red lipstick. And besides, she'll probably get even sicker if she ever finds out where all her bingo chips went."

"What do you mean?" Abby whispered. "Do you know where they are?"

"Well, kinda."

"Tell me. You didn't hide them somewhere, did you?"

"Sorta."

"Where?"

"Nowhere important. God doesn't even know, because he doesn't know anything. You know, he hasn't even made Mommy better. He's never gonna make her better. That's because I don't think he's even real. Have you ever seen him, Abby?"

"Nah."

"It doesn't matter anyway. Mommy's stupid bingo chips are gone and they're not coming back, ever. You need to pinky swear, Abby, that you'll never tell anybody."

"Girls, got everything?" Kneeling, Jane grabbed her daughters by their arms. "Please don't make me turn the car around this morning."

They nodded in agreement. With her hair in a high ponytail, Jane's pink lips stood out more than usual. She was eager to get on the road. She didn't ask either sister to get her a pill; she just wanted her Marlboros and her purse. And instead of taking eight minutes of preparation time, she only took five.

Abigail was happy. Maybe Jane had finally gotten better overnight. Still, they treaded carefully.

"Looks like rain today. You need your umbrellas," Jane remarked, twisting the life out of her pink-stained cigarette butt.

Francine turned up her lip.

"Oh, I'll get them," Abigail said, looking down at her new shoes.

The drive to town seemed slow as dark clouds hovered over the car.

"I assume everything went good last night," Jane said, turning the rear-view mirror. "Both of you were sleeping when I got home. Did you remember your prayers?"

"Yes, Mother," Abigail answered.

"I've been thinking. I know I've been a little short with you lately, but one day you'll see it was for your own good. I just need you two to grow up into decent young ladies. That's all every mother wants." Jane's voice got louder. "Are you listening?"

"Uh... yes, Mother," Abigail answered.

"You need to know that's important." Jane adjusted the mirror again. "Now, Abigail, just because I've been giving you more responsibility, it doesn't mean you don't have to win today. You must always win. Do you hear me? And when you get to the finish line, for heaven's sake, smile. That will show God you're grateful. Besides, you can't be looking like a sourpuss for the school picture, right? What would people think of me, your mother, Jane Moonie, really?"

Jane lit another cigarette. A haze of smoke floated into the windshield.

"And Miss Francine, you have enough on your plate just minding your manners, so please remember them today. Lord, for the life of me, child, spit that gum out. Just how do you expect to stay at the top of your class, chomping like that? Honestly, Francine."

Francine rolled her eyes at Abigail. "Yes, Mommy."

With one spit, the wad landed in her hand.

Looking down at the butterfly necklace, Francine was happy her sister had let her wear it today. A beam of sunrays bounced off the butterfly.

Francine quickly tucked the silver chain under her blouse. She knew her mother didn't need to see that, at least not this morning.

"Okay, girls, we're here. It's a busy day. Remember to mind yourselves, you hear me now?"

"Yes," they answered, grabbing their lunch pails.

Francine shoved the gooey ball of gum back into her mouth.

Slamming the doors behind them, Jane watched them skip their way across the street.

"Good grief," Jane huffed. "Abigail!"

Abigail stopped in her tracks. Searching for the voice, she stood still until she realized it had come from her mother.

"Abigail! Your umbrella!" Jane's voice belted loudly from across the road. "You forgot your umbrella!"

Abigail jumped from the curb and bolted toward the car, her eyes set on Jane's green Chevelle as she dashed across the street. Street noise, laughter, honking horns, and the roar of engines filled the air. Abigail's white shoes slapped against the pavement.

"Abigail! Abigail! Watch out! The car, Abigail!" her mother screamed.

But it was too late. A piercing screech was followed by a crushing bang.

Jane darted from her car and onto the street where Abigail was lying. Pieces of metal were scattered around the girl's small, lifeless body. Like a sleeping infant, her legs were curled into her chest.

Screams shot through the humid air from all directions.

"Call an ambulance!" Jane yelled. Frantic, she fell to her knees. Gently turning Abigail's neck, she cradled her head in her arms. Her hands shook. Jane began to sob. "Abigail, hold on, they're coming. Hold on, Abigail, can you hear me? It's Mommy. Hold on."

Abigail eyes were closed, her skin pasty white.

Gently running her fingers through the child's dark matted hair, Jane watched as red droplets fell in slow motion onto her torn yellow shirt. Looking down, Jane noticed one shoe was gone. She kept stroking Abigail's hair, knowing that help was on the way. But it felt like eternity.

"You're going to be all right, Abigail. Just hold on."

"Mommy. What happened to Abby?" Francine cried as she crouched down next to Abby. "Abby, please wake up. Please, please."

Mr. Hackett appeared and quickly assessed the situation. He dropped to his knees and listened for any sign of breathing. He placed his mouth firmly over Abigail's lips and tried to resuscitate her.

"God, please don't take her," Jane wailed through uncontrollable tears, still on her knees. "Please God, not her too! Not my Abigail!"

Minutes felt like hours. A grey gurney was pushed toward them, accompanied by two white coats.

"Out of the way, everyone!" a voice ordered.

"Is she responsive?" one ambulance attendant shouted.

"No!" Mr. Hackett yelled as Abigail was placed on the gurney and lifted into the ambulance.

Not a second was wasted. The screams from the siren faded into the distance.

"Someone stay with Francine," Mr. Hackett called. Then he and Jane raced toward her car.

Chapter Eleven

Every tick of the clock at the hospital sounded like a giant metronome, yet the hands appeared to stand still. Jane paced the freshly polished beige floor, her hair disheveled. Her lips trembled as Mr. Hackett sat, speechless.

"What's taking them so long?" Jane cried out. "Why can't I see her? I need to see her now."

"Please, Mrs. Moonie, they're doing all they can," a heavyset nurse said. She approached Jane and embraced her. "Listen, I need you to hear this. Your daughter is in good hands and these doctors will do everything possible to help your child. I know it's difficult, but let the doctors do their job, please."

"Well, I need to see her!" Jane gasped between sobs. "Abigail needs her mother! She has always needed me!"

The nurse squeezed Jane's shoulder, then gently let go. Feeling helpless, Jane turned around.

"You have to calm down," Mr. Hackett whispered, his light-colored eyes meeting hers. He surrounded her with his sculpted arms. "It's all right. Randy is on his way."

Jane's sobs began to fade.

Mr. Hackett felt her tears soak through his gym shirt. The air felt heavy as he listened to the slow tick of the clock.

Before long, a small man dressed in white crept through an automatic door and walked toward them. A mask dangled from his neck. He introduced himself as the doctor who had worked on Abigail and then guided Jane to a sofa tucked in the corner of the room.

Mr. Hackett waited nearby as they conversed.

"No! No! No! Damn you, world! Not Abigail too!" Jane pounded her fists into the sofa. "Damn you, God! You had no right to take her!"

Unsure of how to proceed, Mr. Hackett approached slowly. When the doctor asked about Abigail's father, Jane told him that Randy was on the way. Mr. Hackett comforted Jane as the doctor hung his head and walked away.

"I am sorry," Mr. Hackett said, holding her tight. He tried to contain his own tears.

"Jane!" Randy's voice echoed off the concrete walls. Each quick step slammed onto the tile floor.

Jane ran toward Randy and collapsed in his embrace.

The ride home was somber. Jane stared out the window, not realizing whether it was day or night. Randy sat behind the wheel, silent and numb. He wasn't sure how to start picking up the pieces. Glancing at Jane, he didn't know if it was possible. Where would he begin? And what about Francine? How would they tell her that her sister would never come home again? He tried to swallow the lump in his throat.

The walk to the house was lit up like a runway. As they made their way up, two lengthy silhouettes charged toward them.

"Mommy, Daddy!" Francine called, Jenny at her side. "Where's Abby? Is she still at the hospital?"

Randy looked down at Francine and hugged her. He didn't say a word, and Francine could tell there was something different about her father. His eyes were red and swollen. His lips appeared thin and dry, yet his cheeks shone. Her mother wasn't right either. She rarely went out the house without lipstick. And she appeared dazed.

"Does Abby have a broken leg, Daddy? Did she have to stay at the hospital? Where is she?"

Randy noticed the hollowness that had set in Jane's eyes. He knew he would be the one having to answer Francine's questions. His stomach rolled.

In the kitchen, Jenny stood silently. Randy shook his head. Feeling her heart sink, Jenny made her way to Jane. With Randy on one side and Jenny on the other, they maneuvered Jane to the bedroom and closed the door. Neither said a word.

"Daddy, where's Abby?" Francine persisted, pulling at his shirt.

Randy guided Francine to the living room.

"So where is she, Daddy?"

"I have some very bad news," Randy said, taking a breath. He lifted her onto his knee, hesitating as he searched for words. He sensed there was no right way to say this. "Francine, Abigail isn't coming home."

"What do you mean?"

Randy tried to stall. "You know how we all go to church and talk about Jesus?"

"Kinda."

"Well, uh, today Abigail went to be with Jesus, in heaven." He tried to keep his composure. "God needed another angel today, Francine." He cleared his throat. "So he took Abigail." Tears seeped from his eyes.

"Well, how long does he need her for, Daddy?"

Randy paused, feeling a sting in his heart. "Forever, Francine. Forever."

Francine bolted from his knees. Stomping her feet, she threw her hands on her hips. "Well, did you tell him he can't have her forever, Daddy? Abby and me play together! Me and her practice running!" She looked puzzled. "You know, Daddy, she has to get Mommy's pills in the morning, so he can't have her, ever!"

Randy wrapped his arms around her thin body. "I'm so sorry, Francine. If I could change it, I would in a heartbeat, but I'm not the boss."

"Well, who is the boss, Daddy? Is Mommy the boss?"

"No, honey, God is the boss." Randy wiped tears from his cheeks.

"Well, he isn't my boss, Daddy, and he should have never taken Abby! She won't like it and she will be really mad! I want her back!"

Francine sped down the hall, wails of anger erupting. She stomped the floor. "I want her back now!" she screamed as the bedroom door slammed behind her.

Randy stared at Jenny. "I better call Jane's parents."

Chapter Twelve

Francine couldn't believe God would just come and take her sister. Looking at the shiny coffin, she wanted Abigail to wake up. Even if she could just get her attention for a second, to see if she really wanted to go to heaven. She tried picturing Abigail with wings and a sparkling halo. She knew her sister would make a pretty angel.

Looking more closely, she had never really noticed her sister's lips before. They were perfectly curved and pink. On the one hand, Francine wanted to wake her and tell her how pretty she looked. But on the other, she wanted to let her sleep, because she seemed such a perfect angel.

Standing in front of the small box, Francine noticed Abigail's stocky hands as they lay on her embroidered dress. Francine reached into her pocket and pulled out a small wooden cross, carefully tucking it under Abigail's still hand. Then she followed her father down the aisle.

To Francine, it felt like the longest time she had ever been in the church. She was surprised she hadn't yawned. Maybe it was because everyone was crying, and she was not in her usual seat. She glanced at her mother and saw how tired she appeared. She had seen her mother on many bad days, but Francine knew this was the worst day of Jane's life. In the midst of all the people present, Jane wore no lipstick.

Randy put his arm around Francine. "You don't need to cry. Abigail is in a nice place now, and she wouldn't want you to cry." He squeezed her gently.

But as she listened to others sniffle, Francine found it hard not to cry. She kept trying to swallow the dryness in her throat. Father David told everyone how wonderful a daughter Abigail Moonie had been for her short time on earth—and that she had been the best big sister anyone could have. Father David said some nice things about Jesus and the Blessed Virgin Mary, too, and that there was a time to be born and a time to die. She wasn't sure what he meant, but most of the people stopped crying, until he said more nice things about Abigail. Then the sobs started again.

Francine turned around. Among the faces she saw Jenny, Mr. Hackett, Tommy Hall, and his parents. Wendy sat to the side with her head down and an old lady was rubbing her back.

If heaven was such a nice place and Abby was an angel now, why was everyone crying? Francine had many questions. Why had God taken Abby in the first place? She had been happy here. After all, she had just gotten new shoes and was about to win first place ribbons.

Francine found it hard to swallow. Tears filled her eyes as she comprehended that there would be no more races with Abby, no more Abby having her back, and not even one more pinky-swear. Her body shook. The sobs were short and loud.

Suddenly, like a small steam engine, she jerked away from Randy and plowed her way down the aisle, Randy trailing. On her tiptoes, she tried to shake the small wooden coffin.

"Abby, I wanted to let you sleep, but you can't sleep," she said. "Even Wendy's here, Abby. And Mommy doesn't have any lipstick on, so you need to wake up right now. I mean it! Mommy and Daddy need you to come back home."

The mourning grew louder as Father David strode toward her. He motioned for Randy to stay back, and then held Francine and gently placed a hand on her head. Her sobs tapered to silence.

When Deacon Jude approached and put his hand on her back, the cries and moans from the pews began to ebb. Father David nodded as Jude guided Francine back to her seat.

The warm breeze carried a scent of sweetness. Small bursts of cloud were woven into the calm blue background. Beams of sunlight danced gracefully off the glittery headstones. Rainbows of color laced the ground while a mound of black soil was placed carefully to the side.

Francine couldn't help but notice how the box fit the black hole perfectly. Father David stood in front, speaking about the earth again and about Abigail being with Jesus and Mother Mary. Between the weeps and sniffles, you could almost hear the wings of the smallest bird flutter by.

Holding her father's hand, Francine felt tremors from his fingers with each spoken word.

Randy also held Jane's frail waist. The sun's relentless reflection bounced off her brimmed hat, illuminating her pale lips. Grandpa and Grandma Harring stood close by, while Grandpa and Grandma Moonie stood to the side.

Francine scanned for her chance to leave. Slowly, she withdrew her hand from her father's grasp and disappeared into the crowd of murmurs and sobs. With every step she felt a sense of freedom, but with it came a heavier sense of sadness.

The butterfly necklace bounced gracefully off her fair skin as she made her way back to the car. Pulling the door open, she reached in and took out the pink umbrella. Francine folded her legs beneath her as her body sank to the ground. She popped the umbrella open, trying to hide her tears as they spilled down her cheeks.

"Francine, come on!" her father's voice shouted from down the hall. "It's time for school!"

Francine felt groggy as she lazily made her way out of bed. Lately, seeing the empty bed opposite her own made her want to stay there all day.

"You're going to be late again if you don't hurry!" Randy bellowed.

Quickly she dressed and raced down the hall.

"Come on, Francine!"

Francine liked when her father drove her to school, though she knew it was a temporary arrangement. Just sitting beside him in the front seat made her feel older.

Some days they took different routes, and they made games out of counting telephone poles or watching for wildlife. The time with him always went by too quickly.

On other days they talked about Abigail, or how Jane was doing and what was going to be expected from Francine. Those talks always left Francine feeling happy and scared at the same time. She knew she would have Jane's undivided attention soon, but at what cost?

Looking at her father, her heart skipped as she tried to picture him not being at home much longer.

"Everything okay, groovy girl?" Randy asked.

"Yeah. It's okay, Daddy."

Chapter Thirteen

Following the funeral, Jane had an even more difficult time facing the day. As she lay in bed, she looked to Father David, who had stopped by to help her find some sort of peace within.

"You know, God doesn't want you to feel this way," he said. "He doesn't want Jane Moonie to be without hope in her heart. He doesn't want your happiness stolen. Grief is one thing, but to have it consume your life forever, this is not from our Creator." He tried to pour faith into her. "The sorrow you feel now is from Satan. He is trying to steal your joy—any you may have left, that is. This is not your portion, Jane. This ongoing torment does not belong to you."

Father David's white collar stood out in the beige-colored room. His voice was confident and smooth as he placed one hand on Jane's head. Blessing the Father, Son, and Holy Ghost, Jane could feel warmth radiate from his hand—but still she felt empty. The blood that had once flowed through her felt as if it had been drained dry, every fiber withering away.

He raised his voice. "Almighty God, your scripture is our foundation. Your word is our light and the only way." He bowed his head. "I ask you, Father, to pour your blessings onto Jane. Bring her peace and solace with the promise of your words, in her time of need. It is you, Father, who holds the master plan for her life, not Satan. She belongs to you, God. Your word tells us we can never be separated from you. You assure us that your faithfulness towards your children is our shield and rampart. Lord, place this truth and faith into Jane's heart." Flipping through the pages of his Bible, he placed his free hand on Jane's head. "Jane, I am now going to read to you Ecclesiastes 3:1–3: 'To every thing there is a season, and a time to every purpose under the heaven: a time to be born, and a time to die; a time to plant, and a time to pluck up that which is planted; a time to kill, and a time to heal; a time to break down, and a time to build up.'"[2] He flipped through more pages. "His word also says this, in Psalms 73:26: 'My flesh and my heart faileth: but God is the strength of my heart, and my portion for ever.'"[3]

He lifted his head and was struck again by Jane's appearance. Darkness circled her eyes like stamps. They were small and hollow, her skin colorless. It was clear to Father David that Satan's control over Jane was one of pure deceit. It was taking its toll on her, and he wasn't about to give in.

Holding out his Bible in one hand, with the other still placed firmly on her head, he commanded, "Jane, we are going to recite Psalms 23 together. You will draw strength from this." His voice was unshakable as Jane quietly began to speak along in a dry broken voice:

> *"The Lord is my shepherd; I shall not want. He maketh me to lie down in green pastures: he leadeth me beside the still waters. He restoreth my soul: he leadeth me in the paths of righteousness for his name's sake. Yea, though I walk through the valley of the shadow of death, I will fear no evil: for thou art with me; thy rod and thy staff they comfort me. Thou preparest a table before me in the presence of mine enemies: thou anointest my head with oil; my cup runneth over. Surely goodness and mercy shall follow me all the days of my life: and I will dwell in the house of the Lord forever."*[4]

Jane felt like the words dragged out aimlessly, leaving her numb. Father David blessed her and wiped away a tear.

"Jane, understand that Abigail and Julie are both safe and at peace with our heavenly Father now. Scripture assures us of that. You do believe this?"

Weakly, Jane nodded.

"May the Father, Son, and the Holy Ghost fill you with their wisdom and peace today," he commanded, lightly touching her head again. "Another helpful scripture for you would be Psalm 91. You must focus on God now. He is your refuge."

As Father David closed his Bible, Jane drifted off. He turned toward the door, but then glanced back and crossed his chest. He thanked the Father, the Son, and the Holy Ghost. Quietly, he closed the door behind him.

---

2   Ecclesiastes 3:1–3, KJV.

3   Psalm 73:26, KJV.

4   Psalm 23:1–6, KJV.

"See you tonight, Miss Francine," Randy said as he kissed her.

Randy loved and hated these moments. One minute his little girl was beside him, the next she appeared so grown up. It seemed to take mere seconds for Francine and her red lunch pail to disappear into the huge grey school. With long strides, Francine's silhouette vanished. His heart sank every time. He knew, though, that one good thing always came out of her early morning independence: his girl made it in time for the Lord's Prayer.

Randy watched the stragglers race into the school. Soon he had to return to work, and later face Jane again. He hoped she would experience some kind of turnaround soon.

With arms draped over the steering wheel, he hung his head. At times like this he found himself in a struggle to keep his own faith. He knew he had to get back to Jane. Tears welled in his eyes, but still he drove the long way home.

Interlude

Pastor Matthew dabbed the hanky across his forehead as the room fell silent.

"Well, can I get an amen, folks?" he asked with a grin.

"Amen, Pastor."

All eyes were fixed on him. "Now I'm certain most if not all of you have felt your faith compromised at some time in your life."

"That's for sure, Pastor!"

"And I'm sure there are others here right now who are second-guessing the good word!" another voice bellowed.

The congregation got louder.

"Okay, people! We all know the enemy only comes to steal, kill, and destroy. We also know God, light, and goodness go hand in hand. But with Satan, dark and evil go hand in hand, right?" Pastor Matthew patted his Bible. "Yes, and the good book here tells us that Satan is the master of all trickery. He knows the Bible better than any of us. That's right. So if we give him an inch, he will worm his way in and try and steal whatever else he thinks he can rightfully have. His sneakiness is unfathomable! That's why we have to guard our hearts at all times! Gender, age, race, poor or rich... none of that matters. He's going to try and mess with us all at some time in our lives. Cause that's what he does. This scripture right here confirms it! But guess what, people? Our God is and will always be above his dirty name! Can I get another amen?"

The crowd cheered. "Amen."

"Right on, Pastor! That's right!" said a young man who stood off to the side. "We don't have to fall into Satan's trap if we keep ourselves depending on God's word. God will provide armor. Psalms 91 says so! Isn't that right, Pastor?"

"That's right, young man." Pastor Matthew smiled at him. "Now let's get on with the story, shall we? Yes, and then there was young Francine and school. Uh-huh."

Chapter Fourteen

"Attention, class! If you're available to stay after school next Friday to help clean the music room, don't forget to sign the sheet on your way out." Mrs. Barry raised her voice. "I might add, whoever does volunteer will get extra marks on their report card."

Mrs. Barry was so nice that it was hard for even the most rebellious students to turn down her requests. There was a race for the door and the lineup was long. Francine glanced at the queue, then made her way through the noisy crowd into the hallway.

"Francine!" Wendy called. A tunnel of light beamed down the hall, dancing off her shiny dark hair. "Do you wanna hang out with us guys in the schoolyard Friday after school?"

Francine felt blindsided. She had never thought of being friends with Wendy.

She shrugged. "Well, maybe."

"Okay, we'll be there after school. You'll have fun, I promise. See you then."

A wave of excitement came over Francine. But before she had a chance to say anything else, Wendy had already made her way ahead of her.

Through all the heads, she turned and yelled, "Hey Francine, I'm sorry Abigail died!"

The excitement suddenly turned to sadness. Francine missed her sister so much, she could never imagine not missing her.

Making her way to the double doors, the butterfly necklace bounced with each step. The late afternoon had turned hot. Francine saw her father standing beside the car.

"Well, groovy girl, how was your day?" Randy asked.

Francine pulled the door shut. "Pretty good."

"How about the scenic route tonight, Missy? It's somewhere between Whipperton and Whopperton."

She smiled at his joke. "Okay, Daddy."

Francine popped a small purple ball of gum into her mouth and looked intently out the window. The drive was peaceful and bright.

Trying to find the right words, Randy began slowly. "Daddy has to go back to work soon. You know that, Francine?"

"I know, but I don't want you to."

"Well, if I don't get back soon I won't have a job, and we can't have that, can we?"

"Then can I go with you, Daddy?"

"Mommy needs you. And I need you to help her." He waited for a response. "You do understand, groovy girl?"

"Well, sort of. I got to get pills for her now. But you know, Daddy, she still scares me when she puts red lipstick on."

"Well, hopefully the new medicine will help. She has lots of help now, so you don't have to be scared." Randy paused. "You know, Francine, Mommy loves you very much, even though she hasn't been showing it much lately. When you get bigger, you'll understand more. I promise."

Francine glared out the window, and the sleek outline of an animal gliding through a field caught her eye. "Oh, look at the horse! She's so beautiful. All she has to do is run all day. That's what Abby would have liked to do—just run all day. Daddy, do you think there are horses in heaven?"

Randy gripped the wheel and felt his heart skip. "I believe the most beautiful horses are in heaven."

※

"Okay, let's see if you have this down," Randy said as he lined up the pill bottles. "You only get Mommy her pills if she's in bed sleeping. Now, show me Mommy's breakfast pills."

Francine took a blue pill from one bottle and placed it carefully on the counter. Then she grabbed a short white bottle and removed two small yellow pills.

"Now can you show me the one Mommy is only supposed to take sometimes?"

Grabbing a short container, Francine pulled out a little white pill.

"Good," Randy said confidently. "Jenny will be stopping by at lunch to make sure your mother gets her medicine. But this is where it may get tricky, so I need you to listen. If Mommy is sleeping when you get home from school, wake her up and give her another one of these." He pointed to a bottle. "Then, at supper, she gets the very same pills you gave her in the morning, but an extra one of each. Do you understand?"

Francine pointed to the bottles.

Randy nodded. "That's right. Looks like you got it. Any questions, you call Jenny. Okay? Daddy will be home in one week."

Just then, Jane sauntered into the kitchen.

"Hey Jane, we were just going over your medication," Randy said. "Looks like we've got a nurse extraordinaire!"

Jane glanced at the bottles on the counter as Randy gave her a hug.

"All this craziness will be behind us one day," he said. "You know what Father David says: 'This too shall pass.' We just have to believe, right? Someday our daughter will be visiting us with grandchildren. It's all going to be okay."

Francine's eyes opened wide. "Daddy, does that mean I'll have babies?"

"Yes, one day you'll have babies."

Inspired, she skipped her way down the hall.

"Gonna miss you, dear," Randy said, kissing Jane goodbye. "You have all the numbers I can be reached at. Remember, if you're not up to taking Francine to school, she can either catch the bus, or Jenny said she would help out. So don't be afraid to ask her. But it will do you good to get out of here in the morning. I think you should at least make the effort. And you should consider going out at least one night a week." Randy hugged her again. "Francine will be fine on her own for a few hours." He reached for his suitcase and called down the hall, "Bye, Francine! Or should I say, Miss Nurse Extraordinaire!"

Francine charged back down the hall and threw her arms around his neck. "Just how many babies can I have, Daddy?"

"Well, uh, I guess as many as God wants you to have. So let's see. Yep, that probably means as many as you would like." Randy laughed.

"Really, Daddy? Well, I want two girls. Boys don't know anything." Francine thought for a moment. "Well, except for Tommy Hall. Maybe."

"Okay, Miss Groovy Girl. This old dad will see you next week. Remember what we talked about, and mind your manners, right?"

"Yes, Daddy."

Randy carefully guided Francine back down to her feet. "See you later." He gave Jane one last hug and walked out the door.

Francine knew she had a job to do this morning. She had watched Abigail for months and now it was her turn. Reaching as far as she could, Francine grabbed the bottles. Trying hard, she counted out the pills.

"Daddy said two blue pills," she said as she reached inside the tall bottle. Setting them on the counter, she reached for the smaller bottle. "Then one yellow pill."

She lined them up, but something didn't look right. She put her hands on her hips, stepped back, and looked again.

"No, I think Daddy said one blue pill and two yellow pills." Shuffling the pills, she noticed the last bottle. "Um... Abby always said it's good to have a backup, just in case." She dropped the small white pill in her pocket.

"Don't forget my smokes, Francine!" her mother shouted from the bedroom.

Francine made her way carefully across the floor and nudged the bedroom door.

"Thanks," her mother muttered. Reaching for the red package, she assured Francine that she would be ready soon.

Francine had a feeling this might be a good day, at least better than most. She was even done her chores earlier than Abigail had ever done them. Holding her lunch pail, she let the screen door flop behind her and then waited for Jane.

"No. Back there, Missy," Jane spoke clearly, pointing to the seat behind her.

Francine jumped into the back seat. Looking at her mother from behind, she tried to picture her happy. But all she could see was the green scarf wrapped around her hair.

"Did you get that Scouts project done yet?" Jane asked, pulling a cigarette out of her tote bag.

"Nah, not yet."

"You'll never get that badge if you don't work on it, Francine. Hard work pays off."

"I know, but Abby was going to help me."

"Yes, I remember." Jane looked in the mirror to the back seat. "You know how important it is that you also remember Abigail is no longer here, right?"

Francine lowered her head. "Yes, Mommy."

"What day are you supposed to help Mrs. Barry?"

"Uh, I think she said Friday."

"As long as it's not Saturday. We have a lot to do. Like confession, hear me?"

"Yeah."

The drive to school seemed to take a long time.

"Francine." Jane flicked the ashes from her cigarette. "I've been thinking. If you need help with that project, I'll see what I can do. Okay?"

"Thanks," Francine mumbled, smacking her jaws together.

Pulling close to the curb, Jane put the car in park. "I'll see you later. And for the love of God, take that gum out of your mouth!"

Francine grabbed her pail and pushed open the heavy door. She turned to say goodbye and pulled out the sticky wad. When her mother was out of sight, she put the ball back in her mouth, then disappeared through the school door.

"All right, class, settle down," Miss Wartler said. "We have a lot to get through this morning. Open your arithmetic books and turn to page forty-five."

Although the teacher's white hair was arranged neatly, it looked today as if a grey blob had been plopped on her head. And the scent of her tuna sandwiches always hung in the air.

As Miss Wartler made her way to the blackboard, a paper rocket sailed through the room. She turned and scooped up the projectile from the floor. Silence filled the room, and then the snickering began.

Miss Wartler was on a mission. She scouted for clues, her eyes stopping at Steven.

"By just a rough calculation of your marks, Mister Mullen, it seems to me you are preoccupied with some senseless out-of-class curriculum," she said. "Could you please pull out your bottom drawer for me?"

Miss Wartler inspected the drawer and came up empty-handed. She slammed the drawer shut, grabbed the rocket, and headed to the front of the class just as another rocket crashed into her bosom.

"Class!" she bellowed over their laughter, reaching for her pointer and waving it. "I'm afraid no one will be leaving this room until I find out who the culprit is!"

Francine giggled and let out a loud snort, and the sound was caught by Miss Wartler's antennae. Francine hung her head as she heard the click of Miss Wartler's heels approaching.

"Miss Moonie, what do you have to say for yourself? Do you have any more of these?" she asked, holding the paper rockets inches from Francine's face.

Francine tried to straighten out her smirk. "No, Miss Wartler. They're not mine."

The teacher looked satisfied. "At any rate, Miss Moonie, you need to remove that gum at once." She turned and strolled away.

Another burst of laughter sounded in full force. The teacher turned her eyes toward Tommy.

"Mr. Hall," she said, waving her pointer, "open your drawer for me."

He complied, with hesitation. Miss Wartler pulled out a handful of paper rockets, one wide straw, and several small balls. She slammed the drawer shut.

"Mister Hall! I am appalled." She whacked the pointer on his desk. "In my opinion, young men such as yourself should not be spared the rod. In fact, Mister Hall, I would insist on your father using the biggest switch off any old hickory tree he can find on you!"

Tommy tried to contain his laughter, but he couldn't hide his grin. The class fell silent.

"Come with me now, Mr. Funny Man. We'll see just how funny this is when Principal White pulls out the strap."

With the paper rockets underarm, she tossed the pointer onto his desk. She marched out of the room, pushing Tommy ahead of her. The door slammed behind them. The class roared.

"Hey Francine," a voice piped up. Turning, she found herself face to face with Steven Mullen. Steven had the whitest teeth Francine had ever seen. "Heard you're going to be hanging out with us after school on Friday."

"Well, maybe." Francine chomped hard on her gum.

"There are some other kids we don't want there, so mum's the word, got it?"

"Uh, okay."

"Francine, get my pill!" Jane bellowed from the living room. "It's the one that says *Valium*."

Francine took the small pill and walked to the sink. "Be right there!"

She carefully passed the water and pill to her mother.

"Francine, I need to speak with you," Jane said, taking the medication and making a patting gesture on the couch.

Francine sat down beside her. She thought Jane looked better this evening. She wore lipstick again, and Francine was relieved it wasn't red.

"You and I are the only team members in this house," Jane said. "You know that, right?"

She nodded.

"So that means I've decided to give you, let's say, uh, a little more responsibility, including bedtime. Still, I need you in the house every night, as soon as the streetlights come on. Do you think that's fair?"

"Yes, Mommy," Francine replied, snuggling closer to her.

"By the way, if you're going to get the big-girl rules now, you can stop calling me Mommy." Jane placed her hand on Francine's knee. "And maybe now we can finally get that flower project done. What do you think?"

Francine sighed. "Thank you, Mommy... oops, I mean Mother. I love you."

Closing her eyes, Francine drifted off, soon to be startled by the phone ringing.

"Hi, Daddy," she said, answering the call.

"How's my girl?" Randy asked.

She smiled at the sound of his voice. "Good! Mommy's sleeping, and I just woke up."

"Everything good?"

"Yeah, I guess... Daddy, do you wanna know something?" Francine paused. "Uh, I'm going to help out at school tomorrow and Mommy... oops, I mean Mother... is going to let me stay up later now. And do you want to know something else? Mother is going to help me with flowers for my Scouts badge."

"Right on, groovy girl. Miss you!"

"I miss you too, Daddy."

"See you tomorrow."

"Okay, bye. Here's Mother."

"Hi Randy," Jane said groggily, taking the phone. "No, it's okay. That works if you can pick her up later tomorrow."

The conversation faded as Francine made her way outside. Gusts of wind swirled through the raised veranda. The bright sky turned to dark splashes of grey, with hints of orange on the horizon.

Francine looked at the green Chevelle and remembered how much she missed Abby. She opened the door and pulled out the pink umbrella. Twirling it, she skipped her way back to the veranda. Her heart felt heavy thinking about how much she had wanted the Barbie umbrella.

"You know, Abby," Francine said, glancing up at the sky, "maybe if Mommy—I mean Mother—had got me this umbrella, you wouldn't be in heaven now. Mother hasn't been wearing any red lipstick, and she said she will even help me with my Scouts project! So you don't have to worry, Abby."

Spinning in circles, the umbrella turned with her. The red cedars danced to the howling wind.

Francine held the umbrella tight. "Okay, Abby! I'm coming to see you right now!" She leapt off the low veranda, hoping the wind would carry her. But a gust of wind rocked the umbrella, followed by a pop. Francine plunged to the ground.

She pushed herself up and brushed the clumps of dirt from her face. Assessing the broken umbrella, Francine frantically gathered the scattered strips of pink plastic, then raced to the veranda and shoved the pieces behind an old wooden chair. She hoped her mother hadn't seen her crash-landing.

Cautiously, she tiptoed back into the house. There was no sign of Jane as Francine crawled into bed.

Chapter Fifteen

"Francine, I need my pills!"

Francine scurried about, trying to count the pills as she made her way to her mother.

"Lord's sake, child! What on God's green earth is taking you so long this morning? First beauty appointment I've had in ages, and I don't intend to be late!"

Jane snatched the pills from Francine's hand.

Sprinting back to the kitchen, Francine grabbed her lunch pail and raced for the door. As it slammed behind her, she took a deep breath. She could almost taste the freedom as she climbed into the back seat and waited.

It was a somber morning, but Francine's heart fluttered with anticipation about the different kids she would be meeting later.

"Francine, what time did your father say he was picking you up tonight?" Jane asked as a grey smoke ring floated to the back seat.

"Don't know, but he said not too late, Mother."

Jane adjusted the mirror and puffed her hair. "Make sure you do a good job for Mrs. Barry. And what about an umbrella, just in case?"

"I forgot it."

"Well, you can have your sister's, but take extra good care of it, understand?" Jane cranked the mirror towards Francine. "It's in the back."

Francine could feel her stomach turning to lead. Smacking her gum, she knew her chances of skirting the truth were small.

"No, it's not here, Mother. I put it in our bedroom."

"Then you may just have to get wet," Jane snapped as they pulled up to the school.

Francine didn't waste time. She pushed the door closed and darted toward the building.

Jane rolled down the window and watched her disappear. "No running! Do you hear me? And for the love of God, if I told you once I've told you a thousand times, take that gum out of your mouth!"

❦

The buzzer rang.

"Don't forget homework this weekend," Mrs. Barry shouted. "All book reports are due Monday morning. Remember, class. No book reports, no marks. You're dismissed. Oh, but for those of you staying to help clean, I'll meet you in the instrument room."

Francine raced past the music room. Shoulder to shoulder, the students crammed their way out the classroom door. Outside, Francine scanned the crowd and spotted Wendy in the distance. She walked as fast as she could.

Francine nudged her shoulder. "Wendy, I'm here."

"Good. Let's go! We're gonna meet the others out back. I'll race you, Francine!"

From the first stride, Francine knew she was no match for Wendy. Her necklace bounced recklessly in the air while her legs weaved in and out.

"Come on, Francine!" Wendy called back. "You're doing good!"

Reaching the hill, Francine caught her breath. Among the familiar faces were Tommy, Steven, and some she had never seen before.

"Hey Francine, this is Susie and Walter," Wendy said by way of introduction. They go to Sterling Junior High. You know the rest, right?"

"Yeah, I guess."

"Okay!" Walter shouted. "Let's start with hide and seek! We got the whole lake, but the rule is today you can only go as far as the bridge. Everyone got it? Now pick a partner. It has to be one boy and one girl for every team."

Standing straight, Francine looked around and saw Walter approaching her.

"Okay, Francine, you can be my partner this time," he said. "We'll be it to start, and this is home base. Go everyone! Go! Now turn around, Francine. We gotta count to twenty."

Francine heard feet scampering in all directions.

"You all better be hiding, cause me and my partner are as fast as lightnin'!" Walter yelled. "Here we come, ready or not!"

Kicking her shoes off, Francine flew down the hill. She surprised herself by keeping up with Walter.

"You go that way!" he huffed.

The game was over in minutes. Exhausted, Francine made her way back up the hill and flopped down, smiling at Wendy.

"That's it?" Francine asked.

"Yep, well sort of. Walter's the boss, and you'll find that out sooner than later. Nobody jerks Walter's chain."

"Okay, what's next?" asked Tommy.

"Did you bring the smokes?" Steven asked Walter.

Walter nodded. "Yeah, five is all I could get this week. It's someone else's turn next week."

"Everyone has done it so far," Steven pointed out. "Doesn't the new kid in our group have to do something?"

Walter looked at him. "Yep, that will be our golden rule from now on." He turned his attention to Francine. "Your turn next week, so make sure you bring enough for all of us."

She nodded.

Walter stuck a cigarette into the side of his mouth and divvied up the rest of the smokes. Skipping Francine, he reassured her that Wendy would share hers. A wooden match was struck on a stone and before long everyone was puffing away.

Wendy inhaled deeply, then, exhaling slowly, started to choke. Everyone was coughing except Walter. When Wendy passed her cigarette to Francine, she took a small puff and began wheezing. The chorus of hacking amused Walter.

"Francine, you smoke that thing like a little girl! You know what you look like? You look like a piglet with a straw stuck up his little butt!"

Everyone started to laugh, and Francine knew all eyes were on her. She took one last drag, started coughing uncontrollably and staggered away from the crowd. Before she could make it off the hill, she heaved until her ribs hurt.

When the laughter settled, Wendy bolted to Francine. "You don't look so good. You wanna leave?"

Francine nodded. Wendy placed her arm around Francine's waist and took the lunch pail from her.

"You know, Francine, it's always like that the first time. Don't worry. I'll take care of you."

They wobbled away together.

"Same place, same time next week, everybody!" Walter yelled from a distance. "And Francine, don't forget, at least six for next week!"

Standing in front of the school, Francine passed a gumball to Wendy, who studied her.

"You wanna know something, Francine? I would give Abigail my red ribbon, if I could, just to see her one more time."

Speechless, Francine shrugged. She felt sick enough at the moment without having to think about Abby being gone too.

The honk of a car startled her. She turned as a car sped up and stopped suddenly. Grinning, Randy reached over and opened the door. Francine threw her red pail on the floor as Randy reached over and gave her a hug.

"I missed you, groovy girl," Randy said, brushing her hair back. "Everything okay, Francine? You don't look well." He felt her forehead, then put the car in drive.

"Yep. I think I just helped out Mrs. Barry a little too much, Daddy."

"Well, Francine, that was very thoughtful of you to take your turn. I'm sure Mrs. Barry appreciated it."

Francine looked straight ahead: "Yep, I took my turn all right."

Interlude

"Aha," Pastor Matthew interjected. "People, see what I mean about the deceitfulness of the devil? Even on the smallest scale, he's still full of temptation. He already knows young Francine is vulnerable, so the master of trickery keeps himself invisible as he sits and waits, ready to capture his latest victim. Yes sirree, that's his job."

Chapter Sixteen

Randy closed the bedroom door behind him, longing to hold his wife again.

"You know, Jane, this is the best you've looked in a long time," he whispered, taking the comb from her hand and pulling her close. "I miss *us*. What happened to just us, the way we used to be?"

His warm breath caressed her ear as she collapsed into his chest. Neither said a word. Then, as her long fingers glided softly down the back of his neck, Randy guided her onto their bed.

"Francine, remember you have confession later today," Jane said from across the kitchen. "You can wear the dress I made you. Your father and I are going out for a while. And if you'd like, you can have a friend over—but no one stays for dinner tonight, do you hear me? And remember, God and the neighbors are always watching."

Glimpsing at her mother, Francine thought she could almost see a smile forming under her pale pink lipstick. Dressed in white hip-huggers, her high-heeled, red and gold velvet shoes made her look even taller. Francine smiled as her parents walked to the car. The green Chevelle backed out the driveway.

Bolting to the phone, she could hardly dial fast enough.

"Wendy, is that you?"

"Wow, your purple seat is so cool," Francine said as Wendy leapt off her bike.

"Yeah, I bugged my mother a long time for a banana seat! When I finally got a red ribbon, my mother said I could have one." Wendy laid her bike on the grass, realizing what she had just said. She knew the red ribbon should have been Abigail's. "Uh, I'm sorry, I didn't mean to say it like that. Hey, you can take it for a spin if you want."

"Nah, that's okay."

Side by side, they walked up the sidewalk.

"Wanna know something, Francine?"

"What?"

"You know, my granny always says my mother is a cheap floozy. But I don't think it's 'cause I had to keep asking her for my new bicycle seat. I think it has something to do with those big white boots she wears. Granny always says those white boots are the reason I've had lots of dads."

"How many dads have you had?" Francine asked, opening the door to the house.

"Not sure, but Granny always says it's way more than she can shake her walking stick at. Granny also says I need to call my mother by her name, Mary Lou, not mother."

"Uh-oh."

"Hey, Walter might be coming over too, okay?"

"Guess so," Francine said. "Want to see my bedroom?"

As the girls walked, Wendy hoped Walter would behave himself. Her jaw dropped when she saw inside Francine's room. "Holy..."

Confused, Francine asked, "Well, what's your house like?"

"I stay at Granny's."

"Where does your mother stay then?"

"Granny says she's stays wherever she thinks there'll be a new dad for me."

"Oh."

"Yep, Granny told my mother that the only way I could ever live with her would be if they take Granny out in a wooden box. I think it has something to do with the box being made of wood, because that way Granny would never be able to get out of it and smack her a good one." Wendy stared at Francine's bedroom in awe. "Wow! I sure like your room. Look, you even have two beds. That's so cool."

Wendy started to bounce on the neater of the two beds.

"Hey, maybe I could sleep over sometime?" Wendy said.

Francine plunked down on her bed. "You can't sleep on that bed, because it's Abby's and she would be very mad. And quit bouncing. You'll wreck it."

"Oh, sorry. But hey, maybe I can be like your sister now."

"Abby wouldn't like that either," Francine fired back.

"Anybody here?" they heard a third voice ask from outside the window.

Francine and Wendy raced out of the bedroom just as Walter swung the front door wide open.

"Hey, what's everybody up to?" he asked.

"Nothing," Wendy said. "Francine just showed me her bedroom."

"This is a pretty neat house," Walter said, gawking around. His eyes stopped on the collection of medication bottles on the counter. "Do a lot of old people live here or something?"

"No," Francine answered.

"Then why do you guys have all those?" he asked, narrowing his eyes.

"Those are my mother's—to help her feel better."

"Yeah?" Walter picked up a short bottle. "Um, Valium. Think I've heard something about that." He observed the rest of the counter, then set the bottle down. He smirked.

Francine opened the front door and bolted out, Wendy and Walter behind her.

"Who wants to play double-dog dare you, my rules?" Walter shouted. "I'll start first! Um, I dare you to go lick that screen."

He pointed back to the door. Wendy shrugged her shoulders.

"Okay, Wendy," he said. "Don't make me double-dog dare you."

Wendy sauntered to the window and licked it, which brought an explosion of laughter from Walter and Francine.

"My turn now!" Francine shouted, pointing at the bike. "Walter, I dare you to lick your bike tire!"

"What's your bag, Francine? I can't do that!"

"I'm going to double-dog dare you then. Double-dog dare you! Double-dog dare you!"

Walter sensed that if he didn't comply, everyone would soon find out. He walked to the shiny red bike, bent down, and licked the front tire.

The girls erupted.

"Okay, my turn again!" Walter yelled. He pointed to Wendy's bike. "Francine, I dare you to gob all over Wendy's new banana seat."

Francine walked to the purple seat and glanced back at Wendy. Leaning over the banana seat, she let go with a string of spit. She saw Wendy's mouth open wide.

Walter started laughing hysterically. But just as he was about to launch into another dare, the green Chevelle pulled into the driveway. Walter raced to his bike, and with his shaggy head bobbing up and down peddled furiously down the road.

"Who's the kid with the afro?" Randy asked, watching the bike disappear. Jane got out of the car behind him and closed the passenger door.

"Just Walter," Francine said.

"Well, he looks a little old to be hanging around with you, don't you think?" Francine shrugged.

"Anyway, can you help please?" Randy asked. He passed her a bag. Wendy stayed by Francine's side as they walked into the house.

"Put them over there, Francine." Her mother nodded at the counter, then turned to study Wendy. "Now what is your name, young lady?"

"Wendy."

"By any chance are you the girl from Abigail's track and field team?"

Wendy glared at Francine. "Umm, yeah, I guess."

"Well, nice to finally meet you," Jane said as she held her hand out.

Wendy noticed how tall Jane was in her platform shoes. Stepping back, she cupped her hands over Francine's ear.

"So how many dads have you had?" Wendy whispered.

Francine was puzzled. She took a moment, then put her hand around Wendy's ear and whispered back, "Only one, I think."

Francine felt it was time for Wendy to leave, so she walked her friend out the door to her bike and pulled out two gumballs.

"Want one?" Francine smiled as Wendy shoved the blue one in her mouth. "Thanks for coming over. I'll call you later."

"Sure," Wendy said. Lifting her bike, she saw the gob of spit on the seat. "Yuck! Can I borrow some toilet paper?"

※

"Two minutes and we're out of here," Jane said, fastening the last pin to the side of Francine's bangs. "Gotta get these cut soon. Even though you're almost a teenager, Francine, you're starting to look like some kind of ragamuffin. What will people think of me? Honestly."

She brushed the front of Francine's dress.

"You know, your sister kept herself so neat," Jane continued. "I just don't understand. Let's go. It wouldn't look good to God if you were late for confession, would it missy?" She rubbed her pink lips together. "And by the way, if we get out at a decent time, I think we can work on that flower project together. What do you think, Francine?"

"Sure," Francine said. Anxiously, she jumped into the back seat.

Francine never paid much attention to the scenery in Shelbytown. Most days she didn't even notice people's yards. But today she gazed at all the vibrant colors; the late spring flowers looked like they were ready to jump from the bright green blankets they stood on. It was as if they were slowly waving to get her attention.

"Francine, I bought some seeds over at the Five and Dime when your father and I were out earlier. I still can't believe the gumball machines they have at that place. Lord, there must be a lot of cavities in this town. No wonder they call Steven Mullen 'The Rich Kid.' His father probably had shares in those machines long before he became a dentist."

Francine clasped her hands together as they passed the biggest flowerbed Francine had ever seen. Thinking about her merit badge and all her new friends, she smiled with anticipation.

When they arrived, they got out and closed the car doors. Jane lifted her tinted Ray Bans, then stepped on her cigarette butt with her white flats.

The sky looked flawless.

"Thought they were calling for rain tonight. Then again, I only got half the weather report, as usual," Jane said as she flung her purse over her shoulder. "Betcha anything Grandpapa's crops could use some rain."

Smirking, Francine yanked the long dress away from her sweaty legs. Her mother held open the heavy wooden door into the church for Francine and pointed to the booth.

The church seemed unusually crowded, but it didn't matter to Francine; she always maintained that she never saw any kids she knew at church, except for Tommy Hall, and him only once.

Jane nodded toward the booth. "Now don't be in there all evening, you hear? But make sure you tell him everything. We got a lot of work to do tonight, missy. And mind your manners. Away you go."

Francine popped a red gumball into her mouth. She sat inside the hot and stuffy booth briefly before the small window slid open.

Francine wasted no time between chomps.

"Sorry, uh, Father. Uh, I have done something very bad. Uh, I didn't mean to spit all over Wendy's new bicycle seat, but Walter made me." She took another chomp. "And I used to hate Wendy, but now I don't hate her anymore. She's nice. Yeah, she's really nice, just like Abby used to be." Francine smacked her lips. "But when she comes over to play again, can you please ask God to make her stop bouncing on Abby's bed?"

"Child of God," the priest's familiar voice said. "I'm having a difficult time understanding you again this evening. Could you please speak clearer?"

"Mm-hmm," Francine responded.

Father David cleared his throat. "Full of grace, the Lord is with thee. Blessed are thee among women and blessed is the fruit of the womb of Jesus. Holy Mary, Mother of God, pray for us sinners now and at the hour of our death." Then he concluded: "For your penance, I am requesting three Hail Marys."

Francine left the booth and walked slowly to a pew. She knelt, folded her hands, and said three Hail Marys.

Waiting for her mother, she peered through the large stained-glass window facing onto the street. Shadows of vehicles streaked by.

Finally, Jane exited a small booth, went to a pew, and dropped to her knees. Francine heard a cry similar to that of a wounded animal. She felt the sound with her whole body.

Propping herself against the wall, Francine waited.

✽

"How did confession go tonight, Francine?"

"All right, I guess. But Mother was in there for a very long time."

"Yes, Francine, I can tell."

Francine made her way to the kitchen table. "When are you leaving, Daddy?"

"In the morning. I have a big job for the next few months." Randy motioned for Francine to sit on his knee and she plunked herself down. His heart ached, knowing what he was about to tell her. "Francine, you know Daddy has an important job, right? A lot of sheriffs count on me to help them find answers. Understand?"

"Well, sort of."

"Because we're busy right now, I probably won't be able to make it back home for a few weeks. Do you know what that means?"

She shrugged. "Yeah, Daddy. That means I have to get Mother's pills for her, and help with things." Francine frowned.

"Yes, I'm glad you understand, Francine. I'm counting on you."

"Okay, I'll try my best." Giving Randy a puzzled look, she pinched his arm. "Ouch!"

Francine smiled. "Daddy? What's a ragamuffin?"

Tickling her, they both squirmed and chuckled. "Why do you want to know what that is, Miss Francine?"

"Cause that's what Mommy... oops, I mean Mother calls me." Giggling, Francine jumped off his lap and skipped toward the door, not expecting an answer.

"Wait, Francine! Don't you want to know what it is? I'll make you a deal. I'll tell you what it means if you tell me where all this 'Mother' stuff is coming from."

Francine turned to Randy. "Big girls call their mommy Mother, not Mommy. That's what Mommy said."

Jane sauntered past, shaking a seed bag. "I heard that, missy! I think it's time you completed this project of yours tonight."

Randy laughed as Francine followed Jane onto the veranda.

"Okay, Francine, take these containers," Jane said, pointing to a small table nestled against the veranda railing. "Now, take two seeds and place them together in the separate containers. Then cover them with dirt. Got it? I'll be sitting over here if you need me."

Francine took the seeds and gingerly placed them in the holes, then covered them using the scoop.

"How's it going?" Jane asked as she sat on the old wooden chair in the corner of the veranda.

"Good, Mother, but I think I put too many seeds in this one," Francine said, pointing to the container.

Jane peeked over her book, exposing red swollen eyes. "Don't worry. I don't think wild flowers are too persnickety."

Filling the last hole, Francine slapped her hands together. "How long will they take to grow?"

"As long as they need. If they do well, you'll probably have that badge sooner than you think. Don't forget they need water."

"Oh, that's so cool, Mother!" Francine said with joy as she ran back into the house.

"Where you going now?"

"To get some water!"

Inside, she saw her father's clothes spread out on the kitchen table.

"Francine, I've been thinking," Randy said, walking in from the living room. "Maybe Mommy can take you sometime this week to visit with your sister and Aunt Julie. I think it would be awesome for you to see all the flowers in bloom over there at this time of year. Besides, it may give you a little more incentive for that flower project of yours. What do you think?"

"Sure, Daddy. If Mother wants to."

Francine smiled and placed the jug under the tap, then scurried back to the veranda, concentrating on not spilling anything. When she reached the top step, she suddenly stopped. Before her on the table were pieces of the pink umbrella, lined up in a row beside the plant containers.

"So when did this happen, young lady?" Jane snapped.

Francine shrugged. "Don't know, Mommy. Uh, I mean Mother."

"Well, you have one minute to explain."

Still holding the jug, Francine felt her body tighten up. She didn't say anything.

Jane picked up one of the broken pieces. "Well, did you explain this to Father David tonight?"

"No... uh, no, I forgot," Francine stuttered. She took a step backward, trying not to spill the jug.

Jane's eyes turned from red to piercing dark. She grabbed the broken umbrella and started swinging it as she walked towards Francine.

Francine spun around and bolted back into the house.

"You get back here right now, Missy!" Jane shrieked.

Francine burst into the kitchen and threw the water pitcher toward the sink. Missing the mark, it slammed into the cupboard. Streams of water shot across the floor, but she kept running.

"Daddy! Daddy! Help! Please!"

Wielding the broken umbrella, Jane caught up with her just as Randy voice came out of nowhere.

"What's going on in here? Francine, why are you crying?" he asked.

Jane glared at him. "We'll explain later. She doesn't need babying, Randy! She needs a real good lesson. And that's what she is going to get!" She grabbed Francine. "Get the trash bag. Now!"

Francine sobbed as she walked to the counter and reached for the bag. Jane grasped the back of her dress and marched her out to the veranda again.

"Open the bag, Francine."

Crying, she opened the bag.

"Throw the plant container in, now!"

"No, Mommy, please don't," Francine wailed.

"Now, Francine!"

Francine watched the last of the thick dirt, and her hard work, tumble into the bag.

"And now you can finish cleaning this mess." Jane stared at Francine. "There's the rest of the broken pieces, just where you left them. When you're done, meet me in the house."

With the remainder of the broken umbrella in hand, Jane stormed off.

Hoping she had retrieved all the pieces, Francine wiped tears from her eyes and threw the last piece into the bag.

She went back into the house, meeting Jane in the kitchen again.

Jane snatched the bag from Francine's hand and pointed to the puddles of water. "Let me assure you this will be your last stop before bed. Understand, young lady?"

"Yes, Mother."

Francine quivered as Jane tossed a cloth at her.

"Now." Jane stood firm.

"Hey, speaking of now, Jane, do we ever need to talk!" Randy shouted from behind her. He grabbed her arm, pulled her to their bedroom, and slammed the door shut. "Sit down, Jane, we're going to be a while."

Jane plunked herself on the bed.

"Damn it, Jane! For the love of God, do you not know what is wrong with this household? I hate to break the news, but you're what's wrong here!"

Jane sat with her head down.

"You want to know something else? Every dance you have with the devil, you manage to drag everyone around you into it. It's like a damn snowball! And then, when anyone tries to stop or help you, you twirl yourself further into the pit of hell. It's always the same old chapter with you! It's not bad enough we lost one daughter, but you're making damn sure we lose the only one we have left. And do you want to know what's even worse? You willingly keep your guard down." Randy clenched his hands. "So, what the hell is going on here? And here's something else, Jane! Are you ever going to start celebrating our daughter's life, or is this another Julie rerun? You know Abigail needs to see there's a candle still burning down here for her, not some black cloud that has swallowed up her entire existence on earth. Wake up, Jane!"

He walked over to the vanity.

"And what's up with the lipstick?" he shouted, snatching a handful of the tubes. He didn't let Jane get a word in. "You know you scare the hell out of our daughter, especially with the red ones. Get rid of them! For once, can you just practice what you preach? While we're on the topic, what's that phrase you always threaten our girls with? Oh, let me rephrase that, I mean our only daughter with."

The room was frozen in silence.

"You know your famous words about how God is always watching? How come you're the only one who's exempt from that God-fearing statement, anyway?" He took a breath and pointed a finger at her. "Well, here's a newsflash for you—get a new line."

Jane waited for him to finish. Her body felt like it had been thrown into a fire.

"Okay, let me tell you something, Randy. You're the one who got me pregnant—not once, but twice. And then you're never home!"

Before she could continue, Randy cut her off. "Excuse me? Let me refresh your memory about why I'm never home. I'm not here because there isn't a job in this redneck town that could pay me enough to support Jane Moonie's personal pharmacy. And while we're talking about all your stinkin' medication, when was the last time you took any? And don't tell me you *are* taking it, because if you are, then it needs to be changed. I'm serious, Jane!"

They paused for a second.

"Well, is that how you really feel?" she asked. "Let me tell you something else, Mr. Bigshot Randy Moonie. If you weren't so self-absorbed, you might be able to see that this hasn't been easy for me either. And by the way, what was really up with you and my sister?"

Randy's heart pounded at this final dig. His head felt like a bomb ready to blow.

"There you go again, Jane! I'll tell you something: Julie was always there for our girls. She had their backs when I couldn't be here. And from what I can see, that was one hell of a good thing. That's what was up with us!"

He stomped to the door, then turned back and threw his arms in the air. He felt like he had finally lost what he had been trying so desperately to save for years.

He stared at Jane and then dropped his head. "Jane, who is your God anyway?"

Randy walked to the door. Passing the trashcan, he slammed the lipstick tubes inside.

<hr />

Francine's room was dark as Randy tiptoed to her bed. He kissed her on the forehead and whispered, "Your mother's red lipstick is gone, Francine. It's going to be okay now. Good night, groovy girl. Daddy will see you in a couple of weeks."

Leaving the room, he looked back.

"Francine, you did say your prayers, didn't you?"

"I did."

"Good girl."

"Night, Daddy."

Chapter Seventeen

TWO BLUE PILLS, TWO YELLOW, Francine counted meticulously, laying them on the counter.

"No, I think Daddy said one blue pill and one yellow pill, and maybe two white pills," she said to herself. Scratching her head, she looked at the closed bedroom door. "What am I gonna do? Okay, I'll just take Mother some of every pill."

Francine shoved the small collection into her pocket and picked up the short bottle again. It was marked Valium. She shook six tablets from it and shoved them in a different pocket. Then, noticing the red cigarette package, she opened it and silently pulled out six cigarettes, tucking them alongside the six pills.

Tiptoeing into Jane's bedroom, there wasn't a stir. She removed the pills from her front pocket and placed them on Jane's nightstand. Quietly she placed the cigarette package beside them and started to make her way out of the room.

Just then, a groggy arose from the bed. "Francine, you'll just have to fend for yourself today."

Francine turned around, but before she could reply her mother closed her eyes again.

Darting to her bedroom, Francine pulled out the wooden box from under the bed. She emptied the rest of her pockets into it, next to the broken necklace, and closed the lid. She slid the box back under her bed. Slapping her hands together, she sprinted out of the room.

"Mother, do you like this color?" Francine asked, pulling the small brush from the bottle of nail polish.

"Yeah, it's all right. But make sure you put on enough so it shows up. Nothing worse than going through all that trouble of painting your nails and then no one notices."

Watching television with her mother seemed special to Francine, especially now that it was just the two of them.

"Stupid old television. By the time it warms up and gets working right, it'll be morning!" Jane ranted. "Your father says it's because of that old rusted antenna, but I say it's because it's an old junk box."

A grey smoke ring floated across the room.

"Oh, there it is! Finally!"

A hint of enthusiasm radiated from Jane's voice. Tucking her legs to the side, she tried to get comfortable. She watched her daughter slop the brush around and draw it across her nails.

"Francine, you have to put it on in long slow strokes, not circles."

"I'm trying, Mother."

"Now, what in the Lord's name are they parading on television?" Jane sighed in disgust, exhaling smoke. "Shady looking characters. All higher than kites. And sweating and gyrating on a family show! Honest to God! What in the good Lord's name is this world coming to?"

Francine wasn't sure what all the commotion was about. She wanted to peek at the television, but knew better.

"Well, one thing I know for sure, Missy. I'm not having any of that nonsense in my house!" Jane got out of the chair and pointed at Francine. "Girls like you have enough problems. Last thing you need is to see some kind of freak bouncing all over like a swaggering devil. Good Lord!"

Jane walked across the room and yanked the cord from the wall.

"This'll fix every problem we've ever had with the old junk box. Open the door, Francine! Then come back and grab an end," Jane shrieked.

After the television crashed to the ground, she wiped her forehead. Francine looked down at her smudged fingernails.

"Now don't you give any mind to any of this, you hear, Francine? With any luck we'll get one of those brand new ones sometime down the road. The trash men should be here in the morning."

"All right, class, this is the last Friday for room cleanup after school!" Mrs. Barry said loudly, over the bell. "Anyone needing any last-minute marks should seriously consider this opportunity!"

Francine knew she could use a higher mark, but still this wasn't the day to make the effort. She sprinted out of the classroom door. Quickly scouring the crowd of bobbing heads, she recognized Wendy's dark hair.

"Wendy, wait up!"

With her lunch pail swinging, Francine reached her.

Wendy grinned. "Francine, are you coming over to the hill with us?"

"Yeah. It was kinda fun last time."

"Okay, I'll race you there. And whoever loses has to kiss Walter Brown!"

They raced off. Francine knew there was no way she could ever win against Wendy, but she didn't want to have to kiss Walter Brown either. Flying through the schoolyard, Francine bolted awkwardly toward the hill.

"I win, Francine!" Wendy yelled back to her. She plunked down with the others. "Now you gotta kiss Walter."

Walter looked confused. "Francine has to kiss me?"

"Yep," said Wendy, laughing. Soon the rest of the kids joined in.

"Okay, Francine, here's the deal. Just forget about that stupid race," Walter said, rubbing his shirt. "I'll personally let you have the honor of kissing this hunk if you brought what you were supposed to." Walter patted his chest. "I'll make sure you never forget it, either!"

"Ew," Suzy yelled. "Glad I'm not the new kid!"

"Oh, shut up, Suzy! You already had your turn and you know you liked it!" Walter said, grinning.

"Hey, Francine, you'd be better off chewing off old Mrs. Wartler's wart!" Tommy said, laughing.

"You probably wouldn't get as sick!" Steven shouted.

Francine opened her red lunch pail and took out two small bags.

Walter snatched them away. "Give me those! I'm the pack leader here! What I say goes."

Lifting out the cigarettes, he took one for himself and then passed the rest around, one by one. Then he reached into the other package and pulled out a handful of white pills.

"Now, now. What do we have here, little Miss Moonie?" he asked sarcastically. "Could these be Mommy's happy pills?"

Nodding, Francine saw everyone eyeing the pills while lighting their cigarettes.

"Who wants the first candy?" Tommy asked.

Walter waved the bag of pills in the air.

Francine took a drag from the cigarette, aware of all the eyes on her. She shook her head, trying to catch her breath. She gasped and started to cough uncontrollably. Her head spun. Trying to make it to her feet, she knew it was too late. Just missing a pair of black running shoes, she heaved.

Everyone laughed.

"Yeah, Francine, you'll get used to it," Suzy said. "We did!"

Walter held a pill in his hand. "Well, seeing as Francine was the one to bring us these little candies, I think she should be the first to try one. What does everybody else think?"

"Yeah, Walter's right," remarked Steven. "We better see what they do to her first!"

"I don't know if that's such a good idea," Wendy piped up. "Francine is the youngest one here. And what if she can't ride her bike home? What then?"

"Well, guess that means the leader of our pack can take her home, right?" Tommy chuckled. "After all, he wants to be the boss, so he should act like one. Right, guys?"

"Yeah, that sounds cool," Suzy interjected.

"Okay," Walter agreed, holding out his hand to Francine. "Deal. You take the first one, and if I have to, I'll take you home. You know it's a good deal, Francine. After all, you haven't had to kiss me yet!" He laughed.

Francine knew there was no turning back. She took the pill and shoved it in her mouth.

"Yay, Francine! Way to go!" Tommy shouted. "Hey, anybody want to have a game of hide and seek?"

The others quickly agreed.

"You guys know the rules," Walter said. "Me and Wendy will count. Start hiding."

Everyone jumped to their feet and scattered.

"Eighteen, nineteen, twenty! Ready or not, here we come!"

Running from the lake, Walter charged out of nowhere. Tommy tried to catch him, but Walter was several steps ahead.

"I'm home free, you bunch of losers!" Walter shouted.

Wendy was right behind Suzy as they raced toward home base. Suzy knew she couldn't win against Wendy. Steven came from another direction, panting, with Tommy only a few feet behind him.

"Okay, looks like Suzy and Tommy are the seekers this time," Wendy yelled. "Hey guys, where's Francine?"

Tommy shrugged. "Don't know, haven't seen her."

"I haven't seen her either," Suzy said.

"Well, duh, guys, maybe she's still hiding," Walter surmised.

Wendy nodded. "Okay, I think we should all go look for her right now."

Just as Wendy was exhorting everyone to start a search, a pair of red pedal pushers appeared from behind a bush.

"Here she comes!" Wendy ran down the hill to meet Francine. "Francine, are you okay?"

"This game is so cool," Francine slurred, staggering toward them. "You know I love all you guys." She stretched out her arms. "And I love everybody in the whole wide world. I don't ever wanna go home."

Looking around for Walter, Wendy spotted his big hair. He was already trying to make his escape. "Walter Brown! You get back here right now!"

He strolled back, took a look at Francine, and started chuckling. "Everything cool, Francine?"

"Yep, everything is so cool." She giggled. "Do you know I love you? What's your name again? Oh yeah, it's... uh, uh... Walter. Walter Brown."

Walter raised his eyebrows while the others started laughing. Walter and Wendy pulled Francine up the hill.

"Now what are you going to do, Smarty Pants Walter?" Wendy asked. "She can't go home by herself."

"I guess I'll just have to double-ride her home, now won't I?" Walter replied.

Francine tried to balance herself between the mustang handlebars of Walter's bike.

"You know, Walter, you are the coolest," Francine slurred.

"Just hang on, Francine! It's gonna be a bumpy ride."

He swerved, trying to see around her, and then pedaled harder. Gravel pinged from the spokes as they made their way down the dusty road.

"Hold on, and keep your legs up! We're takin' a shortcut!"

Walter turned into the tall grass. The narrow path was hard to see.

"Whee!" Francine shrieked.

Clenching the sides of the handlebars, she swayed back and forth as the grass slapped her face. Soon the bumps became too much for Walter. Struggling to keep the bike moving, he tried to make a hard right turn and veered off the overgrown path. Francine flew from the handlebars as the bike tumbled onto its side.

"You all right?" Walter asked.

Crawling out from under his bike, he saw a patch of rustling grass where Francine lay. She was giggling. He looked down at her red pant legs.

"Oh, wow! I think I found a little pig here," he teased. "Hey Francine, did you really mean it when you said you loved me?" Francine laughed louder. "You know, this would be a cool time to make up for that kiss you owe me."

Francine's laughter grew louder. "You're funny, Walter, but I am not kissing you, ever. Ew."

"Well, I think you are if you want me to take you all the way home."

Francine tried to get up, but Walter shoved her back to the ground.

"So, what are you gonna do, Francine? Go tell Mommy you stole her pills and that's why you wanted to kiss me?"

She tried to get up again, but Walter grabbed for her arm and pinned her down again. She yelled as Walter put his hand over her mouth. Francine bit down hard.

"If you're trying to make me mad, it's working! Quit it! All I wanted was one stupid kiss, but now I think you're gonna be very sorry."

Walter reached for her shirt.

Francine screamed. "Stop it, Walter! Stop it! You're squishing me!"

Trying to get out from under him, she was scared. Walter continued to grapple with her shirt.

"No, Walter! Stop, and I mean it. Now!"

Walter cried out as something slammed into his back.

"Walter Brown! I'm gonna really hurt you if you don't get off her right now!" came Wendy's voice.

Wendy kicked him again and yanked hard at his dome of curly hair.

"Let her up now or I will kill you, Walter! I swear I'll kill you!"

Walter got up quickly and raced to his bike.

"You wanna know something?" Wendy yelled. "If my granny was here, she'd give you a pop-knot right between them evil eyes of yours, Walter Brown!"

Francine sobbed as she got up.

"Are you okay?" Wendy asked, putting her arm around her.

"Yeah, I think."

"It was a good thing you forgot this," Wendy said, handing Francine her lunch pail. Looking at her ripped shirt, Wendy surveyed the rest of her clothes. "Looks like you're okay. I'll walk you the rest of the way home."

Wendy grabbed her bike. Making their way slowly off the narrow path, they saw Walter disappear down the gravel road.

At the top of her lungs, Francine let him have it: "You're the pig, Walter Brown! Can you hear me? You're the pig!"

Interlude

"Now, can I hear an amen?" Pastor Matthew shifted his eyes around the room.

"Amen." The voices spoke in sync, as though it had been rehearsed.

"Pay attention, people. Here we have a child of the Most High whose heart has been bombarded with resentment and bitterness. You know, I don't want that for her. I'm sure you don't want that for her, and I'm certain God does not want that for her either."

He placed his hand on his Bible.

"We know the good book tells us in Exodus 20:12 to honor your mother and father. But we also know the dirty devil has been trying to mess with this child for a long time. He's been trying to slither into any small space he can find. He sees her foundation is crumbling. When I stand here and assess the probable outcome, it doesn't appear to add up to anything good from a worldly perspective. Anyone know what I'm talking about?"

"Yep, bitterness and anger won't just keep you from flying," an old man blurted. "It'll poison you too! That's Satan. He's downright evil, demonic, and a liar. There isn't nothing good about him. And here's something else..." He stood slowly to his feet, leaning into his cane and pointing his crooked finger around the room. "Darn it to heck. I was a work in progress for lots of years. I was young once too, like most of you folks. I had lots of chances to change my ways. But instead, every time I met a fork in the road I decided to go with Satan and dance off into the black horizon with him. Yeah, he is sneaky, and he loved to keep me waltzing all the way down the road to hell." The old man smiled. "Right now, I'm sure he'd love me to dance with him again, but as you can see, I can barely walk."

The crowd laughed.

"Yeah, it took me a long time to get it through my thick skull that it was only about Satan. Satan didn't give a darn about me. No, sir. I thought I had the world by the tail, could do everything on my own. Heck, I didn't need God. If someone peeved me off, I was smarter and would find a way to make them angrier than they'd made me. I always assumed the other person was the sin. I didn't see any difference between the sin and sinner because the enemy kept me blinded. I played right into the devil's hands." He lowered his head. "But what I've also learned is that the good book tells us to love our enemy and the sinner. You see, the sinner is still God's child, but the sin comes from Satan. Why, back in those days the devil had me spiraling downwards quickly. And I didn't even know it. That's how deceitful he is! Yep, he was my partner in crime, sitting right there beside me in that passenger seat, grinning from ear to ear. Yeah, it took lots of years of running my life into the big old ditch to realize I should have never been there in the first place. Folks, believe it when you hear that for every mile of road, there's two miles of ditch. Satan is full of trickery. Yes, sir, there I was, this big macho man with a head as hard as nails and my life was a heck of a mess. But to me that was normal."

He wiped a tear from his worn face as the crowd listened to his story.

"All I can say is, listen up, you young folks. God first speaks to you in whispers, but if he doesn't get your attention, sooner or later he'll wallop ya on your noggin'. Hopefully it's sooner. Take it from me. Our time here is a valuable gift. Don't waste it! An' keep building your foundation on his word with your youngins. You'll see, the rest will fall into place, right where the good Lord intends it be. He is a very trusting and forgiving God. And he'll meet you right where you're at! You can't ever lose with the big guy." His eyes filled with tears as he lifted his cane. "Now that's all I am fixin' to say. The road ahead of each one of you is too dang long and good to be spending time in the ditch with the devil an' a big ole pitchfork."

The old man dropped his head. Wobbling on his feet, he sat down. The congregation stood and clapped.

"Thank you for that, and yes! Amen!" Pastor Matthew shouted. "Okay, let's see what's going on with Miss Francine."

Halleluiahs echoed around the room.

Chapter Eighteen

Francine watched her mother's medication pile up on the nightstand. Counting her pills was an endless job, and Jane rarely even came out of her room anymore. Francine's father didn't come home much anymore either, although Father David and Jenny checked in on Jane regularly. Grandma and Grandpapa Harring were too old to attend, though, and had finally given up a few years back.

Francine knew her mother needed her medication, but most days she also suspected her mother wouldn't even notice if she left. If that wasn't bad enough, Francine realized she had just painted her own lips red.

"Oh man, this used to be Mother's crazy color," she said out loud. Looking in the mirror, she knew she didn't need a reminder of how things had gotten to this point. She scrubbed the red from her lips.

The phone rang, startling her.

"Yep, it's me. I can hardly wait! Got the bus schedule right here," she said, answering the call. It was Wendy. "Are you sure you still want me to come? Yeah, I know California is a long way. But it's going to be so worth it!" Francine snickered. "Looks like it's going to take a couple of days. I'll call when I get to Santa Montrose. I can't wait to see you, Wendy! Okay, bye."

Francine grabbed the red lipstick tube and tossed it in the trash. Glancing at her reflection again, she felt every childhood recollection impede her. The more she tried to elude the memories, the more they tried to make themselves known. Looking into her familiar washed-out eyes, Francine knew the memories weren't about to leave. She only hoped she could finally run from herself, but at this moment in time there was no place to run. She froze. The eyes staring back held her captive.

Francine's thoughts flooded. Face to face with the tainted image, desperate, she tried to sift her way through a tangled web of memories. A flicker of her sister's smile and an empty pew flashed by. Her body quivered. She clenched her hands.

The memories were still unstoppable. Her heart pounded at the recollection of past voices. One by one they invaded her mind, eagerly latching onto each other.

She closed her eyes, longing for some sort of peace. Trying to focus with each breath, little by little her thoughts slowed.

Carefully, she opened her eyes again to her reflection. A glimmer of relief overtook her.

She examined the remainder of the lipstick tubes. Reaching into the trash, she pulled out the red one.

"What the hell. I'll try anything once. This one's for you, Mother."

Francine sighed, opened her mouth wide, and slid the red tube softly across her lips. Then she smacked them together.

"How do you like me now, Jane?" she whispered into the mirror as she analyzed her reflection. Then she scooped up the rest of her makeup and made her way to the door.

In the background she heard her mother yell, "Francine, I need my pills!"

Francine never even turned around.

"Oh, believe me, Mother... or is it Mary Lou? Whatever. I would never have followed you here if Granny hadn't died." Wendy grabbed her sweater. "As far back as I can remember, you've always said, 'Yep, this man's the one for sure.' Right. Just how many guys have you tried to lure in since the first time you said that? Ten, fifty, a hundred? How many, Mother?" She kept on ranting without taking a breath. "You know what the problem is with you? They're all just too damn smart for you!"

"I was only doing it for you, Wendy." Mary Lou sobbed, wiping her eyes. "My whole life has been for you!"

"Oh please, Mother! Spare me! Every guy you've been with leaves you worse off than the last one. You know it and I know it. You're so high and dry, I can't believe you haven't cracked right down the middle by now! Really!" Reaching for the door, Wendy turned back. "And here's something else before I split. At least I'm making something of my life. And I'm capable of keeping one good friend!"

Wendy was on a roll and wasn't ready to stop.

"I know you never liked Francine, but the truth is she's probably the sweetest, most honest girl anybody could call a friend. And don't worry, Mother, she would never steal any of your slime-ball boyfriends, if that's what your problem is with her. She wouldn't lower herself!" She caught her breath before delivering one final slam. "Oh, and just in case you're wondering, Mother, for the record, yes, I am in love with Max. Yeah, Max, my pimp! But you wouldn't know what real love was if it slapped you in the face!"

Wendy stomped out, slamming the door.

"So what exactly do you want from this job, Miss Moonie?" Max asked, his eyes fixed on Francine's tight Calvin Kleins.

"Uh, just a new purpose in life I suppose," Francine answered, repositioning herself on the sofa.

"Woowee! Looks like Wendy's little friend is on fire. Now, guess I got me a fine long-stemmed daisy here, 'bout to enter into a wild pasture." Max ran his hand slowly through her hair. "Did your friend Wendy mention the rules here?"

"Rules?"

"There's no shortchanging me. You got to work the hours, with regular disease testing and minimal drugs. And if some psycho makes you feel unsafe, you get the hell out. Now I didn't say uncomfortable, I said unsafe. There's a difference, understand?"

Francine nodded. Getting closer, she could see why Wendy was head over heels for him. She looked for something wrong, anything, but the more she studied his face the more she saw something right.

His warm breath swept across her face.

"You know, most daddies like to find out what they're investing in, but I think you and I are gonna have a different kind of understanding here. Whew, look at you, girl. It's easy to tell I need to win your heart first. Mmhmm. But don't get me wrong, I'm still your boss. So let the chips fall where they will, beautiful. You'll come to love and respect me in no time. It's gonna be so ridiculously easy. Cool with you, Miss... uh, Miss...?"

"Uh, it's Miss Frankie. Yeah, that's the working name I've picked. Is that okay?" She lowered her head, timidly.

"Can't say I ever had a Frankie before." Gazing into her eyes, he whispered, "I think Ching-Ching would be more suitable, don't you?" He twirled her hair around his finger. "Yep, one of a kind. That's my girl, Frankie. You know, Daddy likes money."

Max threw his head back on the sofa and let out a gentle roar. Feeling more at ease, Frankie started to laugh too, contributing a huge snort.

Startled, Max jumped forward, still laughing. "What the hell was that, Miss Frankie?"

He kept laughing as he tried to get the words out. Frankie shrugged, grinning as he wrapped his arm around her and took her face in his hand.

"You know, baby doll, with a laugh like that, you're either gonna make me or break me!" He kissed her forehead, got up, and walked toward the door. Slowly he turned. "Yeah, Wendy's got her work cut out with you. Think this is gonna work out mighty fine."

"Okay, Francine, you do it like this." Wendy grabbed the red steel pole and began to shimmy her way to the top. During the ascent, her plastic fishnet stockings looked like silk, and her snowball tanktop made her moves even more mesmerizing. Wendy's thick, sculpted legs were flawless. As her dark hair floated in the cool air, she clutched the pole and began to slide back down, arching her back gracefully until she reached the floor. "It's that simple, Francine. Now let's see what you're made of."

Both girls laughed.

"I can't do that, Wendy!"

"Well, Francine, I hate to break it," Wendy said, lighting a cigarette, "but you have to get on this pole and make it happen. At least you have a chance to broaden your horizons. Look, here's the bottom line: the more versatile you are, the better you'll live, and the more you'll have to fall back on. Besides, it will keep you in shape." Wendy glanced at the pole. "Or, if you want, you can forget about what I'm trying to tell you and you can just crawl through life working the grungy beat, hustling in seedy alleys and worn street corners. And oh, did I mention, loneliness is a freebee that comes with any grimy street job? Then, for all the long, scuzzy tricks, you'll turn most of your money over to some creepy pimp who'll never give a crap about you in the first place. With most pimps, you'll only be their meal ticket. You're only trash to them. Max is an exception.

Understand what I'm saying? Francine, believe me, you never want to be just a survival prostitute."

Francine scrunched her mouth and nodded.

Wendy took a breath and continued. "Respect Max, but don't get too close to him either. There isn't a girl here that wouldn't give their eyeteeth to shack up with him. Just do your job. He'll make you feel special, but all that's required of you is to do your job."

Francine paused. "Not sure I understand."

Wendy took a long drag and exhaled slowly. "What I mean, Francine, is although Max and I go back in time, I finally earned the responsibility of bottom girl. Don't let the title fool you, though. In any other profession, I would be called the top dog. Yeah, someday when we decide to fold our jobs I think there's a damn good chance Max and me will tie the knot. I'm sure you got that impression when you met him, huh?" She blew the swirl of smoke from her mouth, not waiting for a response. "Remember, when it comes to daddies you lucked out with your first one. You got the cream of the crop. Max is only doing me this favor. Realistically, he won't be your pimp forever. Sure, girls respect him and like working for him, but the competition is heavy. Younger and prettier girls show up here all the time. You may be younger than most, but you're still older than some. And remember, when you're in the game with Max you'll never be above him. It's always his game. He runs the show, understand?"

Wendy flicked her cigarette.

"He commands respect, seldom demands it. That's why his girls want to be the best they can be. You know, there are a lot of pimps out there beating their girls to a pulp. You don't do what they say, cheat them on their coin, or get just plain lazy, you got a lot of trouble coming your way. It can be a real hellhole out there, but with Max it's different. If you do what you're told and let him make all your decisions, you'll never want for anything. His girls become family. Food, a roof over your head, clothes, drugs, whatever you want, you'll get it, Francine. All that should make you never want to mess up. The truth is it can be good and scary at the same time. Get my drift?"

Acknowledging her, Francine nodded.

"Yeah, with Max it'll be your own damn fault if things start messing up," Wendy said. "So it's totally up to you."

Francine stared at the pole, studying it inch by inch. "Okay. I guess I'll give it a try."

"Hell, it's about time." Wendy sighed as she made her way back to the pole. "You know, I was in the same boat as you. The stage is yours."

Francine wrapped her hand around the cool pole as Wendy kept talking.

"One of the reasons Max got this pad in the first place was for this huge reinforcement pole." Wendy snickered. "Hey, what the hell, when you get busy, you'll start to appreciate this ugly pole. It's even good for your brain. You're gonna learn to love it, Francine. I did!" She eyed Francine's Calvin Kleins. "Not sure how those jeans are going to slide, but I guess we're about to find out."

Assessing the objective, Francine thought she could wrap her long arms around the pole at least twice. She tightened her lanky legs around the polished cylinder and started to claw her way to the top. Exhausted, she put one hand over the other.

"You're doing great, Francine!" Wendy directed from below. "Keep going! Steady. Easy does it!"

Francine's arms were shaking.

"Awesome, Francine! Now nestle into the pole! Push your boobs into the pole! Push your shoulders back! Don't let go! Get those legs up closer to your hands! Keep arching, Francine! Come on! Okay, breathe in! Now come down slowly... slowly, Francine! Keep your grip, but slide your hands at the same time!"

Francine could feel her palms burning. Her arms were weak, her legs numb. Trying to maintain her grasp, her grip began to loosen. She grasped the pole tighter as her chin hit the steel. Pulling her legs upward, she was now turned around. With her legs above her, she tried to regain some poise. With tangled arms it was too late. She was coming down fast—face first.

Wendy reached out, trying to save her from total disaster, but it was too late. She hit the floor with a plunk, her legs folding clumsily behind her.

"I guess that's the end of my work-out career," Francine said. "Ouch."

"Not if I can help it! This is only the beginning."

Both girls rolled onto the floor, laughing hysterically.

"You may have a long way to go," Wendy said, "but look at the bright side. You can't go any lower."

"Yep. Gives a whole new meaning to hitting rock bottom, I suppose," Francine said, looking at the pole.

"Hey, if you keep this up, you may be riding buses for a very long time."

Francine twirled her chain. "Can't believe I still have this old butterfly. She and I have been through some weird things together."

"Well, if you want to know the truth, I can't believe you still wear that piece of junk!" Wendy laughed.

Francine sighed as she stroked the butterfly. "Yeah, I know."

"So... what do you really want out of life here?" Wendy asked, staring at the cratered ceiling tiles as Francine lay beside her.

"Never really thought about it much." She paused. "Guess I don't need any reminders of that black hole of Shelbytown, that's for sure. I secretly wished every day would be the day my old lady finally came to her senses. Didn't matter how many times I stood in that stinking hot booth confessing all my crap to a strange voice, practically nothing ever changed. As far as I can tell, God is not a nice God, and that's if there even is one. Who knows? Maybe there is and I just made him mad from the get-go. Still, as far as I can tell, I was brought into this world by the strangest mother ever. But now it's time to finally get a move on. Yeah, that's why I'm here. Hey, do you believe in God?"

"Naw, not really, but my Granny did. Still, I never thought this would be my life either. But I gotta say, if need be I can still outrun any girl on the strip. Hell, I could give any psychopath a run for his money. I'd be the one hunting him down!" Wendy sighed. "I guess built-up frustration has to go somewhere. Yep, right here to amazing Santa Montrose. It's a good thing I got some of Granny's blood in me. She sure had a lot of love for being so damn stubborn."

"Nope, you never were a pushover, Wendy," Francine said. "That's what I've always liked about you."

"Keep hanging out with me, Miss Frankie, and I'll show you what you've always had inside you, though you never knew it!" Wendy gave Francine a nudge. "By the way, I like your street name. I think you and me, or should I say Frankie and Lollie, are gonna be just fine."

Wendy laughed, getting up from the floor.

"Hey Francine, someday that is going to be Mrs. Maxwell Cardosa to you."

"Okay, this is our dime millionaire rack," Wendy said, standing in front of a long line of clothes and shoes. "It's pretty much self-explanatory. Feel free to use anything in this room. But after you've worn it, it gets put back on that rack. When you start making money, you'll want to buy a lot of your own things."

Francine felt overwhelmed. "Wow. But will this stuff fit us taller girls?"

"This place is like a trashy Fifth Avenue store. Don't worry, Francine. Max wants to make money too. He'll do you right, so chill out."

They walked towards a huge shelf. Wendy pulled out a curly red wig and pair of thigh-high boots. Turning, she walked back to the rack and picked out a lace dress.

Looking at the arm full of clothes Wendy had chosen for her, Francine was in awe.

"Uh, do you always help us girls like this?" she asked as Wendy started handing her clothes.

"Only when you're new to the stable. That's what I get paid for. Besides, when you get to know Max, you'll understand." Wendy picked up a cropped cashmere jacket and lifted it. "Oh, cashmere has always been my favorite! These clothes are only suggestions. If you don't like it, feel free to switch up. Jewelry is over there."

Wendy pointed to a white vanity on the opposite wall.

"Thanks," Francine said. "Hopefully I'll get the hang of it sooner rather than later."

"By the way, there are a couple of guidelines for new girls here, though none of them are carved in stone. Depends on how much money you want to make, I suppose, and if you want to keep Max happy. The first is a no-brainer: if it bags, sags, or if you think it makes you look like Mary Poppins, don't even think about wearing it. And if you think it's too tight, it isn't. The second one is: you're responsible for your own makeup and personal hygiene." Wendy flung the clothes at her. "You can figure out the rest. Good luck. You'll get to know what most of your customers like anyway by how many tips you get. Trust me. You'll do good."

Wendy started to leave the room, then turned back.

"Hey, almost forgot. A good rule of thumb is that there's never any point in being poor and looking poor. And any lines, highs, or whatever you need before work comes right off the top of your pay. I'm sure Daddy explained, right? No special treatment."

Francine looked down at the fire-engine red smothering her arms. "Sure, I'm cool with everything."

"Great," Wendy replied, disappearing down the hallway.

Chapter Nineteen

Francine clicked her way to the lounge in the eerie quiet. Trying not to twist an ankle, she took long slow strides through the entrance.

"Wow," came a calm voice from the corner. "Ching-ching. Daddy's got one sweet looker. Mm-hmm."

Every step she took towards Max made her more nervous. The harder she tried to steady her feet, the more difficult it became. Trying to take confident strides, she felt her ankle bend and nearly lost her balance.

Max raced forward and grabbed her arm. "Easy does it, Frankie baby. You're gonna do just fine."

Francine felt relieved when she reached the sofa.

"Hey," Max whispered, putting his arm around her shoulder, scanning her up and down. "You know, a lot of girls have come through this door, but I gotta tell you, there is something real special about you." He brushed his lips across her cheek.

Francine felt a little awkward and a little safe at the same time. His deep green eyes were like soft daggers. His dark hair spiraled onto his shoulders, effortlessly complementing his eyes.

"You know, baby, Daddy is expecting big things from you. Remember, the street is your stage. Bottom line is this: anything you don't feel safe doing, don't do it. Got it?" He brushed her red curls back. Francine took a breath as she struggled to hear each word. Max pointed to the back of the room. "Whatever you need to start the night, it's all back there. But remember, Frankie, the candy store ain't free. Everyone pays their way. I don't need to partake in fake highs. My girls are my highs." Max grinned. "I'm gonna tell you straight up, baby doll, what I tell the rest of my girls. A little of that monkey junk goes a long way. Too much of a good thing, that's when problems happen. And when problems start, it costs Daddy money, understand?"

Max slid his hands gently to her waist.

"Yeah, I understand, Daddy."

Francine made her way to the back of the room and saw a small mounted cabinet with a long table sprawled under it. A disarray of paraphernalia had been spread over the table. Trying to focus, she stood silently.

"Need some help, Frankie?"

Francine turned and saw Wendy walking towards her, a curvy mirage of black and gold. Francine was struck by her beauty.

"Think you may just want to start small, Frankie," Wendy whispered. "And if you can't find it on the table, backups are stored in the happy cabinet up there." She reached across the assortment of small containers, her gold bangles clanking. "Here, this one is a good starter. We've named it Snow White."

"Okay, that one's cool," Francine said as Wendy handed her a small pill.

"Listen, Frankie, there's nothing to worry about." Wendy looked back at Max. "It's time to let go of the nerves, hear me? We've got you covered tonight. Max is letting me do you a favor. It doesn't happen often. So because it's your first night, and unfortunately a full moon, I'll be on the strip with you. Other girls will be wanting to steal your territory, so I'm gonna help you out with that too. But only for tonight. Got it?"

Francine nodded.

"Besides, Max can't be everywhere at once. He's got a lot to girls to turn out. For tonight, consider yourself lucky. Real lucky."

Feeling a sense of relief, Francine smiled. She swallowed the pill.

"Okay, let's blow this stand," Wendy said. "Bills won't get paid standing here, and neither will Max."

She felt a squeeze from behind.

"Now, go bring Daddy home the payday, Frankie," Max said.

Strutting toward the door, Wendy looked back at Max, giving him a nod. "Everything good?"

"Yep, everything is cool, Lollie. Everything is so cool."

※

"Got it, Francine?" Wendy asked, as they made their way to the boulevard.

"Think so."

"Now get yourself together. You got to do this first night up right, understand?"

"Sure, it's cool. You know something, Wendy, I think your street name really rocks. I wish I had thought of Lollie." She giggled. "Yeah, I just know we're gonna be a good team. Hey, maybe one day we can turn our lives into a book or something. We could call it *When Lollie and Frankie Do Downtown*. Sounds like a total page-turner, don't you think?"

Wendy flicked her cigarette ashes into the night air. "Sure, but let's not get carried away. One night at a time is gonna be about all you can handle for now. Believe me." She tried to stay confident as she glanced at Francine. "Max and I have told you a lot, but there are a couple more things you need to know. Are you listening?" She blew a smoke ring at the sky.

"Sure, fire away."

"Sometimes the other girls will want to shove you off the strip. It's a big problem between pimps. And since there's been lot of crap going down on the other end, a lot of girls just don't want to work there anymore. So they're coming this way. I know what you're made of, Francine, so I know you ain't gonna make that your problem, right?"

"Nope, don't worry about me."

"Oh, and when a potential customer pulls over, he ain't asking for the time. He's asking how much for your time. Got it?"

"Cool. Got it." Francine giggled. "That's what I've always liked about you, Wendy. Oops, I mean Miss Lollie Paulie Pops. You're always right to the point!"

Glancing at her, Wendy wondered if Francine was ready for her debut. "Okay, good luck." She pointed up the boulevard. "I'll be hanging around by the old Playhouse Disco if you need me. Oh, and make sure you get dropped off back here. Right, Francine? And make sure you use your working name too."

Francine nodded, noticing a car circling slowly nearby.

"Looky here," Wendy said excitedly. "I think you may have your first customer! Good luck."

A dark-colored Toronado edged its way toward Francine. Approaching, she knew she was ready to take on whatever the night brought.

A few minutes later, she closed the door behind her. The car's taillights soon faded into the distance.

At the sound of footsteps, Wendy turned and recognized Francine's tall frame making her way across the street.

"Hey, Francine, I didn't think it could be you this soon," she shouted while looking at her watch. "You're supposed to be making Max money!"

"Oh, I got paid all right!" She laughed, boots in hand as she neared Wendy.

"What's wrong with you?" Wendy asked. "And why are you barefoot? He didn't feed you any more monkey junk, did he?"

Francine tried to speak through her laughter.

"What is it, Francine?"

The more she tried to stop laughing, the more her words broke up. "Good tip. Really, really good tip."

Waiting for an explanation, Wendy remained silent.

"Well, after I saw he was sporting more frills than Mr. Frederick of Hollywood…" Francine started to laugh again. "Okay, I'll put it this way: it was the most relaxing fifteen minutes of foot massaging I've ever had!" She snorted. "The dude loved my toes! No one's ever liked my toes."

"You better have enjoyed it, because chances are no one will ever do that again!" Wendy looked to the sky. "Least not 'til the next full moon."

Francine was in hysterics. "Just the tip was worth it. Wow!" She pulled the crinkled bills from her laced top and waved the money through the night air. "Yep, Miss Frankie here is going to be hitting the bigtime very soon."

Wendy stared up at the florescent moon. "That's why I'm here tonight, Francine, that's why I'm here. Think it's going to be a crazy night."

Just then, they heard the roar of an engine behind them. A pickup truck pulled over and Francine jumped in.

✿

The darkness had a soothing but eerie calmness. The moon began to fade and a light breeze swirled through the truck's half-open window.

Returning to the strip after another trick, Francine shut the door behind her. It didn't take long for the truck to disappear.

She spotted an empty bench across the road and walked toward it. It felt welcoming to unzip her snug boots, kick them off, and sit. She flung her head back and slowly counted the dimly lit stars.

Francine tried to remember the last time she had even noticed a star, or thought about her sister. Scanning the sky, she wondered if Abby was looking down at her. Exhausted, she felt a tear trickle wetly down her cheek. She didn't have to guess what Abby would have thought about her new career. She knew. She took a deep breath and closed her eyes.

"Francine!"

Her eyes jolted open and saw Wendy's shimmering black-and-gold figure getting closer.

"Come on, Francine. You done good for your first night."

Getting up slowly, Francine reached into her bag and pulled out a wrapper. She shoved the gum into her mouth as Wendy reached for her hand and gently squeezed it.

"Max is gonna be happy with you, girl. Now let's go home."

Francine rolled over and glanced at the clock. Hearing distant footsteps in the hall, she knew she had overslept.

"Afternoon, Francine!" The cheery voice rang through her room. It came from an unfamiliar face: a petite blonde, scantily dressed. A ray of light spotlighted her figure in the door, revealing perfect teeth. "Max asked me to get the rest of you girls up. There's going to be a meeting in the common room in one hour flat. He needs us all there."

It was no secret that Francine had slept well.

The blonde studied her tangled hair, then added, "Even if you don't get your crap together in an hour, doesn't matter. Come anyway. Max wants us all there, pronto."

"Sure. I'll be there," Francine said, yawning.

Looking around, Francine didn't recognize all the faces. Either she had never seen these girls before or they just looked different out of their working clothes. Most seemed comfortable showing off their almost naked bodies. She felt awkward in the midst of such confidence and poise.

"Coffee's fresh. It's over there." The slender blonde pointed to a small counter and sauntered past Francine in a pair of bikini underwear.

Francine took a breath, feeling overdressed in her long cotton skirt.

"Hey," said a voice from behind her. "Had a good night I hear."

Francine turned to look at the dark, curvy newcomer. "Yeah, guess you could call it that."

"Well, don't let that first night fool you. Maxine, is it?"

"Actually, it's Francine." She tried to ignore the girl, but she sidled up shoulder to shoulder with her.

"I don't know if anyone told you, but you'll eventually realize that, out on these streets, you're no more important than the rest of us. And we all have our own regulars. Oh yeah, as for Max, he has his favorites too. But we earn that. Got it, Francine?"

Francine turned toward her, noticing the girl's stunning eyes.

"Uh, I got it," Francine said as she watched the girl mosey away. Her steps were light.

"Okay, ladies," Max bellowed from across the room. "Time to start!"

Francine grabbed her coffee and made her way to the couch, still feeling uncomfortable by everyone's state of undress. There were so many different-shaped bodies congregated before her, including a long-haired redhead with a black eye and swollen lip who sat by herself.

Wendy, dressed in a short satin robe, sat beside Max.

"Grab a seat, everyone!" Max said. "It's time for me to talk and you to listen! So here's what's going down. We have some crazy dudes out there thinking they own my property. Get my drift? They even think they can slap Max Cardosa's ladies around like ragdolls. But that's not how it's gonna work here. No one slaps my women around, not even me." He patted his chest and looked at the redhead. "Not gonna stand for it, got it? No one lays a finger on any of you."

On a tangent, he swung his hand in midair, pointing to different girls.

"Not on you, not on you, and not on you!" He stopped at Francine and stared at her. The room fell silent. "And definitely not you. Okay ladies, we got some serious business to take care of today. You all know by now that I don't take kindly to violence against women, especially my beautiful women. So I'm offering each of you protection. It will be your decision to accept it or not, and that shouldn't be hard to decide." He walked confidently to the dark curvy girl, stroked her hair and placed his finger on her chin. "My money is my money and I haven't budgeted for medical bills, or body bags, so it's up to you. I don't know if it's one lone sick douche ranger, or a pack of wolves working for other pimps. Doesn't matter. Talk has it someone wants you girls off the street. However it's rollin', it's lookin' like a total whack job. The long and skinny is this has potential for a real bad outcome, if it's not nipped. I don't need anyone hurt."

Max locked eyes with Francine. Trying to dodge his stare, she turned at Wendy—but Wendy's eyes were fixed on Max.

Francine lowered her head. She could hear Max's footsteps getting closer, then saw his suede shoes in front of her.

"Hey, baby doll, I'm talking to you," Max said in a low tone.

Francine looked up. A feeling of guilt brushed over her as his deep emerald eyes danced up and down her body. Mesmerized, she couldn't think, let alone move. He placed his hand under her cheek and caressed it.

"This means you, beautiful. Do I have your undivided attention now?"

Francine felt her face flush. Shaking her head, she again looked at Wendy.

"Is there a problem answering the question, Francine?" Max asked.

Francine took a deep breath. "Nah. It's cool with me, Max."

He knew he had won her attention. "Good girl," he said as he sauntered back toward Wendy. Francine heard hushed talk around the room. "Okay, my beautiful women, we got the cream of the crop right here." Standing behind Wendy, he wrapped his arms around her and kissed her neck. "So listen up. You all know where Wendy stands. She has earned her way to the top. Anyone who disrespects her deals with me. I must say, that would be kind of ironic, cause the only reason she has her important job in the first place is cause of all your respect for her. Right?"

The girls cheered.

Max kissed the back of Wendy's head and ran his hand through her hair. "If you have a problem, my girl Wendy will assess it first. That's part of her job. Now hear this, girls: I don't want any of you to come crying to me with petty concerns. Don't have time for it, especially when my name is being run down on the streets by no-good skuzzy pimps. No, Max Cardosa will never be a has-been. Got it, ladies?"

Mumbles filled the room.

"Well, what if some guy rips us off and it's not our fault?" the curvy girl blurted out. "Does our tip kitty have to make up for it? What then?"

"You're the keeper of your own bod and my money, temporarily, so you're responsible for your own solution. Got it, Jamie?" Max said. "At the end of the day, my only need is my money and what you owe me. Just like I said, Wendy's here. Feel free to whine to her about your petty problems. All I'm saying is that serious problems are gonna have serious consequences."

Max reached into his pocket and pulled out a handgun. He pointed it at the floor.

Undeniable

"Ain't no one gonna mess with my girls. Nobody. And wanna know something else, ladies?" His eyes shifted across the room. "Daddy has more where this came from."

The rumbles got louder.

"Whoa! Now calm down, ladies. It's just a little Saturday Night Special. They're a dollar a dozen. They're inexpensive and disposable, but most important, they could save your life." He studied their faces and continued. "Shhh, shhhh, ladies. Come on, settle down. You know you're gonna have other options. You don't think Daddy would just hand you over a piece of sweet heat to pack just for the hell of it, do you? Not forcing anything on any of you, but hear this: Max Cardosa ain't going down without a fight, and neither are my girls. Got it? Listen to me. I'm not saying everyone's gonna need it, but hot damn, we're sure gonna be ready for it, if trouble comes knockin'. Understand? Just remember, the only thing you need to soak into your beautiful brains is that this little baby only warrants a life-or-death situation."

He waved the weapon in the air.

"There's no turning back with this little princess," he said, sliding the gun back into his pocket. "Remember, the pigs will know nothing. All right, gonna wrap this thing up. You fine ladies are gonna make me some nice ching tonight. You're dismissed."

Francine's skirt felt like it had been glued to her legs as she stood up. The jabbering in the room was loud. She tried to get to Wendy, but the curvy brunette—Jamie—nudged her out of the way.

"Hey," Jamie said, looking Francine up and down. "I'm not sure why Max had you show up at the meeting. Don't think you'll ever amount to much here. For that matter, I'm not sure why he even hired you. Oh, that's right, I think I heard he was doing Wendy a favor or something like that. Well, good luck."

Francine could feel Jamie's breath on her cheek.

"Max should save the protection for the ones who really matter," Jamie whispered.

Dumbfounded, Francine knew she had to take a stand. "Jamie, is it? Uh, I really don't need any more monkeys hanging off me. You see, that's the only reason I'm here. Just trying to shake the last of them loose, understand? Tell me something, Jamie, have you ever considered just going back to your porch?" She smiled, then gave one final dig. "Oh yeah. And apparently I do matter. Just ask Max."

Jamie threw her chin in the air and stomped her way through the crowd of girls.

"Hey Francine, everything cool?" Wendy asked, coming up from behind.

"Sure. It's just great. Other than dodging stupid flying monkeys. I think I'm good now."

"Are you talking about Jaime? Hell, don't worry about her. She's turned less tricks than any of us, and she's probably been here twice as long. Don't think Max is too impressed."

"So why doesn't Max get rid of her?" Francine asked.

"We aren't sure, but if you ever figure it out, let us know, would you? We're all dying to know." Wendy grinned. "Hey, I know you're off tonight. I'll be hanging around, tidying up some lose ends for Max. If you're up for a little pole practice or just feel like hanging out, it's our PJ night. You're welcome to join us. It usually turns into a good time. Besides, where else can you have a serious gab session while splitting a gut?"

"I'll think about it."

"You've gotta enjoy these times, cause soon Max will have you working hard, believe me." Wendy grinned again. "Hey, would you promise me something?"

"What's that?"

"Get rid of that frumpy granny skirt!" Reaching around, she snapped the back of Francine's bra. "And while you're at it, lose that stuffy thing too. It doesn't matter how big or small those things are, all girls need to breathe, especially on girls night off! You'll learn."

Francine went back to her room and flopped on the bed. Closing her eyes, she thought about her parents. She remembered her father's nickname for her, Groovy Girl. One part of her wanted to laugh, the other wanted to scream.

"Groovy Girl, hooker," she said aloud. "Groovy Girl, hooker."

Though it seemed much of Francine's past life was a twisted maze, she could still recall clearly the footsteps that had led to her present circumstance. She wasn't sure how she felt about her father anymore. She had adored him for being her rescuer, part-time. Although his hands had seemed to be tied, it crossed her mind that if only he had tried a little harder, he could have taken the chains off her. After all, he was half the reason she had come into this world to being with.

Francine couldn't help but wonder where he was now and who was left with the dreadful job of counting her mother's pills. She closed her eyes and drifted off.

The hand felt warm and soothing against her forehead. Waking up, the eyes looking back at her were undeniable. Like daggers in a sea of emeralds, they shot through her.

"Hey beautiful. I don't like you sleeping the day away. I know the first night can leave you wiped out, but you need to get out with the girls. Soon that will be a rare opportunity." Max ran his hand down her neck, then kissed her cheek. "Is everything good with you, Francine?"

"Sure," Francine replied.

"That's my girl." He ran his hand up her leg. "You did a fine job last night, my beautiful little ching-ching. Wendy said she's expecting you tonight." Max looked at her skirt and chuckled. "I think this is why I like you so much. You know, my other women wouldn't get caught dead in this thing." He kept laughing as he pulled the skirt up. "It just shows me that you got more guts than all of them put together. Now that's something to be real proud of."

Francine grabbed his hand. "Stop it."

Max grinned, not taking his eyes off of her. "You know, baby doll, there are only a few things I have never really liked to share. One of them is you. But unfortunately, it's always business first. At least for now."

Max winked.

Uncomfortable, Francine sat up. "Uh... well, uh, Wendy and you are..."

"Shhhhhhhh." Max brushed his fingers across her lips. "Daddy don't want to hear no flack. Not today, not tomorrow, not ever. I knew you were something special from the first time I laid eyes on you. But I know I have to share you, at least for a while. It kicks me right here in the heart, but that's the way it's got to be. For now." Max pressed his fist into his chest. "Hey doll, I waited a long time for something this special, so we gotta play the game right. Understand?"

"What about Wendy?"

"Shhhhhhhh. Tomorrow will take care of itself. Just trust me, baby doll. I'm Max Cardosa. Everyone trusts Max Cardosa." Slowly, he reached into his pocket, pulled out the gun, and drew her chin toward his. "You are the most inexperienced, or should I say newest, of all my girls, so this is what it has come to. Are you cool with it? This is what's going down, until things settle down out there in our territory." Max's voice turned soft.

Francine stared at him in disbelief.

"You see, Francine, all you have to know about this little gem is how to load it and how to fire it. That's it." Max reached in his other pocket and pulled out a handful of brass shells. "Shove these in the mag, like this. Put mag in gun. Then pull back on the slide. Locked and loaded. To unload, you drop the mag. Pull back the slide and the round ejects. Empty." Max calmly handed her the shells. "Now you try it."

Trembling, she took the gun and the shells. She held it in her left hand and reached for the mag, loading it. She pulled back the slide and chambered a round. Nervously, she aimed the gun at Max.

"Are you crazy? What are you doing? That thing's loaded!"

"Just making sure you're paying attention, Mr. Cardosa. That's all." Francine laughed as she lowered the gun and emptied it.

"Yep, just like I said, more gonads than all my other girls put together." Max laughed. "Good girl. Daddy knew it wouldn't take you long to catch on. Not only have you got it going on, you got the brains too. Your momma and daddy must have been real shakers in their day. They sure taught you good. Yeah, Max Cardosa has finally hit the jackpot!" He kissed her cheek. "Now, tuck this little gem away and make sure it goes with you whenever you're turning a trick. Got it, doll face?"

He pressed his lips against hers.

Chapter Twenty

"Hey, Francine, come on in and join the party," Wendy threw open the door and put her arm around Francine. "Better late than never. You know most of these girls, don't you?"

Francine glanced around the room and recognized a lot of the faces. A couple of the girls were sprawled out in their undergarments while two more were engaged with the pole. The redhead with the swollen eye sat in the corner crying, her head on a brunette's shoulder.

"I forgot to introduce myself earlier, but my name is Angela," the petite blonde said, holding out her hand. "Want a toke, Francine?"

Francine hesitated. "Uh, I'll pass for now."

"Well, what's your beverage of choice? You know the unwritten rule here: nobody leaves sober on girls night off." Jamie smiled as she approached. "We've got a tall, fair, and handsome Tom Collins with a crispy dill. A Juicy Lucy—with one extra large swirl stick, I might add. Ooh, there's also a Harvey Wall Banger a la carte. That comes with two olives and a juicy slice of orange, your choice. Oh, and our all-time favorite, a Ginny Gin Gin, she'll make you sin. So what's it gonna be, buttercup?"

"Uh, I'll take one of those gins on ice!" Francine said. "Make it a double. Thanks."

"No more long chin for Jim when his woman's drinking gin," a slurred voice somewhere belted out.

Smiling, Jamie handed Francine the glass. "Glad you could make it, Maxine. Oops, sorry. It's Francine, isn't it?" She leaned in and whispered into Francine's ear. "Yeah, us girls are all friends here, you know? And don't know if you heard, but whatever happens here on girls night stays here, right?"

The girls sat on the floor in a circle. Francine joined in, folding her legs under her on the shag carpet.

"Now where were we?" Wendy asked, smiling at Kelly, one of nicer girls in the group.

"Okay, so this rich-looking fossil pulls up in his Cadillac," Kelly said. "It was sporting the coolest stripe I've ever seen on a luxury car. Anyway, he pays me, so, duh, of course I'm going to get in. Like really, I got my Tina Turner wig on and I'm feeling good, ready to rock the night. It's still pretty early, but it got dark quick. Oh yeah, it had been raining, too. Anyway, he takes me to the drive-in." She pauses, reacting to the moans and giggles of the other girls. "Excuse me, but could you please stop laughing, at least 'til I finish the story? Thanks. Well, of course no one is going to be at the drive-in on a rainy night, right? So that's where he took me." She looked around the room and laughed. "Well, girls, that's the end of my story."

"No friggin' way!" A chorus of groans punctuated the silence. "Come on, Kelly, tell us what happened next."

"Okay, settle down and I'll tell you," she said, trying to contain her own snickers. She waited for a moment. "So, it's like dark and all, it's pouring, and I'm with this rich old dude, sitting in his fancy Caddy. Then he asks me to take off my fake-diamond-studded boots. So I did. And then, and then and then! Okay, that's the end."

The boos grew loader.

"Okay, cool your jets, would you? I'm getting there!" Kelly shot back. "Well, anyway, there was a gas leak."

"No way. So what did you do?" Angela asked.

"Well, I plugged my nose. Okay, it wasn't that kind of gas leak, not from the car or anything like that. You get my drift?" Kelly could hear moans through the laughter. "Now listen. I think the dude had... what do those sophisticated people call it? Flatulence, that's it! But it was bad and it filled every pocket of air in that gorgeous Caddy. I'm telling you, it could have choked a dead cow!" She tried keeping a straight face as the laughter grew louder. "Listen, would you? Anyway, the guy looks at me. You know that deer-in-headlights look, right?"

"Yeah, yeah. We know!"

"Okay, so now he knows he has to take me back. He's drivin' the bloody thing like he stole it! We head back. But no sweat off my butt, because I already got my money. He loses either way, right?" Trying to gain some composure, she cleared her throat. "Now he drives me back, just off the strip, and he doesn't say a word the whole way. So when he drops me off, well, it's more like I have to do some kind of tuck, drop, and roll. I need my boots, right? So I grab them and then he shoots me this dirty look. Honest, he looked like Satan, only worse. Anyway, I slam the expensive door behind me and then yell as I banged my hand against the window, 'Thanks for the cash, fart face!' So there I am, sitting in front of this beat-up disco joint, putting my boots back on, when I see something all over the bottom of one of them."

Francine started laughing. Wendy too. Soon the room reverberated with laughter and screams.

"Just tell us! Tell us, please!" Wendy said. "It wasn't! Not dog pooh, Kelly. Was it? Ooh, tell us it wasn't!"

Seized up with hilarity, Kelly couldn't speak, but she nodded and the girls went crazy.

Francine grabbed her stomach, rolling onto the floor. Wendy's drink tipped, soaking Kelly's hair. A piece of ice flew out of Jamie's mouth and bounced off Francine's headband.

"Okay, everyone!" Kelly called over the laughter. "That's kind of the end, but it kind of isn't."

"Please, don't tell us anymore."

"Well, just one more thing, and I promise that's it!" Kelly said, trying to catch her breath. "So about a week later, this car pulls up behind me. I turn around and wouldn't you know it, it was the same black Caddy with the same silver stripe. When I turned my head, I guess he got a look at me and lost it! He tramped the Caddy down the boulevard, his taillights disappearing faster than a hot Georgia sunset. And then he does this chewy around the corner and vanishes, never to be seen again, that is until I see him with Jamie!" She laughed again. "I swear it's all true!"

"You've got a big mouth Kelly!" Jamie fired back.

"Hey, who needs another drink?" Wendy asked, turning her empty glass upside-down. "Well, whoever does, hand your glass to Kelly. After turning us into a bunch of babbling hyenas, I think she owes us at least that much. Right, girls?"

Still laughing, the girls passed their glasses to Kelly.

"Hey, I think it's pole time, girls," Jamie said. "Can someone turn The Disco Queen up?"

Grabbing Francine's arm, the girls walked toward the pole in the middle of the room.

"Come on, Francine," Jamie said. "Show us what you're really made of!"

Francine embraced the pole, tightening her grip and wrapping her legs around it. As best she could, she worked her way to the top in her cotton shorts.

Her hands burned, but that was only half the challenge. With every inch, she felt her stockings heat up—and her legs wanted to go in the opposite direction. Determined, she kept climbing.

"Way to go, Francine," someone yelled over the music. "You can do it! Pose for us!"

Soon Jamie joined in on the fun, her curves on display as she made her own ascent up the pole. She arched her back and flung her dark hair back. Slipping off her silk robe, she let it fall silently to the ground.

Halfway up, Jamie started singing. "I work hard for my money, so you better treat me right!"

Francine clutched the pole, her arms becoming more and more tired.

"Come on, Francine!" Jamie called. "Just sing two lines and I'll let you back down!"

Not wanting to give in, Francine knew she had no choice, especially with Jamie below her.

"I work harder than Jamie does for her money!" Francine blurted out. Fatigue setting in quick, she felt her hands loosen. "Get out of my way, Jamie. I'm comin' down!"

"Hey, Francine, I think your mommy's calling you back to your toy box!" Jamie laughed, clinging to the pole just below her.

Francine's attempt to remain aloft failed and she slid uncontrollably down the pole—into Jamie, who crashed to the floor with a thud.

Francine picked up the silk robe that lay beside her on the floor. She giggled, waving it at Jamie. "Think you forgot this."

Snatching the garment, Jamie snapped, "We all know what's on the bottom of your boots, Francine."

Jamie made her way to the door.

"Hey Jamie, the party's just getting started," Wendy said. "Where are you going?"

"Max is expecting big things from me tomorrow. Got quite the schedule this week, so I think I'll call it a night." The door closed behind her.

"Okay, friends," Kelly slurred, holding her glass in midair. "Let's all have a dwink on Jamie and her very loooong schedule!"

"You know, every time Max gets a new girl here, Jamie freaks outs," Angela said. "That's a given with her. Guess she's scared of anyone stealing her regulars."

"Well, she should be scared," Kelly said. "She doesn't have many! And from what I can tell, most of us wouldn't want them anyway."

Francine chugged her drink back. "Well, think I'll have one more for the trip back to my room." She hiccupped as she wobbled to the table.

The chatter was soon drowned out by the voice of Tina Turner. Angela tucked her thumbs into the front of her pajama bottoms, thrusting her hips while Kelly attempted the Charleston with sloppy footwork. Francine joined the others, spinning in circles and showing off disco moves that had never made it into society.

"Hey, ladies," Max's voice shot from across the room. "I need your attention!"

Max walked to the stereo. The sound of him pulling the needle off the record jolted everyone as the room went silent.

"Girls, I think we should wrap this thing up. It's getting late and I need you all to be on top of your game tomorrow. Business has been going down and I need all my girls sharp out there!"

Moaning came from all directions as the girls tipped back their glasses.

"Let's go," Wendy yelled.

Max motioned to Francine. "Everyone goes except you."

One by one, the girls staggered out, laughing and singing, trying to get one more dance in. They jerked their shoulders and swayed side to side. Arm in arm, they ambled down the hall.

"Did I do something wrong?" Francine asked.

"No," Max said as he guided her to the pole. "As a matter of fact, it's not what you did, Francine. It's what you didn't do. Heard you had a problem with this beast of a thing again tonight."

"Really now? Did baby Jamie tell you that? Well, just for the record, Daddy, I did make it to the top. The very top."

"I believe you. I just needed to see if you were all right, doll. You know, you're very special to me, and I think you understand there's something bigger going down between us." He kissed her gently. "Okay, beautiful, I think it's time for you to go now, too."

Max walked her to the door and kissed her again.

"Yeah, my breathtaking doll," he said. "That's what you are. Now get the hell out of here before we find it's too late, doll face."

"See you tomorrow, Daddy. Gonna do you good. Promise."

"Well, don't forget the little gem," he ordered, forming his right hand into the shape of a gun and pointing two fingers into the air.

Francine giggled as she strutted away. "I won't."

Chapter Twenty-One

Francine touched up her makeup, then added one more dark layer to her eyes. She studied her reflection and gave her lips a final smack.

"That should do it," she muttered, walking to the shelf with the wigs. She selected the wild-child blonde wig. "Yep. I think it will be this one tonight. Now, boots or shoes?"

Rummaging through the crowded rack, she stopped at a pair of high-heeled patent-leather shoes.

"Bingo."

Francine ran her fingers over the spiked heels, then, arms full, fumbled through the dress rack, grabbing a mini. She pulled it on and slipped into the heels. Her shoes made a clicking sound as she walked across the floor and pulled the gun from her drawer. She loaded it and slid it in her handbag.

With long strides, she strutted into the lounge. The loud background chatter turned to silence. She knew all eyes were on her.

"Whew! Now who do we have here? A little hot fox!" Max's voice rang out.

"Hey, Francine, need a little something to kickstart your night?" Wendy asked as she walked toward the cabinet full of pills and alcohol. "Looks like you may have a busy one, girl."

Wendy pulled back the curtain hiding the goods and peered inside.

"Not sure which one I want," Francine said. "Well, how about the same as last time?"

"Sounds good. Snow White it is." Wendy handed her the pill.

"How about chasing it with a gin?"

"I don't think that's such a good idea, Francine. Why don't you treat yourself when you get back? But remember, nothing's free here."

"That's cool," Francine said.

Wendy looked toward Max and gave him a thumbs up.

"Okay, baby girl, the night belongs to you," Wendy said, laughing. "Show them what little Frankie's made of. You gotta keep my Max happy. He needs all the money he can get for that big mansion he's gonna buy me—or should I say, Mrs. Wendy Cardosa." She hugged Francine. "Keep safe. See you tomorrow, Miss Frankie."

Beginning to feel light on her feet, Francine pulled a wrapper from her purse and calmly walked towards Max.

He embraced her tightly. His heart pounded against hers. His warmth felt good.

"You packed the gem, baby doll?"

"Yeah, it's all cool." Francine sighed. "See you in the morning, Daddyoes."

The strip was quiet. Francine wondered if she would even make enough to buy her favorite package of gum, let alone earn enough for Max. Yet in a way it didn't really matter; she felt a sense of calmness float through her veins.

Francine scoured the street. She saw Jamie on the next corner, trolling for customers in her white thigh-high boots.

As the red ash from Jamie's cigarette trailed through the dark, Francine looked into the night sky at a lone star. She thought of Abby and clasped her hand tightly around the butterfly necklace.

Before long, a car approached. It first headed toward Jamie, then circled back toward Francine. Jamie watched as the car window rolled down beside Francine.

"Hey, gorgeous, I got some time to kill," the man inside said, waving a handful of bills. "Wanna split the strip for a while?"

Francine smiled. "Sure."

"Just a minute," he said, grinning as he made his way around the vehicle and opened the door for Francine. He walked back to his side and got in.

"Okay, baby, let's lose this strip." He laughed, looking her up and down. "You new here?"

"Pretty much."

"Don't worry, gorgeous." He paused as she got in and closed the door. "I'm gonna take good care of you, just like I've always taken care of the rest. You can count on that."

From his profile and the way he spoke, Francine sensed he came from good stock. She wondered why someone of his stature would be out looking for girls like her.

But that wasn't her problem. She imagined that he must have someone of similar pedigree waiting at home. One thing she knew for sure: whoever he was, this guy was going to be late having that nightcap with anyone.

They rounded the corner and Francine noticed Jamie still standing there. Realizing what had just happened, Jamie glared as they drove past.

As they sped off, Francine knew she would have to face Jamie's wrath.

"Same time, same place next week?" the man asked as the car pulled back up to the curb.

"Sure. My pimp has me working this area for the next few weeks, so I'll see you around. Somewhere." Francine got out and shut the door.

As she watched him drive away, another vehicle stopped beside her. Francine got in.

The lights of the city began to retreat as they left the strip. The smell of pine from a cardboard deodorizer on the rearview mirror permeated the car. A gold scorpion dangled from a leather bolo lace that hung from the man's neck. Despite his gruffness, he spoke in a gentle, captivating voice.

"My name is Rosco. What's yours? Angel?" He stretched out his arm behind her.

"No, actually, it's Frankie."

"Must say, that suits you. I haven't been in this area much, but I'm sure glad I am tonight." He laughed, gazing into her eyes. "May just have to change my route."

After they returned to the strip, he opened the door for her, reached for Francine's hand and guided her out. Her heart fluttered. Finally she felt a sense of belonging. But she knew the only thing that really mattered was earning Max's respect. Even still, if it meant conflict with her rivals, that was the way it would have to be. Nobody was going to stop her now. Her customers were even starting to mean something to her. Rosco had proved that. She could see her ticket to freedom. Her head swirled with anticipation.

Weary, she made her way back to the house. With her heels in one hand and her purse swinging from her shoulder, she nudged the door open. From down the hall, she heard faint voices in the common room. Remembering Wendy's words, Francine headed straight for the happy cabinet.

With the sun beginning to rise, she made note of the fact that she had never before had a drink at dawn. Her life had changed, but in a strange way she now knew she could get used to it.

Wasting no time, she tipped the glass back.

Every fiber of her being knew she had earned the right to sleep the day away, so she made her way to her room. Her bed welcomed her as she closed the door and flung her purse onto the chair. Still holding her shoes, she caressed the spiked heels.

A knock sounded at the door. She opened it and found Jamie standing in the hall.

"Hey, can we talk a minute?" Jamie asked, still in her white thigh-highs.

"Suppose, as long as it's brief. I had a long night."

"I know," Jamie said, pushing her way into the room. "This will only take a minute."

She let the door close behind her.

"So, now you're stealing my regulars too, are you?" she snapped.

"It's a free for all as far as I can figure."

Jamie's voice rose. "Not with my regulars it isn't! I think you should hand over at least half of your tips from the night. Think that's more than fair for stealing my guys."

"That's not gonna happen. Get the hell out, Jamie."

Jamie grabbed Francine's wrist. "Not until you repay me, thief!"

Reacting, Francine seized Jamie's hair and slammed her head into the wooden door.

"Hey, Little Miss Trouble Maker," she whispered into Jamie's face, pulling her hair tight. "I think it's about time you know something about me, so listen, and listen carefully. First of all, I'm not a thief. And really, I have never taken kindly to being harassed and bullied, especially by a sawed-off know-it-all little runt." Francine brought a shoe up and pressed the polished heel against Jamie's neck. "Oh, by the way, while I just happen to have my shoe up here—it's Jamie, isn't it?—do I act like I miss some stupid toy box?"

She twisted the heel into Jamie's cheek. Shaking her head back and forth, Jamie's eyes grew larger.

"That's what I thought," Francine said softly. "Oh, there's just one more thing, little darlin'." She turned the shoe and pushed it hard against Jamie's throat. "If you ever so much as breathe another word about my old lady, I swear I'll kill you. Understand?"

Jamie nodded.

Satisfied, Francine lowered the shoe and stared into her Jamie's eyes. "And whatever happens in this room stays in this room, got it?"

Jamie bolted out the door.

Francine closed the door and dropped her shoe. She took off her wig and threw it onto the chair. She was exhausted, but she knew she still had to play by the rules.

She walked to the bathroom and took a shower. Warm water caressed her skin as she reached for her necklace, wrapping her baby finger around the silver chain.

"Yep, Abby, it's all gonna be all right. Pinky swear."

Chapter Twenty-Two

FRANCINE DIDN'T KNOW WHERE THE TIME HAD GONE; THE LAST MONTHS HAD FLOWN by. Earning her way with regulars took the pressure off, but it was mostly their generosity that helped her climb the ladder so fast.

Her new life seemed surreal, except for the constant uneasiness that stalked her. The darkness that came with it gnawed slowly at her soul.

Francine knew the time had come to face her invisible predator. It was time to make *the* phone call. If not for her sake, than for her father's.

She took a deep breath and picked up the phone.

"Dad?" Francine asked, her quiet voice trembling.

"Is that you, Francine?"

Hearing her father's voice, a tear trickled down her cheek. "Yeah, it's me. Didn't think I would get you at home. How is everything in Indiana?"

"It was a whole lot better with you here, that's for sure." Randy's voice cracked. "Are you doing all right?"

"Yeah, Wendy and I have good jobs here in Santa Montrose," she said. "We got a place and everything is totally cool. Still, we work a lot of weird hours. Just doing what it takes to get by. You know how that is, Dad."

"I do, Francine." Randy paused. "We have a new doctor in town now and it's looking promising for your mother. You know, it would please her if she knew you found a church to attend." He cleared his throat. "Before I forget, the store downtown where Mrs. Tasker works, it's finally closing its doors. When I heard the news, I went in and bought the nicest umbrella they had left. Old Mrs. Tasker helped me pick it out. She said to say hi. She wanted to know if you ever made it onto a movie set. Anyway, the umbrella is lying on your bed back here."

"Thanks, Dad." Francine caught her breath. "Tell Mother I haven't found a church yet. Seen lots in my travels, but I'm still looking."

"Well, your mother and I will pray you find one soon. We haven't stopped praying, Francine, and we won't. And don't you stop either."

Francine held the phone from her mouth, trying to swallow through the lump in her throat. "Is Father David still coming around?"

"Yeah, he's been visiting her over at the short-term facility where they're getting her medication straightened out. Even Father David is seeing a difference in her." His voice broke again. "She's home every weekend, you know. Her spirits are good considering the house is empty."

"I'm pretty sure they know how to dispense pills over at the Regional Care, Dad. And I'm glad someone is seeing a change in her." Francine could feel her heart pound as wetness glided down her face. "I'm sure Jenny must visit too. She's always been good like that."

Several long moments of silence passed between them. Francine hoped he couldn't hear her sniffling.

"Well, I just thought I would call," she said, "but I really gotta go now. I'll call again."

"Okay, Francine." Randy cleared his throat again. "You need anything, call. You'll always be our little girl. You know that, right?"

"Sure, Dad. I really have to go now. Bye."

"Bye... groovy girl."

Francine pressed the receiver down and twirled the black cord. She tried to catch her breath as the tears fell faster than ever.

"Anyone got dibs on the snakeskin boots tonight?" Francine asked, making her way into the common room.

"It depends," Kelly said.

"What do you mean?"

"Well, if that guy who's beating the crap out of us likes snakeskins, then I think I pass on them, forever."

"Is there something new I've missed about that jerk?" Francine asked.

Wendy came over, overhearing their conversation. "Didn't you hear? Another girl was beaten up a few nights ago, on the other side of the city," she said. "But rumor has it that she probably had it coming."

"As if anyone ever has that coming."

"Well, I think her street name was Marla, or Maple. Something like that." Wendy shook her head. "Anyway, I heard she had been pimping for that creep who sometimes used to sniff around here, until Max put an end to it. Anyway, apparently all hell broke loose over there. I heard he kicked her butt down the street. I feel sorry for her. It sounds like she just took her chances and went to turn a trick with no one having her back. Poor girl. Heard they don't know if she's gonna make it."

"Does anyone know anything about this creep?" Jamie asked, joining them. "Like what he looks like or what he drives?"

"Well, some think there might be a couple of psychos out there," Kelly said. "Some of the other girls gave different information. None of it's really adding up. One girl says a truck, another says a car. Makes it hard to figure out." She paused, looking around from face to face. "Hey, what do you call those guys who imitate something?"

"Copycats," Wendy said.

Kelly nodded. "Well, all I can say is that I hope the first guy doesn't start doing some really gruesome stuff. That could be very bad for all of us. Hell, it scares the crap out of me! How about you guys?"

"Like totally," Francine piped up. "We're all just trying to make a living. What other job do you go to where you don't know if you're gonna come out beat up, or even worse? It's crazy. As far as I can tell, the risks that come with this damn job are the worst. Well, unless you work for the mob or something like that."

"Unfortunately, there isn't a lot we can do about it except take our chances," Wendy said. "I know that firsthand. Usually you don't see it coming. Still, it's damn scary. Guess we just gotta play the game the way Max tells us, and protect ourselves." She paused, wrapping her robe tightly around her waist. "Hey, I know we're all carrying some kind of protection, but let's make a pact right now to really look out for one another."

Standing, all the girls huddled in a circle, stretching out their hands and forming a chain. Jamie reached for Francine's and gave it a light squeeze. Francine didn't bat an eye; she kept her focus on Wendy.

"I'll take this one," Wendy said. "Okay girls, repeat after me: Because we are all sisters here..." As instructed, they repeated each of Wendy's sentences. "We will always have each other's best interest at heart. If I see, hear, or smell any trouble coming my sister's way, I will do everything I can to help her because that is my duty as a sister." She smiled. "Okay, girls, let's have three cheers."

They all raised their hands and swung their arms in midair. "Hip-hip-hurray. Hip-hip-hurray. Hip-hip-hurray!"

Jamie hugged Francine. "Hey, Francine, I just want you to know that if I ever need someone to have my back, I sure hope it's you. I really mean it, Francine."

"So be it, Jamie, but if I ever need someone to have my back, I sure hope it isn't you. You'd get us both killed."

Jamie lowered her head. "Yeah, you're probably right on that."

"Wowee!"

They all turned to acknowledge Max as he walked into the lounge and leaned against the wall.

"Now that's what I like to see," Max said. "My beautiful chosen ones all together. It makes me feel good when I see all my women gettin' along, and I know you all have each other's back, no matter what. That's a real fine thing." He took his time surveying the girls. "But don't expect any more special treatment from me, got it?" he said, breaking out in a wide grin and crossing his arms. "You girls got everything you need to do your jobs damn good."

Chattering amongst themselves, they started walking out of the room.

Max grabbed Francine as she approached the door. She felt his palm on her cheek.

"How's it going, doll face?" he said, moving his hand to his chest. "You're lookin' mighty fine. You gotta remember somethin' for me, doll. My heart comes before any of your regulars. Understand? It's my game. I own it and I own you, remember? Yeah, you and me are gonna be together for a very long time."

Looking Francine in the eyes, Max pressed his lips against hers.

"Hey, what's up you two?" Wendy asked, approaching quickly. She scanned Max and then turned her attention to Francine. "Something here I should know about, Francine?"

"Uh, nope, don't think so," Francine said, looking to Max.

"Well, that's good. That's the way it's supposed to be between best friends, right?"

"We're just taking care of a little business here, Wendy," Max said calmly. "Isn't that right, Francine?"

"Yeah, sure. That's all."

"Good." Wendy wrapped her arm around Francine. "Now, if you have anything bothering you or need anything, that's why I'm here. Isn't that right, Max?" She ran her finger across his lips. "Right, baby?"

"Yeah, that's right, Wendy," Max said. "That's why you're here."

Wendy put her arm around Francine as they left the room together.

The fake snakeskin boots appeared classy. Between the boots and the butterfly necklace bouncing loosely around her neck, it seemed like a tossup lately as to which gave Francine the most luck. At this rate, one day soon she would be able to afford her own snakeskins.

Sighing, she headed out.

The sounds of the street romanced Francine. She felt more and more comfortable in her surroundings.

Dusk descended as she looked across the street and saw other working girls—she didn't own the entire corner this night, but she was good with that, confident with the customer appreciation list she kept in her brain.

"Hey Frankie," a familiar voice spoke as a car pulled up. The window rolled down. "Am I surprised to see you or what?"

Turning, she saw the gold scorpion sparkle against Rosco's dark muscle shirt.

"Boy, I didn't think I would see you again so soon," Rosco said. "And definitely not tonight. Well, are you getting in or what?"

Smiling, Frankie slid onto the seat. She placed her velvet purse on the floor and closed the door.

"Wow! It must be these lucky snakeskins," she said, grinning. She threw her leg up on the dashboard.

"That's real nice, Frankie, but my dash isn't a footstool." He guided her leg down. "We need to talk."

"Everything okay, Rosco?"

"Can't say that it is," he answered as they drove further away from the strip.

"Rosco, maybe tonight isn't a good night then. I'm cool with that." He kept silent, kept driving. "Where are we going? I've never been this way before."

"Somewhere we can be alone, just you and me."

A flicker of light swept across his face. Francine recognized that something had changed since the last time she'd met him.

"Just how many regulars do you have now, Frankie?"

"Enough to keep my bread buttered, I suppose."

"Well, don't you think I'm good enough for you, all by myself?"

"Uh, what do you mean, Rosco?"

"With what I pay you, do you think you need to be out hustling all the time?" he asked. "Besides, I had a little visit from this Max guy. He wants me to stay the heck away from you. I told him I don't think I can do that. Besides, I don't even know how he found out we're regulars now, you and me." He glanced up at her. "I don't know why you're so overdressed tonight if you weren't expecting me."

"As a matter of fact, no, I wasn't expecting you. This is my job, Rosco. But don't get me wrong; I'm still happy you showed up."

"Didn't your mother teach you anything, like how not to dress when your man isn't around?"

Francine started to tense up. She glanced out at the beach as they drove along the highway. She knew they were completely alone out here.

"Rosco, I don't like you mentioning my mother, remember? And where are we going?" Her voice cracked. "You're making me nervous."

He broke into a grin. "Well, you told me you like surprises, Miss Frankie. Remember?"

"Not tonight. Just take me back now, please."

"Sure, I'll take you back. But not yet."

She noticed the sweat on his forehead. "Come on, Rosco! We can talk on our way back to the strip."

"Don't think so. And what's up with that Max dude? He ain't after my blood for no reason. What did you tell him about me? And just how serious are you two, anyway?"

"I didn't tell him anything," Francine said. "And we're not serious at all."

The waves crashed to shore as the car rolled to a stop.

Rosco clenched the steering wheel. "I'm tired of games, Frankie. One night you wanna be with me, the next I find you down the strip, waiting to be picked up by some stranger. I thought when you left me last time we had an understanding."

"Well, we do. But this is my job."

Calmly, he reached across and ran his fingers through her hair. "The game is over. You're my girl. Nobody is going to stop us from being together, not even Max. Understand? There's something special about you. You know, I haven't felt this way about no one in a long time."

As he pulled her closer, Francine began to tremble. "Rosco, you know I like you, but I'm not ready to settle down with anyone just yet. For the first time in my life, I'm with people who care about me. I've waited a long time for this, and I can't just throw it away. At least not yet."

She watched his face for a reaction.

"All right, Frankie, settle down. All I want is for you to prove to me how much I mean to you," he said, taking her by the arm. "That's all."

Francine tried to get away, but as she heard another wave crash into the shore she knew there was nowhere to go. Rationalizing, she understood that her only chance was to give in.

Chapter Twenty-Three

"SEE, THAT WASN'T SO BAD," ROSCO SAID SOFTLY, BRUSHING THE LONG HAIR FROM HER face. "All you needed was a reminder to show you how much I care for you. That's all. You don't need anyone else. You're mine, Frankie."

"Please take me back now," Francine whimpered. "I swear I won't say a word to no one."

"Say what to who? You fell in love with me and I fell in love with you, a prostitute... a hooker? That's so sad, too bad, but come on, Frankie, don't you want anything else out of life?" He stared at her hard. "Here I am, good enough to give you a chance to change your ways and make something of yourself. You know, I can see one day, if you don't stick with me and me alone, it's gonna get bad for you out here. Where will you run to then? Home to Mommy? You know she's not even gonna want you." His mouth curled into a grin. "She'll know she didn't teach you any good thing, won't she?"

Rosco laughed as he adjusted his belt.

Francine's whole body shook.

He cupped her face in his hands. "Now, who did you say you're gonna tell about us here tonight, huh? Is it Max you're gonna run to?"

"Just take me back!" she begged. "You have my word, I won't tell a soul. You and I can be like strangers for a while, and then start this whole thing from scratch. We can fix it and start over. Then, in time, we can be together. I swear."

"Strangers?"

"Well, no, I didn't mean it that way... honest."

Rosco hung his head. "Wait a minute," he whispered. "After putting my time and money into you, giving you my heart and showing you how much I love you, now you're telling me we can just act like we're strangers?"

"No, that's not what I meant," Francine cried. "I... I just meant you and I could let things cool down for a while. And then we can start to see each other again."

"I don't think that can happen. From the first time I saw you standing on the boulevard, I thought for sure you were something more than a good time. Don't know how I missed that by a mile. And if I did, tell me something. Does your mother know she raised a whore? Cause that's all you are then, Frankie. And living like this, you'll never be anything to anybody. You can't even respect yourself. Bet your mother is real proud of you."

Francine reached for her purse and frantically pushed the door open.

She ran as fast as she could in the snakeskin boots, convulsing in fear as she heard his footsteps behind her.

"Come on, Frankie! I was just kidding. We can't just end it like this."

Rummaging through her purse, she pulled out the gun, her hands shaking uncontrollably. The waves kept crashing in the distance.

"That's not what I think it is, is it? Now, Frankie, come on. You don't wanna do that. All I want to do is help you. Just throw the gun to me." His shadow was getting closer. "You know I was just kidding. You know I love you, Frankie, and would never hurt you. I only want what's best for you."

Step by step, he advanced. Trying to hold the gun straight, Frankie put her finger on the trigger and pulled.

The shot rang out in the darkness. Not knowing if she'd hit him, she aimed once more, desperately trying to steady her grip. She fired again and again as echoes rang out.

The shadow fell to the ground with a thud.

Frankie fumbled with the gun and dropped it in her purse. She felt ready to collapse, but she instead she ran. Her purse swung violently as she plowed through the brush. Desperate, she tried to make her way to a clearing. She struggled up an embankment, her heels sinking into the sandy soil.

Frantically, she crawled to the top. Through the darkness she saw a set of headlights coming toward her. Waving her arms anxiously, the car sped up and roared past.

As she staggered along the road, more headlights shone at her. The beams were blinding.

Finally, a car stopped.

"I need a ride!" she cried out, trying to catch her breath. "Please! It's my boyfriend! He's gone crazy! You have to help me!"

The driver, a young man, analyzed Frankie and acquiesced. "Okay, get in."

"Thanks. You have no idea, but you probably saved my life," she whimpered as she settled in and he started to drive again.

"You're kidding, right?" he said as he pushed down on the accelerator.

"Where to, lady?" he asked.

"Anywhere on the strip."

He noticed her ripped dress. "Are you sure you're alright?"

"Yeah," Frankie replied, trembling.

"Well, that have must have been one hell of a fight," he said. "Tell me something... the jerk didn't just leave you out in the middle of nowhere, did he?"

"No, not really. Uh, I... I think he's still back there."

Finally, Frankie saw the lights of the city ahead. She knew her feet would soon be on familiar ground.

"What do I owe you?" she asked a few minutes later as he pulled up to the curb.

"Nothing, lady. Just take care of yourself, okay?"

Frankie slammed the door and walked wearily up the street. Feeling the butterfly bounce lazily across her bosom, she tried to muster her last reserves of energy.

She made her way home, desperately making sense of the night, knowing how close she had come to cheating death.

Chapter Twenty-Four

The lounge was nearly empty. Glancing at the clock, Francine knew she had some time to herself before the others started straggling in. She kicked off her boots and quickly made her way to the happy cabinet. The bottle felt good on her lips as she tilted it back; coughing, she wiped her chin. She took another gulp.

She knew she could never mention a word to anyone about what had happened—and she knew her life would never be the same. Nothing could ever change it. Nothing.

One of the few people she had come to trust was dead now. Her heart sank as she took one last gulp, slamming the bottle down on the table.

"So you decided not to show up again, God," she murmured.

Francine pushed herself away from the table and weaved out of the lounge. Turning, she pulled off her boots and threw them at the wall. She flung her purse over her shoulder and staggered down the hall.

That night, Francine had nightmares about being chased. Her eyes burned as they opened to the sound of a faint voice.

"Hey, Francine, wake up."

She awoke to find Wendy standing by her bedside.

"Just thought I'd check in on you," Wendy said, setting down the snakeskin boots. "Max and I were a little concerned because no one saw you come in last night."

"Um, yeah, got in early I guess." Groggily, she brushed damp hair from her face.

Wendy sat down on the side of the bed. "Okay, that's cool. Are you feeling okay?"

"Yeah, I guess. What time is it anyway?"

"9:00 a.m.," Wendy picked up the ripped dress and examined it. "Well, maybe you're all right, but this dress sure isn't! And what the hell is all over your boots?" She reached for Francine's hand. "I think you need to talk to me. I'm listening."

Wendy shut the door quietly when she left Francine's room, anguished over her friend's plight. Of all the girls to get into a mess like this, it had to be Francine. Knowing Francine's life had been one long train wreck, Wendy had always tried to have her back.

Wendy knew how easily things could spiral out of control. She also knew that Max was part of the mix. Although she had plans to be with him, he had a special fondness for Francine. She wondered if this latest development would push Max closer to Francine, or if he would ditch her for good.

Either way, it was going to be a sad situation.

"So what do we do, Max?" Wendy asked later that morning, nestled in his arms. "That's probably the dead guy they found on Sunset Beach last night. You know, this could seriously damage Francine for the rest of her life. Then what good would she be to you—or anyone else, for that matter? And what if she stops bringing in the money? Then what? We've got our dreams too, baby." She wiped away some tears. "I know she's my best friend and all, but really, Max, you don't have to do me any more favors. Honestly." Wendy quivered.

Devastated, Max gently nudged her aside. "I cannot let that girl go, Wendy. That's not the answer, at least not right now."

He knew he had to make a decision, but at the moment he just wanted to hold Francine and tell her it would all be okay.

Wendy embraced him again. "Don't worry, baby. It'll work itself out. It always does."

Max straightened up. "Get the girls together. There's a meeting in one hour. Everyone shows. Well, except for Francine. Let her sleep. God knows she needs it."

The lounge buzzed with whispers as the girls made their way in.

"Okay ladies, listen up!" Max bellowing, calling everyone to order. "We got serious business going down. I need your attention now."

Scantily dressed, most of them were still half-asleep as they took their seats.

"All right. Word on the street has it that some creep got shot last night. And it could very well be the sicko who's been stalking you girls. Whatever. All I know is that there was a guy shot dead last night, and I'm not getting good vibes." He paused to listen to the girls' chatter, then cleared his throat, zeroing in on Jamie. "Shut up, Jamie! You were working last night, sure, but you still got some time you can't account for. So you don't need to be shooting your damn mouth off about Francine. Got it? Man, I'm getting sick of you." He turned his attention back to the group. "Now, I know I gave some of you protection to use. You need to keep that protection—until something changes. But if the pigs come knockin', you need to get rid of that protection, pronto. Understand? If Wendy isn't available, I will be. Just turn it over to one of us, fast, and we'll look after it. Now, in saying all that, the pigs can't come in without a warrant, so don't be inviting them in. Hear me?" Max's eyes scanned the room. "One more thing. If you suspect or hear anything about a murder, anywhere, keep your mouths shut and just take care of your own damn business. Or I'll send you down the road! I'm not having any more trouble. Do we have an understanding, girls?"

The girls nodded.

Swaggering to the door, Max finished his speech. "That's it. Now go get some sleep. I got bills to pay!"

With her head over the toilet bowl, Francine hoped her flu would end soon. It was dragging her down. Exhausted, she made her way back down the hall.

"Francine, wait!" a voice yelled from behind.

Looking back, she saw that it was Wendy.

"You know, Francine, you haven't been looking so good this last while. Max and I think you need to see a doctor."

"Wendy, I'm too drained to see a doctor right now. "

"We know. That's why you need to see one. Actually, Max and I have been talking and we decided to make this easy for you."

"What do you mean?" Francine asked, rubbing her stomach.

"Well, you're suspended from work, starting now, until you're checked out. It's simple, Francine. You need to see a doctor. Besides, we don't need anyone else getting this bug, right?"

Pondering the ultimatum, Francine sighed. "Okay, guess it's your call. Get me the damn appointment then."

Francine went back to bed, hoping the sickness would soon run its course. She placed her hand on her stomach and closed her eyes.

The florescent light was almost blinding. Considering her mother's plight, Francine hadn't had a lot of reassurance regarding the medical field. Somehow the white coats always made her feel worse.

"Miss Moonie, the doctor will see you now," a voice rang from behind the desk.

Francine struggled as she kicked off her flats.

"You heard the doctor," Wendy said. "So now what?"

"I'm in a hell of a mess, that's what." Francine threw herself onto the sofa.

"Well, it's your decision whether to keep it or not, but you know you can't have it both ways. There's no time for a baby with this job. And as for the other problem, don't worry. Chances are no one is ever going to find out you were with Rosco that night." Wendy noticed the dark circles under Francine's eyes. "If you want my opinion, here it is. I think your biggest obstacle right now is figuring out what you're gonna do with the kid. Nope, I wouldn't want to be in your shoes, but you've got to make a decision soon. You heard the doc. Not much time, if you're thinking what I'm thinking."

Francine sat speechless.

"Okay, these are your options," Wendy continued. "They're simple. You can either make this situation temporary or permanent. That's it. It's up to you."

"Thanks." Francine sighed. "Just give me another day or two to think about it."

"Sure," Wendy said. "Oh yeah, almost forgot. Max wants to talk to you. I think it's about that gun he lent you. He said something about things starting to heat up here with questions from the pigs. Apparently they've been snooping around asking about us girls and where everyone was the night Rosco was shot."

"All right," Francine muttered.

"Another thing. Don't know if you heard, but Max was a little uptight that night. I guess the more he turned you out, the less comfortable he was getting. I know he's been real happy with all the coin you've been making for him. Can't say I blame him for worrying. He's got a lot on the line with you. Anyway, get some rest, Francine."

Francine was despondent. She twirled her silver chain with one hand and gently placed the other on her stomach. Awash in emotions over her pregnancy, she also had to contend with the fact that she may soon have the police knocking at her door.

Maybe the easiest thing to do was to just turn herself in. Even if it meant letting down Max and disappointing Wendy, the writing was on the wall. The thought of having a child born in prison also weighed on her. Francine knew she would never survive that.

She had to make a decision.

"Max," Francine shouted as she made her way down the hall.

"How you doing, doll face?"

Sizing her up, Max saw she wasn't up for questions or advice. But time was running out.

"A ghost would look darker than you," he said, wrapping his arm around her shoulders. "I need to talk, baby doll, just me and you. Meet me in the back room in fifteen. Okay?" He kissed her on the cheek and left.

Jamie greeted Francine at the kitchen entrance. "Still not looking so hot, Francine. You all right?"

"Yep, just trying to shake this thing," she said, walking to the counter.

"Sure. Must be one stubborn bug," Jamie whispered, gently touching her shoulder. "Hey, you know that guy who was shot? Rosco DeFranco? They say he was a real decent family man. Rumor has it he was living the dream. Well, at least up until his wife and kid were hit by a drunk driver out on the interstate a few years back. He hasn't been the same since. Guess he just never could get his life back together, poor guy. Think he had a pretty sad life the last while, at least from what I've been hearing."

Francine felt a jolt of sorrow pierce her heart. "Uh, really? That's too bad."

"He was one of your regulars, wasn't he?"

"Yeah, guess you'd call him that."

"I guess no one knows for sure why he was shot. Or if they do, they're not saying. Someday it will all come out. Creepy, isn't it?"

"Haven't been thinking much about it," Francine replied, looking at the clock. "Oh man, I'm gonna be late. Gotta go."

"Francine, lock the door," Max said. "I don't want us to be disturbed."

She flipped the steel bar and turned to look at him.

"Come, sit here." He pointed to the sofa. "Okay, gorgeous, I'm gonna get to the point." He gently flipped her hair back. "I heard from Wendy that you got yourself in a bit of a jam. You know, Max doesn't like it when one of his girls ain't doing well. I heard that Rosco dude is probably the kid's father. Is that right, baby doll?"

Francine hung her head.

Max sighed. "Okay, now that I got that out of the way, I need to know what your plans are."

"Uh, well, I talked to Wendy and she thinks it would be best if I don't go through with it. I have a little money tucked away, so I was thinking maybe I could head to Mexico and get it taken care of down there. And maybe after it's taken care of, I could get my job back. Well, that's if the cops don't pin me first."

Francine started to cry.

"It's okay, doll. I'm blaming myself for what happened. I didn't want to send you out that night, with everything going down, and I know I was a little late sending Wendy out to see if you were okay. I'm sorry for that. Max Cardosa let you down, and I'm sick over it. Now look at the mess I got you into. Wendy and I've been talkin' and she thinks it's your best bet to be out of sight, out of mind for a while, baby doll. We both agreed Mexico is a good option under the circumstances. At least for now. She's checked with the clinic there and they can get you in pronto. No fuss, no muss. Less stress for everyone. Can't beat the price and they'll really look after you down there. I can help foot some of the bill. Hey doll, before you know it, you'll be heading back to your job and into daddy's arms. No, Max doesn't leave any of his girls hanging, especially Francine Moonie. Get that, doll?"

"Thanks." Francine sobbed as Max tenderly kissed her.

"You know, beautiful, when you get this behind you, things will change around here. That's a fact. The future is ours. We just have to wait for the smoke to settle. Leave it to me."

"Sure."

Looking into his emerald eyes, she was even more mesmerized than the first time their eyes had met. She knew it wasn't right, but her heart flickered with a small burst of hope.

"It's gonna be fine, Francine. I'm certain I know more of what's going on here than you," he said. Embracing her, they walked to the door. "Oh, I almost forgot, doll, I need the gun back. You don't ever wanna be caught with that, especially at the border." He gave her a squeeze. "But I'll give you something a little less dangerous, just in case. A top of the line knife. It's rare, so just respect it. But use it if you have to. Got it, doll?"

"That's cool," Francine muttered.

Opening the door, Max kissed her again. "You'll always be Max's girl, Francine. Remember that. I'll be here waiting for you, Mrs. Francine Cardosa."

Francine nodded. Walking down the hall, she wiped her cheeks.

The early morning rays danced across the windshield.

"Are you sure you got everything, Francine?" Wendy asked as they pulled up to the glass doors at the bus depot.

"Yep, think so." Francine looked around, watching the people bustling in all directions.

"You know the number, right?" Wendy asked, holding back tears. "I'll be here for you anytime. Just call me."

"Sure, Wendy. You're gonna be so sick of hearing from me, you'll probably end up yanking the damn cord out of the wall."

"You got the backup from Max, right?"

"Yep. Right here." Francine patted her bag.

Wendy opened the car door and walked around to the passenger side to meet Francine.

"Oh no," Francine said. Getting out of the car, she adjusted her bandana and twisted it tight around the crimped short wig. "I forgot to pack my comfy shoes. These ones will be killing me in no time."

Wendy laughed, looking down at her feet. "Well, you can have mine if you like."

"Sure, those would look good on me. But what would I do with my toes?"

"Uh, maybe you could just fold them up!" Wendy joked. Francine tried to laugh. "Some things just never change with you, do they? That's what I've always loved about you. You're like the sister I never had. Promise me you'll call."

"Sure, promise."

Hugging each other, Francine heard Wendy's sobs.

"Everything's cool, Wendy. Like I said, you may even have to move just to get rid of me."

"Okay, you better get going. Remember, any problems, you know what to do."

"Totally."

Francine held out her finger, looking Wendy in the eyes. She hadn't pinky swore in years. Cautiously, she locked fingers with Wendy.

"Pinky swears," they whispered, standing face to face.

"Now, get going before you really make me cry," Wendy said.

With her purse over her shoulder, Francine walked to the depot door. Turning back, she held up her fore and baby finger and tried to smile. "It's gonna be okay, Wendy."

Chapter Twenty-Five

FRANCINE FOLDED THE SOFT GREY STICK OF GUM, THEN SHOVED IT INTO HER MOUTH AS the glass door closed behind her. Beads of moisture trickled down her painted brows, stopping at her eyes. She regretted not buying the more expensive mascara in the shiny pink tube. Her eyes stung, but counting pennies had become crucial, even it meant she wouldn't look her best temporarily.

Though Max had been generous with his time and plans for her well-being, Francine wanted him to be even more proud of her. Embracing full independence was the right thing to do. That meant taking nothing more from him, not another penny, at least for now.

"Next!"

The voice from the ticket booth bounced off the drab walls of the bus station. Francine felt that if she didn't make it to the front of the line soon, she might faint and disappear through the old cracked floor.

The wearier she grew, the more confused she became as she stared at the endless line of people. Were all these people leaving the city, she wondered? Francine was surprised. She had believed most people loved it in Santa Montrose, where the sun was blinding and the coast sparkled like polished diamonds.

One thing seemed certain: no one was leaving for the same reason as her.

Francine studied the frail woman in front of her. The old lady's hair looked like it had succumbed to lethal amounts of hair gel in its day. Scrunched stiffly on the back of her head, the mop showcased the woman's tanned turkey neck; her tube fingers clenched a faded handbag.

Turning, the lady offered her a grandmotherly smile. Francine smiled back. She only hoped she could make it to half the woman's age. Under present circumstances, she would be satisfied with surviving at least until she got the bus ticket in her hand.

As she wrapped her fingers around her silver chain, the voice echoed again.

"Next!"

The small booth was in sight. It blended in with the rest of the decor, dilapidated and lonely. Glancing around, Francine's heart sank. She had never been in an asylum before, but if she had, she knew it would be a dead ringer for this place. A string of memories fought for her attention. Focusing on the butterfly swinging silently from her neck, a wave of calmness swept over her.

"Next!"

This time the voice was clear. An old man in front of her clutched several tickets in one hand.

Cautiously, she scanned her surroundings. With all that had happened to her, Francine's thoughts raced. With all that had transpired she was learning the importance of being ready for any surprises: an attack from a lunatic or from some prehistoric, demonic carnivore. Anything.

Interlude

The crowd snickered and moaned. At last, a woman wearing a bright floppy hat stood. She adjusted her hat and waited for the crowd's attention.

"Now tell me, ladies," she began, smiling as her hat swayed from side to side. "You've no doubt been in a situation like Francine's, where you anticipated the very worst. Believe me, I'm no exception. I've put God second on my list, bottom of my list, or just left him off my list! Yes, many times I knowingly made it harder on myself when I pushed God aside, just to give the devil a foothold. Has anyone here done the same thing?"

Hands raised timidly across the room.

"I can give you an example," she added. "If you would like?"

Pastor Matthew nodded and smiled. "We're all ears, Mrs. Murphy."

"It's kind of similar to the time my mother-in-law planned a three-week visit with us." She smiled at the man next to her. "My husband and I had been yearning to go on a pleasure trip, but soon discouragement set in, knowing his holiday would be well over by the time his mother left us. Then, about a week into our visit, we gave some consideration and decided that maybe it was time to rearrange our priorities. So my husband and I removed everything from our list, and put God at the very top. And we prayed. Miraculously, two days later we were on the pleasure trip of our lives. Out of the blue, my mother-in-law decided she wanted to spend time with other family as well. Lo and behold, we were taking her back to the airport after just one week! Now, I don't think a single person here can tell me that wasn't God at his finest!" Mrs. Murphy laughed. "I might add, my husband ended up having a wonderful time just skirting the beautiful countryside. Why, every end always comes with a brand new beginning. Yes, God is mighty good!"

The crowd cheered.

"Well now, Mrs. Murphy, I believe my story is sounding a little dull compared to yours," Pastor Matthew said, grinning. "Thank you for sharing. Even God shows and finds the humor in things. So, now Francine has finally got herself to the ticket booth. Let's hear what she's up to next."

Chapter Twenty-Six

"Where to, ma'am?" the old man in the booth asked.

"Tijuana."

"Is that roun' 'r one way?"

"Round."

"Think you made a good choice, lady," he said in a cracked voice. "Not many people want to stay in Mexico this time of year. Travelling alone?"

"Yep, sort of." Francine glanced down at her slight belly pouch.

Quickly, she sorted through her bag and pulled out several small bills, placing them on the counter. The old man swooped up the money without counting it and handed her the tickets.

"Things aren't the same in Mexico as they are here, young lady. If you're going to Tijuana to find a male friend, be dang careful who you trust. Too many young girls with round tickets never come back." He pointed his crooked finger. "You hear me now? Keep your wits about you, girl. You'll be on the 7:45 bus. It's a little behind schedule."

Nodding, he pointed to the waiting area.

Francine felt nauseous. The oversized bag was heavy and the strap on one of her stilettos felt like it had been branded onto her ankle. She clicked her way across the floor and plunked down into a chair. Relieved, she knew that at least she could relax now. After all, she'd been in worse situations.

Kicking off one shoe, she grabbed the chain that rested on her breasts and drifted off.

"You're not taking my daughter!" a voice bellowed.

Francine's eyes jolted open. To the side, she saw a woman holding a crutch. A young girl was clinging to her, her face buried in the woman's bosom. A scrawny dark-haired man hovered over them, his arms swinging through the air as he yelled.

"You ain't takin' my girl, yah hear? She ain't goin' nowheres, an' you ain't goin' nowheres either. Yah hear me? All ya do is sit on that big fat rump your momma giv' ya. Now git up off it and git home and cook me up some fix'ns. Do ya hear me, woman?"

The girl sobbed as her head jerked back and forth.

"No!" the woman hollered. "I will not go back there 'til Maddie gits the operation she needs! If she doesn't git it, Bruce, she'll end up like your mother, not hearing a dang thing anybody says to her! Just let 'em do it!"

"Margareet! It'll be ov'r my dead body! You ain't takin' her down there!"

The man grabbed for the crutch and yanked at Margareet's shoulder, but she wouldn't budge.

No one flinched at the ruckus except a middle-aged man who had his nose buried in a thick book. Francine could only see the top of his black fedora, when, through the commotion, he lowered the book. Standing up, he made his way toward the unruly man.

Agitated, Francine sprang from her chair. Wearing one spiked shoe and carrying the other, she bounced her way across the floor. She clumsily skipped past the man in the fedora and approached the bossy husband, pouncing in front of him, stopping suddenly. Face to face, she stared at him. His eyes were empty. Like a mother bear protecting her own, Francine let him have it. With one hand on her hip, she swung the stiletto like a machete.

"Who do you think you are, mister?" Francine demanded. "Yeah, do you think anyone here needs to listen to your bullcrap? Besides, do you know what you're doing to your kid?" She impatiently waited for his response, but he didn't say a word. "Men like you are cowards! Parents like you should be left on an island somewhere, anywhere, with a... a bamboo shoot growing up their cowardly butts! Hey mister, want to guess how fast bamboo grows?"

Francine waited for an answer.

"Say, I'm talkin' to you, Mr. Father of the Friggin' Year! Do you know how fast they grow, you dweeb? Well, in case you've never heard, they grow real fast! Mister, don't say a word. You sure had plenty to say a few minutes ago, didn't you, you loudmouth? Do you know what the problem is with you? Hey, I'm talkin' to you, spazz." The man tried to stare her down, but Francine glared back at him. "Seriously? Do you know what your problem is?"

Before he had a chance to answer, she let him have it again.

"The problem with you is that you needed to meet someone like me a long time ago! Leave the lady and kid alone. Got it? I've got connections, and you really don't want me to use them. Understand?" Stepping back, she whispered, "Go bag your face, you coward."

As the man stood, silent, Francine could feel her blood racing. She studied his scrawny frame. Wiry whiskers curled into the corners of his thin lips. She knew there was no backing down now. Holding her shoe in midair, she was ready for whatever was to follow.

The man took a step back, then another, and another, until he disappeared. Francine sighed, then turned to Margareet and placed her hand on her shoulder. Francine noticed the girl's tattered dress and let her stiletto drop to the floor. She extended her hand to the girl, who glanced shyly up. With her finger, Francine stopped a tear from sliding down the girl's cheek.

"It's okay, baby," Francine said. "You know, sometimes a girl has to be tough. Really, I was a kid once, too. You're going to be all right."

Margareet smiled approvingly. She didn't need to say a word; Francine could see the appreciation in her eyes.

Picking her shoe up, Francine hobbled across the floor and glanced back. The middle-aged man, who had cautiously kept his distance, now knelt in front of the woman and young girl, his fedora perfectly in place. He had one hand on the girl's head, the other wrapped around his book. He had the poise of a professional. Francine speculated that he might be a mental healthcare worker of some kind.

She squeezed her necklace as she tried to block the memories knocking at the door once again.

With each step she took across the station, a recurring picture came into focus—she had once been that little girl. The circumstances may have been different, but it was still the same crap. At least the mother had her daughter's back, Francine thought, sighing as she recalled that the only protection she'd had at that age had been taken from her. At times like this she missed Abigail.

A fissure in the past had now opened and memories began pouring through. Francine tried to make sense of one image from her youth: the cold pew in church that had been such a big part of her world. It had never held up to its promises. As far as she was concerned, it was just a chunk of shiny wood.

If there really was a God, she realized that she would just have to accept that he was mad as hell with her. After all, confession meant you were supposed to tell the whole truth. But worse, if God did exist he would know how many times she had slid her mother's green bingo chips into the gum machine outside the Five and Dime. To make matters worse, she had also broken the silver handle when the whole apparatus fell into her hand one day.

If there was a God, Francine imagined he would find some type of payback for her past indiscretions. In Shelbytown, and now Santa Montrose, Francine had made sure he had seen it all.

Her heart pounded as she made her way across the floor.

"Please don't let there be a God," she muttered as she returned to her chair.

Francine picked up her bag and noticed her gum packet on the floor. Her wallet had spilled out too. She picked them both up as she dusted off.

"Figures," she said to herself.

She remembered from past experience that whenever she got fired up about something, somehow her anxiety came back, biting her right when it would annoy her the most. She opened the gum wrapper and tossed her wallet back into her bag.

By intervening in that argument, she believed she had done the right thing. She had stood up for the little girl. Francine's heart was good with that.

As she kicked off her shoe, she noticed every eye in the joint staring at her, but she didn't care. Moments like this made her realize that at least one good thing came from being raised by a crazy mother: a thick skin.

With one hand clasping her silver chain, the other slowly caressing her stomach, she closed her eyes.

When she awoke after a short time, the room was full. A young mother with two small children sat across from her. Francine guessed they were on vacation. Looking more closely, the girls appeared identical. They wore blue plaid dresses that made their red sandals stand out. The only discernible difference between them was their hair. One had tame locks with a long French braid, held together by a huge blue ribbon. The other had unruly pigtails with two green ribbons. Francine admired their mother's effort to give them their own subtle identities.

Sitting patiently, the mother was reading the girls a story.

She felt happy for them but sad at the same time. The mother's face glowed with contentment. Just looking at her, Francine could tell she was head over heels for her girl's father. It was impossible to hide.

But unlike the mother and her twins, disgust dripped out of every fiber of Francine's own being. Why? She looked down at her swollen tummy, stroking it. Although she felt she was doing the right thing, times like this made her second-guess herself. The confusion never lasted for more than a second, though.

Reality came trudging back into her thoughts. She wished she could just jump out of her skin, back to freedom.

It would be great to have something from Max's happy cabinet to dull the pain.

Francine slipped her shoes on and grabbed her bag.

"Come on, you stupid bus," she groaned. "Like totally, this kid will be all grown up before you even get here."

The station was getting louder and hotter. The pink tie-dye bandana wrapped around her head was starting to make her fake, crimped hair feel even more lifeless. She wished she could ring the sweat out of it, but she had already drawn enough attention to herself. She felt like people were still watching her.

She noticed an awkward man sitting a few seats away. He looked too mature to be sporting a light-colored ponytail. His dark handlebar mustache appeared to offset his hairstyle—in a bad way. Yet the combination of them miraculously complemented the stone-washed T-shirt that clung to his pumped shoulders. It was obvious he considered himself a star in his own life.

Francine looked at him. He looked at her, then away. Francine turned her head again and glanced back. He did the same.

Studying him a bit at a time, she wondered if she knew him. After all, she'd had a lot of clients and it was almost impossible to keep them straight, unless they had left her a huge tip. Scanning her memory, she wasn't sure. It didn't matter anyway, because half of her clientele were nobodies. The only challenge about her job was making every Joe Blow feel like a somebody, even for a short time. When it came down to it, most were just people like her, trying to get through life.

As Francine tried to forget the stranger, it crossed her mind that maybe he was an old client and had been secretly following her to reward her with the huge tip he had forgotten to give her at the time. She giggled, then realized she wasn't thinking straight. She was hot and tired. She wanted to get on the bus.

"Bus 7:45 Tijuana is loading at the east corridor" came a muffled voice from the loudspeaker.

"Like totally friggin' time." Francine sighed, picking up her bag.

Her silver chain swayed in sync with each stride as she made her way to the exit. Sweat trickled down her neck.

Francine could deal with almost anything now, knowing she was one step closer to getting her life back. As long as the troopers didn't catch up with her.

She saw several familiar faces in the line. The fedora man was helping the young girl and the woman with the crutch with their luggage. The mother and the twins stood behind Francine. Scanning the backs of heads in the lineup, Francine also saw the scraggly ponytail.

"Ew," she muttered. "Don't know why, but that guy gives me the creeps. And now he'll actually be riding the same bus as me? Like totally bad luck!"

Also in the line was a young lady with wide-rimmed glasses. She wore a dress with cherries on it and looked out of place, yet she exuded confidence.

Francine squinted, trying to examine the other passengers. Her eyes widened when she saw one man in particular. She thought it was the abusive father she'd encountered a while ago; he was standing at the back of the line and her creep meter started to spin. She tried to get a better look, but her view was suddenly blocked.

"Crap."

She sighed. It had been a long day.

"Hell, I just want to get to Tijuana and back," she whispered to no one. "That's all this girl wants."

"Hello, miss," a gravelly voice in front of her said. It was the middle-aged man in the fedora, the hat pointed directly at her. He had a quality of gentleness. It all fit together so comfortably—his round face, the avuncular smile, and the fedora.

"I see things have settled down a bit," she said. "That was quite the little ruckus back there. Such can be our lives at times."

He laughed. "I'm John. It sure seemed to take this bus a long time to get here," he said in a jovial voice. "I'm heading down to the border for a conference. I must admit, there were a couple of times I thought I might be walking to the conference."

His disposition appeared more patient then most. She wasn't sure if he was going to say something nice about her defending the lady and kid, or maybe give her crap in a nice way. One thing she did know, he didn't fit the profile of any of her clients. That meant he was probably just a nice guy without an agenda.

Francine popped some gum into her mouth. Then, with some hesitation, she made eye contact with him. He had the calmest eyes she had ever seen.

"Yeah, my name is Francine. Don't think we've met before," she said reluctantly. "Have we?"

Before he could answer, the line started to move.

Francine felt her temperature rise. John was such a polite man; she only hoped he didn't recognize her. She wasn't sure why she felt this way, because he meant nothing to her. In a quandary, she guessed he would have had her back if she ever needed help. Francine couldn't recall many people ever having her back.

The cool air felt welcoming on her clammy skin. Francine knew she was pushing her luck by hoping she could get a couple of seats to herself.

Toward the back of the bus, she spotted an empty row. She knew most people wouldn't intentionally pick out a seat anywhere near the restroom, but most weren't in the shape she was in. She just wanted to be alone. Besides, a few short rows from a stomach sanctuary was a good place to be, at least for now.

Exhausted and nauseous again, Francine hoped no one would sit beside her. She knew from experience bus passengers could seem like the nicest people for a while, then turn into annoying babblers. She didn't understand why some people just couldn't shut up. Besides, she would hate to have to hurl with someone sitting close by. Still, she knew she would if that's what it came to.

She adjusted her damp bandana, sat back, and took a deep breath.

Francine glanced up the aisle and saw the twins and their mother take their seats. Margareet and her daughter took places a few rows ahead of Francine.

John ended up sitting across from her. Francine tried to see where the ponytailed stranger went, but she couldn't spot him—until she turned her head. She held her breath as he looked at her, scanning the rows of seats. Then he turned back around.

Closing her eyes, she silently and dramatically enunciated the words "Thank you" as she managed to escape the awkwardness of having to sit by a weirdo for hours.

Chapter Twenty-Seven

"Is this seat taken?" a soft voice asked.

Francine groaned and hesitantly opened her eyes. "No, it's all yours."

The lady pushed her glasses back and sat down. Lifting a binder onto her lap, she tucked her purse beside her. It was Miss Plain Jane in the cherry dress, looking all quiet and reserved. Francine hoped those words would also correspond to their conversation.

"Great," Francine mumbled.

To Francine, she looked somewhat refined, with a dazzling charm bracelet wrapped perfectly around her wrist. She noticed a modesty about the woman, both in the length of her dress and the small cross that glittered from the dress's neckline.

Regardless, Francine was too tired to care. As long as she didn't start talking about saviors or sinners, it could possibly work out all right.

Out the corner of her eye, Francine noticed the woman search through her binder. Hoping she wouldn't strike up a banal conversation, Francine peered out the window. But she couldn't stop thinking about that cherry dress. She knew there was no way she could ever wear a red cherry dress. It would be just plain wrong; she never thought of herself as the wholesome farmgirl type.

Francine started to giggle. Trying not to look at the lady, her giggle became louder.

"It's all right to sit here, isn't it?" the woman asked.

Francine tried to regain her composure, avoiding eye contact. "Yes, it's okay. Sorry, but I've had quite the day. When I'm in this state of mind, the giddiness just has a way with me."

The woman stared at Francine. Then, face to face, they started laughing.

"Well, I've had a rather long day, too," the woman said, pushing back her oval-shaped glasses. "But probably not as long as yours!"

Black streaks ran down Francine's cheeks as she started laughing again. The lady could not speak. Pointing to her own cheeks, she hoped Francine would get the hint.

Slipping off her bandana, Francine wiped her cheeks with the damp piece of cloth.

The stranger sighed with relief. She leaned back and placed her purse on her lap.

"Well, after all this, I guess I owe you a proper introduction. Hi. My name is Anna." She held out her hand. "And to be frank, I do have a mother and father, and I wasn't hatched in a cabbage patch, nor was I conceived in some far-out spaceship. But that's probably contrary to what you've gathered to this point."

Francine laughed. "Yeah, good to meet you, I guess. And for the record, my real name is Francine, though most of my colleagues call me Frankie. I help people mostly with life issues. It's ironic, since I clearly have a few of my own!" She laughed again. "Doesn't mean I'm not good at what I do, though. By the way, presently I don't have a mother or a father. To be honest, I would probably have been better off being hatched in a cabbage patch. Most of my life, I've felt like I was living in some kind of twilight zone!"

"I work for the state as a program coordinator," Anna said as she relaxed. "I mostly work with unwed expectant mothers. Although the job gives me a lot of satisfaction, I must admit I've been known to ignore my nametag and wear my heart on my sleeve." She sighed. "At any rate, a training opportunity came up at a women's facility just outside of Tijuana. My boss signed me up and now here I am! I don't really mind, though. I'll never be blessed with a family of my own..." Her voice cracked. "I'm all right with that. I'm convinced God has his own purpose for my life. He didn't give me good role models by mistake, so I certainly don't mind spreading the love!"

"Awesome." Francine slipped the bandana back over her head. "I wish my story was as sweet as yours. You see, I don't really have a story, at least not one I would feel good telling anyone." She hesitated, reaching down and twirling the silver butterfly chain around her finger. "Well, except I did have a good role model once. She was my older sister. Yeah, Abby sure could make me laugh! I wish I could say my mother was a good role model, but I'd be lying. Hell, my teacher Miss Wartler set a better example. Still, I remember that lady and her face wart."

Francine touched her nose and giggled.

"Really?" Anna asked.

"Yeah, I haven't thought about that woman in years. I remember her hair was white for years, and then overnight it just turned blue. Still, she kept a tight bird's nest on top. And when she tried to get her point across, she would come up beside you, raise her voice, and the spit would fly. We never tried to dodge it because that would only make it worse. Then, when she was finally finished, she'd slam her book shut and smile at you like nothing ever happened. Boy, us kids loved to hear the sound of the book closing because that meant the rain shower was over."

Anna held her stomach as she howled with laughter.

"Even around Halloween," Francine went on, "rumor had it she would fly this electronic broom to school. We kids believed anything. Yeah, we all thought we would get a glimpse of it, especially Tommy Hall, but none of us did. Then one day Tommy brought an old corn broom into the classroom and left a note on it that read 'The Wart Mobile.' Tommy told us Miss Wartler found out he left the note and kept him after school. Apparently she chased him around the room screeching like an old witch. He told us he screamed as she gouged him with the broom. Finally, when he just about got to the door, Miss Wartler caught him. We weren't sure if Tommy was telling us the truth until he rolled up his sleeve the next day and showed us his nasty scratches. From that day on, none of us ever breathed another word about brooms or stupid witches. Except I'm sure we all kept secretly looking for her parking space every Halloween. Now that was creepy, just like a lot of my life. Plain creepy."

"Well, I sure hope I never leave that kind of trauma with anyone!" Anna exclaimed. "And I'm most certain I will never wear a bird's nest, either. The last thing I would ever want to be is someone's bad memory."

Francine let out a snort.

The noise on the bus started to dissipate as they left the city behind.

A voice came over the speaker. "We will be picking up in Daly City, then onto San Lateo for a short layover. Please be courteous with the restroom and enjoy your ride."

It seemed to Francine like she had drifted off for hours when she finally opened her eyes to rustling papers. Anna was studying some kind of chart, carefully flipping pages back and forth.

Francine started thinking about a man she was falling in love with, a dead man, and an ongoing murder investigation. Taking a deep breath, she tried to think of all the friends she had made since moving to Santa Montrose. Wendy was her best friend, and even Jamie had become almost likable.

Switching her focus to the future, she thought about the doctor who would perform her surgery. Would he even speak English? Francine grunted as she felt her stomach flop. She only knew she was desperate and wanted it behind her.

She reached into her bag and pulled out a wrapper. Shoving the gum into her mouth, she grazed her stomach.

"Your stomach bothering you, Francine?" Anna's pleasant voice asked.

"A little, I suppose. I had a touch of that flu that was going around. Nothing major. Actually I've been feeling a lot better lately."

"Hey, Francine, you never told me where you're headed."

Francine thought quickly. "Oh, nowhere really, I suppose. On my days off I just like riding buses."

"Really?"

"Well, seeing as you asked, I'm going to Tijuana too... for, uh, a small female procedure. Money is a little shy now that I'm not working. I don't have insurance, so I decided to have it done in Mexico for half the price. It's quite urgent. Apparently, if I don't have it done soon, doctors say it will probably ruin the rest of my life."

Anna gasped as she watched Francine's eyes fill up.

"Yeah, Anna, this could be grody to the max if not taken care of pronto. It's been stressful leaving my job and all, but a girl's gotta do what a girl's gotta do. I'll definitely be back to my old self in no time. This trip is going to be so worth it."

Holding her silver chain, Francine lowered her eyes.

"I certainly hope it goes well for you," Anna replied softly.

Francine sighed. Glancing over, she couldn't help but notice a sunbeam dance around the small gold cross that hung from Anna's neck. It was mesmerizing. Looking down at her own necklace, she thought of her sister.

Francine heard the bus gearing down and knew they were approaching Daly City.

"What do you think of butterflies, Anna?" Francine asked quietly, lifting the chain off her shirt.

"They're rather lovely, free-spirited in their own kind of way," Anna said, studying the butterfly. "I would say your butterfly is vintage. Somewhat unique, and look at those unusual wings. What a marvelous piece." Taking a closer look, she leaned in. "Just stunning. Look at those colors! The links in the chain are beautiful too. Now where would a girl get something of that caliber?"

"It was my sister's, handed down from my Aunt Julie, which came from my mean great-aunt Almeda. My sister Abby was totally awesome, though. She was never supposed to lend this butterfly necklace to anyone, not even me. My mother would've had a major fit if she knew any different." Francine sighed. "But Abby let me wear it sometimes. The day of her accident, she wanted me to wear it until after track was over, for good luck. I've often thought, if she had of been wearing it at the time of the accident, our fates may have been reversed. It's kind of my good luck charm now."

Anna was stumped. It sounded like her sister had died, but Francine hadn't come right out and said it. "Well, your sister has left it in very caring hands. Lucky you, lucky her."

Francine kept talking, as though she hadn't heard the comment. "Yeah, if our mother knew I had it, she would probably roll over in her grave, if she's gone now. Then again, I've heard only the good die young."

Francine took a breath.

Anna tried not to show her shock. Having immense respect for her own mother, she had trouble comprehending what she'd just heard.

"Wow, really?" she exclaimed.

"Yeah, really," Francine said softly.

For a second, the silence was overwhelming. Anna couldn't believe the hatred Francine harbored in her heart for her mother. She would have liked to have handed her gold cross to Francine, because it had given her a sense of serenity through the years. But she felt that would be overstepping their new friendship. Turning her head away, Anna closed her eyes and touched the shiny cross as she prayed silently for peace for her new friend.

Chapter Twenty-Eight

NEW PASSENGERS WERE TAKING THEIR SEATS AS THE BUS STARTED MOVING AGAIN. Francine watched a pregnant lady take her seat. With her back swaying, the woman carefully maneuvered her wide frame into position. Sighing, Francine was reminded that she had better things to do with her life.

"How are you doing?" a man's voice asked from the aisle. Looking past Anna, Francine saw John standing there.

"I'm fine," Anna said as she turned to Francine.

"Yep, we're doing good," replied Francine. "So far the trip is flying right along."

Feeling a little embarrassed, Francine wondered if he had overheard their conversation earlier.

"Won't be too long now until San Lateo," he said, "but with these rough roads it may seem a lot longer. I've taken this route before and pretty much know it like the back of my hand. Most secondary roads are just that. They never take priority. The recent floods were hard on some of these California coastal roads. The state's never kept them up like the main freeways."

The bus lurched as it hit a pothole. John laughed as he grabbed Anna's seat.

"The further back on these buses you go, the rougher they seem to ride." John chuckled. "Still, any excuse for a good stretch is good for me. By the way, I like your crucifix, miss. I bought one just like that, but my mother liked it so much I ended up giving it to her. Bless her soul."

Francine's heart pounded, her nausea returning. How could things go so bad so quickly? Somehow the subject had turned to crucifixes and mothers. She detested both. Wishing the bus would sink into a pothole, she knew it would be less of a hassle if she could just get off and make her own way to the border, even though it was still a long way off. She stared out the window. The bus roared, her stomach rolled.

She noticed John head towards the restroom.

"Thank God," Francine mumbled.

She glanced at Anna and saw the woman smile as she looked down at her open binder. Francine threw her head back on the headrest.

"Well, I told you you hadn't seen the last of me," a voice bellowed from the aisle. It was the abusive father Francine had yelled at in the depot.

Francine and Anna shared a nervous glance.

Making his way up the aisle, the man stopped and glared at Francine. His rope suspenders stood out over his baggy pants. He stretched his neck past Anna, leaning in and focusing on Francine.

"This time, lady, you stay to hell out of my business, if you know what's good for you!"

Francine's body straightened.

"Is that the guy you had words with back at the depot?" Anna whispered.

"Yep," Francine replied, not taking her eyes off him.

"Leave my business to me," he said. "You understand, girl? Don't want any more trouble than there has to be. Ya hear me now?"

Francine felt her throat tighten, and she couldn't say a word. Locking eyes on him, every sense of her being knew he meant what he said. He then shifted his glassy eyes and sauntered away.

Francine tried, inconspicuously, to get a glimpse of where he was sitting.

"Hey, ladies, if you're going to use the facility, you may want to hold off for a while." John's voice rang from the aisle. "The line has already started."

John was almost face to face with Anna as he took his seat across from her.

"Thanks, John. Guess we can wait." Anna smiled, but then turned back to Francine. "You know, we don't need any problems here. Tell me you're not going to do something that you'll regret."

"Depends. How do you define regret?" Frankie replied, suddenly irritated. "Does it mean never coloring outside the lines? Does it mean never standing up for what you believe in? Does it mean going through life without being heard? Does it mean always putting up with someone else's ignorance? Just what the hell do you mean? You know what, Anna, I've learned one thing for sure: if you're willing to stand at the bottom of a hill all your life, you're just asking to be crapped on—or worse, run over! You know, crap always runs downhill. Yes, crap, Anna! Can you say that word, or does that shiny cross dictate your vocabulary too?"

Anna was dumfounded. "Francine, all I want is peace and an uneventful trip. That guy scares the heck out of me. He's on a mission, and I certainly don't want to be a part of it, and I don't want to see anyone hurt. Remember when that fellow tried to assassinate Reagan last year? It doesn't matter who you are, out of sight and out of mind is just a good place to be. Can you not see that?"

"You know nothing about me and what I've put up with, Anna," Francine huffed, glancing at Anna's cross. "This is where I draw the line. I'm definitely not in this world to win some prissy goodie-two-shoes award!"

Francine was trying to stay focused on the abusive father as he sat motionless in his seat.

Then she let Anna have it again. "Sounds like you came from that white picket fence crap where Mommy baked sunshine cookies, read you princess stories, and told you how great you were going be. And you mentioned you couldn't have kids? Well, do you want this one?" Francine laid her hand on her stomach. "Oh, I can see it right now, Miss Anna Whoever. You wouldn't be able to stand all the joy! Yeah, that would make your life just about too perfect, like totally over the max!" Francine caught her breath. "Hate to say it, but I think your God screwed up again!"

Francine's stomach rolled. Anxiously, she clenched her necklace as she reached for her bag. Shuffling things around, she pulled out a silver wrapper. Shoving the gum in her mouth, she chewed frantically, still never taking her eyes off the man upfront.

Anna felt a chill wash over her body. Trying to comprehend the anger that just came out of Francine's mouth, her body felt numb. Baby? Francine was going to have a baby? Stunned, she tried to focus. Now it was all coming together. Doctor, procedure, Mexico.

Anna's heart skipped. Maybe she had lived a somewhat sheltered life, but she knew one thing for certain: she had never experienced anyone with such sadness. Not to this degree.

Francine craned forward, unwilling to let that monster out of her sight. At the first sign of trouble, Francine knew she would be in full throttle. She could almost taste the victory, remembering the weapon she had stashed in her bag. Her bandana heavy with sweat, she wiped moisture from her face and arranged her hair.

Anna was tense as she stared at the chart on her lap. Francine felt badly, but thought it was too late to take back anything she had just said. Still, she had meant every word, and besides, looking at the cherry dress, Francine figured it was about time for Miss Anna to get a glimpse of the other side of the pasture.

The wiry father sat still. From his seat, he looked like any other passenger waiting to reach his destination. Francine was relieved. Though she didn't want more trouble, she wanted him to realize that, in her eyes, a cruel parent had no place in this world, not even slithered under a rock. She analyzed his gestures and, feeling more comfortable, knew she could let her guard down, at least temporarily.

She closed her eyes, put her hands on her stomach, and drifted off.

"Francine? Francine, are you awake?" Anna's voice whispered.

Francine didn't know how long she had been asleep. She tried to remember where she was; her eyes stung as she tried to focus.

Turning to Anna, the haze started to clear.

"Yeah, I am now," Francine said. "Why?"

"Well, the driver announced that we're stopping for a short layover. He said there's a place close by where we can get a bite. What do you think?"

"Yeah, totally sounds good," Francine answered, trying to shake off her drowsiness.

Anna reached for her purse and left the bus.

❀

The roadside diner resembled a shack. Not only did it look like something from a 50s B-movie, through the dusk the green flashing neon sign read "Famous Greasy Spoon."

Francine and Anna made faces at each other.

"Well, if it's bad food, at least it sounds like it will slide down easy," Francine said, sighing.

"Yeah, it could be way worse. The sign could read 'The Famous Greasy Armpit'!"

"Eww," Anna gasped as Francine laughed.

The lineup was long and the noise of clinking dishes hung in the background. Francine wondered whether the food was good or the travelers just desperate to eat. But Francine's stomach turned when the smell of burned grease reached her. She looked at the faded menu on the wall, then turned to Anna.

"A burger, tomato juice, and pickle" was all she said before disappearing into the restaurant crowd.

Anna, always curious about life, tried to take everything in. The group of people before her was diverse in race, age, and size. She saw the mother with the crutch, with the young girl, and smiled. She had learned years ago from her grandma that God always disguises himself through others. Even if things appeared odd or unfair, she believed God was still there.

"Next!" a voice shouted.

"Yes, may I have two burgers, one tomato juice, one milk."

Anna placed the money on the counter.

"Your order will be up shortly," the waitress said, pointing to the far end of the counter. "Next!"

Anna tried to exit the line. As she bumped into people, she cordially apologized until she found some space for herself. Glancing up at the spoon-shaped clock on the wall, she wondered why Francine was taking so long. Anna knew Francine had recently made some new acquaintances, but she also knew there was a good possibility she was on her knees in front of a toilet.

"Hey," Francine said, startling her. She held her pink bandana and her face had turned a paler shade of white. "Sorry I took so long, but I got talking to that John dude. You know, the guy from the bus?"

"Oh yes, the nice man," Anna said.

"Hey, I also managed to sneak in a small conversation with that bully. You know, the one who has the nice wife and sick kid."

Anna glared at her. "Francine, you didn't. You need to avoid that guy. Are you insane?"

"Well, maybe sometimes, but at least he knows I'm definitely not his number-one fan."

The waitress called from the counter: "Two burgers, juice and milk up!"

Anna grabbed the tray, and she and Francine found a corner table.

Francine couldn't get to the food quickly enough. She snatched up her burger and started tearing into it, knocking over the glass of juice.

"Crap! Why does this bogus stuff always happen to me?" Francine said, frazzled. She shoved the last of a crisp pickle in her mouth and tried to wipe away the juice that had splattered everywhere.

A frown creased her face as she glanced down at her soggy shirt.

"I'll be right back," Francine muttered.

Anna saw that Francine wasn't doing well. She grasped the gold cross that lay against her dress and closed her eyes. "God, please make everything right for Francine."

Savoring the peace, Anna found it difficult to open her eyes.

"This place is a dump. If I could only puke one more time," Francine sputtered between gags.

As she rose, carefully, her butterfly necklace clanked against the toilet. Lifting her leg, she maneuvered the handle with her foot. The toilet flushed.

At the sink, the reflection in the mirror jolted her. She ran her fingers through the crimped hair as her stomach turned again.

"Girl, you look some kind of worn-out trollop," she mumbled back at her reflection. She looked at her shirt. "Not to mention a dirty one."

Francine tried to scrub the stains from her shirt.

When she opened the women's restroom door, the voices outside were loud. A mob stood at the entrance of the men's room.

"Someone call an ambulance!" a man shouted.

"He's not responding. Doesn't look good," another interjected.

"Ambulance is on its way!"

Francine tried to get past the commotion. As she neared the men's restroom, she felt all eyes on her. A guy with a bushy beard peered at her; she could smell his breath as she tried to pass.

"Hey girl, you okay?" he asked, looking at her shirt. "You know anything about the situation here? Is there anyone else in the ladies room?"

"Not that I know of, but then again I wasn't looking for anyone else!" Francine snapped. She felt the stares as she pushed her way past him.

Sneaking a peek into the men's restroom, she saw dark-colored pants and a small pool of blood on the floor. Francine felt her anxiety mounting.

"I gotta get out of this hellhole now," she said out loud, frantically barging her way back toward the restaurant.

Francine looked for Anna and located the woman's dark-framed glasses in the distance. Approaching quickly, Francine wondered if anything fazed her new friend.

"Come on, Anna! We got to leave here, now!" Francine said, grabbing her bag and bandana.

Anna complied, hurriedly leaving the table.

"What's going on, Francine?" Anna asked, looking up at the clock. "All I know is that you go to the restroom, and exactly twenty minutes later all heck breaks loose back there. Then you fly up here, acting like someone was just murdered or something. Are you all right? Is there something I should know?"

"Well, as a matter of fact, there is," Francine said abruptly. "There's a man back there in the men's room. Wait a minute, let me rephrase that: I'm pretty sure there's a dead man back there in the men's room!" She took a deep breath. "At least he looked dead."

Anna gasped, but before she could get another word out Francine grabbed her.

"Come on!" Francine ordered as they fled out the door.

Trying to catch her breath, Anna was agitated. "Is there something else I should know while we're on the subject of dead people?"

"Yeah, there is." Francine huffed as they sped across the parking lot toward the bus. "First of all, never believe a clock shaped like a friggin' greasy spoon, okay? Second, don't ever buy cheap mascara. And third, don't ever let anyone tell you that crap doesn't run downhill! Now come on! Let's blow this joint!"

Sirens were screaming in the parking lot.

"Stand back, stand back," a guy yelled as two men in white maneuvered a gurney and several pieces of equipment through the door of the restaurant. Charging across the scantily lit parking lot, firefighters and policemen converged on the scene as people gawked.

To Francine, it felt like the bus was miles away.

"Wonder how they're all going to fit into that tiny little restroom anyway?" Francine wondered. She tugged at Anna to move faster. "That would be a hazard in itself."

"How would you know about the men's restroom?"

"If it's anything like the women's, it's small. The women's was so cramped there was really nowhere for me to throw up, except pretty much on myself." She looked down at her shirt. "That place was the worst grunge bag I've ever been in, and I've been in a few."

Francine rustled through her bag as they walked, her hand brushing against the steel blade Max had given her. The more she thought things over, the more she regretted the way Max always told her what to do. But she was torn; she knew he had her best interest at heart. Max was clear that he didn't want her to get into a jam in this crazy world without something that could save her life.

Scouring the bag, she pulled out a silver wrapper. Anxiously, she shoved the gum into her mouth.

"You need a chew too, Anna?"

"Definitely not now. Besides, I'm trying to quit," she said sarcastically.

Things seemed unusually quiet on the bus as they made their way down the aisle. Taking their seats, Anna took her turn next to the window.

"Guess we're a little early," Anna said, trying to sound optimistic.

"Looks that way," Francine replied. There was only one other passenger. She leaned back, closed her eyes, and placed her hand on stomach. "Come on, Tijuana."

Chapter Twenty-Nine

"CAN YOU BELIEVE WHAT HAPPENED BACK AT THAT JOINT?" A LOUD VOICE ASKED.

Francine straightened up, startled as she realized the bus was loading again. Shuffling people had started filling the vehicle.

"Yeah, not good at all," another voice remarked. "That guy was a total nutcase. From what I saw, it looks like the dude finally met his match!"

"For sure, a pretty nasty clock-cleaning, I'd say."

"Man, what a way to go. Especially at that joint."

Further away, a woman's voice distracted Francine. "Look, Lacey!" said the mother of the identical twins. "Why can't you be good, like your sister? You are so lucky your father isn't here!"

"But she took mine," said Lacey. "It was my candy. Give it back!"

"I have had enough of you, young lady," the mother growled as she yanked her daughter's pigtails.

Making her way past Francine, Lacey frowned. Her sister followed silently, chomping in delight as though a candy store had just landed in her mouth. Francine knew her sister was never going to see that candy again. Guiding the crying Lacey into her seat, the mother slammed the other child onto her lap.

"Next time this bus stops, neither one of you girls are getting off, understand?"

"Wow," Francine remarked to Anna. "And here I thought I made my great-aunt Almeda look good."

A small tunnel of light shone down on the open book in Anna's lap. As she pushed her glasses back, Francine saw that the woman was in full concentration.

"I've certainly come to know that a lot of things in this world aren't always what they appear to be," Anna replied, shifting her eyes to Francine's shirt.

"So, you have it all figured out, do you, Anna?"

"Apparently not, from the pointers you gave me on the way back to the bus." They laughed. "Hey, Francine, I'm sorry for the things you've been through. I honestly can say I don't know what it feels like, because I've never been in your shoes. And speaking of shoes, I don't know how you can wear those things. They look like weapons. And would you mind changing that shirt? To put it bluntly, it looks like a bloody mess."

"Probably a good idea," Francine answered, looking down at the blotches smeared across the shirt.

The only thing on Francine that looked to have escaped trauma was the butterfly necklace. It hung perfectly, resting overtop the pools of stains.

Francine sighed. Knowing she had packed too lightly was the least of her worries. She picked up her bag.

"I'll be back shortly. Save my seat," she smirked.

When the door closed, she lifted a fresh shirt from her bag. She pulled the soiled shirt over her head.

Something hit the floor with a clunk, followed by a tumbling wig. Francine reached down and, quickly grabbing the knife, shoved it back into her bag. Next, she grabbed the wig and tousled it until she had it looking almost normal again. She tugged it back on her head, scrunched up the stained shirt, and heaved it in the bag.

Opening the door, Francine heard the plea of a small child.

"Mommy, Mommy, where's Daddy? I want Daddy."

Looking up the aisle, Francine saw the woman with the crutch and the young girl. A uniformed man was escorting them off the bus.

Francine took her seat again beside Anna.

"Now that makes me feel a lot less nervous," she said, looking at Francine's clean shirt. She shifted her gaze to Francine's hair. "Are you all right? Looks like you just spun out of a twister."

Francine glared back at her. "Tell me something, Anna. Have you never had a bad hair day in your life?"

"As a matter of fact, I've had many. But through the years I've managed to leave most of my concerns with the good Lord, including bad hair days." Anna grinned, her eyes returning to her book. "I would never have dreamed I would be on a bus heading to Tijuana. But then again, I'm not the one with the master plan." She placed her hand over her cross. "What I'm saying is, if it was all up to me, I would never have had the pleasure of meeting you."

Francine rolled her eyes. "Well, by the time you leave this bus, Anna, you will probably wish you had never met me."

Anna hesitated. "Francine, what if you were to learn somehow that butterflies actually do come from God? And what if he has the very reason in the palm of his hand for why he chose you to wear that necklace, the one you so adore? Then would you at least consider that there are no coincidences? You know, you have nothing to lose if you choose to believe in that."

"Look, Anna, if you stay on the God kick again, I'll have to leave." Francine's tone grew more serious. "In case you didn't notice, I can manage my life just fine without having to believe in some invisible dude lurking around me. Believe me."

Anna sighed as she looked at Francine's twisted hair. "Yes, I've noticed."

"May I have your attention, ladies and gentlemen?" a voice asked from the PA system. "This is Detective Taylor. Tonight you are probably aware there was a serious incident at the Greasy Spoon diner. I could hold this route up, but instead I have decided to do a routine investigation while in transit. If anyone saw anything unusual, please come forward with your information. It will be kept confidential. In the meantime, I will be visiting each of you in your seats. Please have your identification ready. No one gets off this bus until this task is completed. Thanks for your cooperation."

Mumbles and whispers were heard all around.

"Wow. These fellows don't mess around, do they?" Anna remarked.

"A serious incident. That doesn't sound so good," Francine said. "But I suppose murder would sound even worse. Wonder who he was?"

"Well, how would I know? It wasn't me who saw the body!"

"Anna, all I saw were pants and blood. That's it."

"Very well. It will all work out in the end," Anna replied. "It always does."

"I'm not sure who the guy was, but I've sure run into my share of left-field people since leaving Santa Montrose," Francine said, glaring at Anna.

"Excuse me, ma'am," the detective's husky voice interrupted. "I need to see your identification, and your friend's, too."

Anna and Francine lifted their identifications from their wallets. The detective sorted through the papers.

"Are these your current addresses?" he asked, pulling out a black book and pen. "Just routine, ladies, but I'm required by law to document your information." He turned to Anna. "What's the reason for your travelling?"

"I'm on my way across the border to help coordinate a training program," Anna answered eagerly.

"Yeah, Detective, and I'm on my way to Tijuana for a small procedure." Francine sighed. "You know how expensive healthcare is in the land of the free. Well, I would much rather spend my hard-earned money on other things."

"What's your profession, ma'am?" the detective asked Francine.

"I'm in the fashion industry, selling girl stuff."

He studied her picture. "Well, I guess that would explain the different hair in your photo. Okay, ladies, there's one last thing. Did either of you see anything that may help us with our investigation?"

Anna looked at Francine.

"Nope, I didn't see a thing," Francine said. "Don't even know who the guy was. Sorry, can't help you."

"Miss Moonie, is it?" the detective asked, flipping slowly through his notes. "Some persons are saying you and the man found in the diner restroom had a confrontation back at the bus depot in Santa Montrose. Other individuals claim you had another run-in with him before he was found. Are you sure you don't know anything?"

Francine could feel the blood rush to her face. "Are you telling me *that* was the guy, Detective? The dead guy?"

"How do you know the man is deceased, Miss Moonie? I can't recall me ever stating that."

"Well, he sure looked that way," Francine said, feeling anxious.

"According to state law, we are unable to release his name yet, dead or alive. But for your satisfaction, Miss Moonie, yes, that could be the man."

"That coward bully?" Francine blurted out.

"Is that all you saw, Miss Moonie?"

Francine chomped down on her gum. "For sure, but I got to tell you, Detective, he probably had it coming. The way he was carrying on with his wife and all. And that poor kid of his. I bet a guy like him had more enemies than a heroin junky has needles. Still, I suppose it will be bad news for someone."

Anna cleared her throat, trying to get Francine's attention. When Francine looked at her, Anna's big eyes were fixed on her.

Undeniable

"Well, ladies, if you remember anything, please contact me," the detective said. He reached into his pressed breast pocket, pulled out a card, and handed it to Francine. "Uh, Miss Moonie, there's just one more thing. If I didn't know better, I'm almost certain we've met before."

His voice sounded so smooth. Francine's heart started pounding.

"Nope, can't say we ever have," she said. "A lot of people say I just got one of those faces."

The detective nodded as he made his way to the next row.

"Oh crap," Francine whispered.

"What on earth is going on, Francine? He seems to know you from somewhere. You certainly were spilling it out."

"What does that mean?" Francine glanced at the card and shoved it in her bag. "That guy doesn't know me from anywhere!"

She pulled out a silver wrapper and shoved another stick of gum in her mouth.

"Please, Francine, for your own good, let me tell you something," Anna said intently. "That Detective Taylor seems to think you know more than what you're saying. Can you not see that? What I know for sure is that I don't want to be an accomplice to anything. And yes, I may have lived a somewhat sheltered life in your eyes, but this may be turning out to be a little too public for my liking! And it's not like it's any of my business or anything, but I'm not sure what you were doing back at the diner. Regardless, I still believe there are no coincidences. And speaking of coincidences, do you really believe your baby was just some ill-fated luck of the draw? Look, I don't know your circumstances, but from what I've gathered, I think you're not sure who you really are!"

Anna flicked at Francine's hair.

"You change your hair, your story, and practically your skin," Anne continued. "I have to hand it to you, girl. You are the quickest chameleon I've ever seen. But then you also have this notion that you have to save or butcher the world. And if that isn't crazy enough, you try and do it all at the same time! Like I said, it's not my business, but who are you really hiding from?" Anna looked at her intently. "You're not going to like this either, but I'm almost certain I know who. Don't you think it's time to slow down and just give yourself a break?"

Anna took her cross in her hand and held it tightly. She knew she had said too much.

Francine stared into the distance. "Okay, you win, Anna," she muttered. "Just to clear the air, you're right. For that matter, you're probably always right!

You with a silver spoon hanging from your mouth, how could you not possibly be right? Well, I can handle myself just fine, even when I run into people like you, coincidentally."

Anna sat up straight. She knew she had drawn the line with Francine and it was time to take her hands from the wheel. Her advice didn't seem to be helping. From Anna's past experiences, she knew there was only one thing that could help Francine's troubled soul. And that would be in his time.

"Are you finished yet?" Francine asked, wrapping her butterfly chain around her finger.

"Yes, I believe I am."

Anna glanced slowly down at the mound of papers.

Snatching her bag, Francine stood up. "Guess it's time I go find myself a new conversation. This one seems a little worn out. Excuse me."

Anna discreetly observed as Francine moved over to talk with John. She could hear Francine giggle and then let out a snort. John roared with laughter.

"I guess that's just how it goes in life, Francine," John said with undeniable enthusiasm. "We're all only one bus ride away!"

Anna wasn't sure what their topic was, but she could tell Francine had taken a shine to John. Her intuition told her there was something different about him, but she couldn't figure it out. What she did know is that John would be guaranteed a rather odd, yet interesting, conversation.

Anna closed her eyes. Holding onto her cross, she prayed quietly. "Dear God, thank you for this turbulent introduction with another one of your splendid children. Although Francine may be a mystery to me, I know she's no mystery to you. Dear Lord, please have her reconsider her health crisis. Thank you for being such a loving God. Amen."

Anna opened her eyes and gently kissed her cross. She felt reassured that her new friend was going to be all right.

Looking beyond the frayed fabric of the seat in front of her, Anna noticed Francine had moved on and was taking up residence with another man. He was wearing one of the biggest cowboy hats she had ever seen. Anna snickered and wondered just how long it would take for him to hit one of Francine's nerves.

"I see y'all had a disturb'nce back thar' at the diner," came the voice from under the hat.

"Oh, it was nothing, really," Francine said. "Is this seat taken?"

"No, ma'am, help yourself." The man pointed to the empty seat. "What's yer name, young lady?"

"Francine," she answered, sitting down.

"Y'all must have some mighty strong roots in yah, from whud I saw. I'm Har'ld." He tipped his hat and held out a calloused hand. "Can't wait 'til I git this her' old man's back end off this bus. Think it wud a bin a li'l easier jus' ta ride my horse southwards. But if I buys a car on the other side of the bord'r like planned, the horse would have to leave her ther'." Harold chuckled. "Fer sure, I knew'd it wud a been a darn lot quicker thin the three days on the road ridin' buses. So whad's a gal like ya doin' travellin' alone through this country anyway? You know'd, if you wuz my daughter I'd kick yur bu'hind all the way ta Cucamonga. Well, that's if ya'd had no good reason fer bein' on this her' bus to starts with."

Francine smiled. She wasn't going to get a word in. But that was all right. She was tired of defending herself. She welcomed the peace that came with a one-sided conversation.

"Yeah, me and the Mrs. wuz blessed with a boy. He's a natur'l-born cowboy. Still, he had some of them ther' things, think you'd call 'em egzastra'bations of becomin' one of them ther' ottornies of the law and such. Me and the Mrs. never discouraged his dreams, though. Weez seen wuda brog'n spir't can do. Tell me, miss, ya ever had your spir't brog'n?"

Harold looked curious.

"Not that I remember," Francine said.

"Well, let me tells ya, if ya ever saw a horse with a brog'n spir't, you'd know'd it fer sure. It's a purdy terr'ble thing. There ain't no peace wer'ev'r them horses go, after that happ'ns." Harold shook his head. "Yep, it's a real bad thing."

Fumbling with her bag, Francine found another chew.

"So, what do you do for a livin', miss?"

Francine chomped on her gum. "Ah, Harold, guess you could say I help people in crisis. I guess you could call me an emotional rescuer or something like that." Francine yawned.

"Miss, as long as yu's 'r good at whatcha do, and like doin' it, it'll pay off fer ya down the road. Fer sample, take this big ole fancy hat her'. Ernest won it in one of those ther' annual pig-wrasslin' comp'titions. Just like anythin' in this ole world, you just have to keep at it. Practice pays off. This her' hat is a remind'r. Ain't nud'n' easy 'bout hard work!"

Harold tipped his hat.

Francine grinned. "Well, I guess I'm getting pretty good at what I do. I've had practice and now my customers just keep coming back."

"Lordy, sure wud'a bin nice fer ya to meet my boy! You wud'a bin a good inspir'tion fer him. Yeah, me and the Mrs. talk 'bout him lots, even though he's purdy much grow'd up. Some of the neighbors say the Mrs. talks too much, though." He laughed. "Yeah, heard 'em say back ther' at home, she's got a mouth on her like the back end of a Whipp'rwill, and that's pudd'n it nice. Though my Dor'thy is a real good Christian lady, yid never wanna cross her. No sirree! She's just proud of her boy, that's all. Wezz hop'in he settles his saddle soon. You know, I think you'd be a fine one fer Ernest. Far as I kin tell, ya got that purdy head of yor's on straight as a row of horses lined up for the trough. Yes, ma'am, I can tell yor ma and pa did right by you. Heck, Ernest would treat ya as if you wuz a queen. He'd prob'ly even take you to one of these her' bus trips. An' if he gits his otternie paper, the good Lord only knows wer' him and the lucky Mrs. would end up!" Harold winked. "Anyway, ya may jus' be too dang prurdy even fer that ther' kinda life, young Miss."

Francine stared ahead, trying to comprehend his words. She appreciated the temporary distraction, until her stomach rolled again. That triggered her escape.

"It was nice talking to you, Harold, but I must get back to my friend." She tried to sound joyful. "Have a good trip."

"Nice meet'n ya, miss," Harold replied, tipping his hat. "If ya's ever in Jackson, look us up now, ya hear? The last name's Langwire! Har'ld an' Dor'thy Langwire. Still be mighty happy to intr'duce ya to 'er boy."

"Sure, thanks."

Francine made her way slowly down the aisle.

Almost everything appeared surreal now, except her butterfly necklace. She glanced at the strange faces. Two months ago, she never would have dreamed of being on a bus with such odd people, heading for Mexico. She was starting to believe that if there really was a God, this trip proved he had reached his wit's end with her.

Her stomach felt heavy as she peered through the darkness. Margareet was cuddled back up with her sick daughter, who was asleep. Margareet's eyes were swollen, her expression empty as she stared into the distance. Francine could see her pain and wanted to console her, but she knew she couldn't. Thanks to

Jane, Francine had learned at a young age that pain was transferable. She realized that if she extended a hand to this woman, especially in her present state, it could be detrimental. Francine knew neither the woman nor her daughter needed more pain. She kept walking.

Then she saw the young mother with her twins. They were also sleeping, sharing a seat as their heads bobbed with every bump in the road. Francine smiled at their undeniable sisterly love, and she recalled the candy tantrum they'd had earlier.

Next she saw the man with the scraggly ponytail talking to Detective Taylor. First he glared at Francine, then smiled through his handlebar mustache. She tried to get past him quickly.

Her bag grazed a jacket which was flung over his seat. It fell to the floor. Not looking back, she stepped over it. Francine felt there was something creepy about the guy, but at the same time intriguing. Considering her emotional state, Francine found it bizarre that she would give the weirdo any space in her brain.

Exhausted, she made her way toward Anna again.

Anna's eyes were closed and she had moved to the aisle seat. Papers had been placed on the seat next to her. It was clear she didn't want to talk anymore.

"Looking for a place to sit?" John asked.

"Thanks," Francine said, taking the aisle seat next to him. "Looks like my partner in crime is getting some rest."

"I'm awake now," Anne said, having overheard. "That must have been some conversation you had with the cowboy up there. And by the way, I am not your partner in crime."

Francine scoffed. "Hey, Anna, maybe it's time for you to settle down."

"What do you mean by that?" Anna asked, sighing.

"Well, the cowboy's name is Harold. Don't let the hat fool you. He's on his way to maybe buy a car south of the border or something like that," Francine said, pointing up the aisle. "He has it all, and he's right there, waiting for you. You just have to walk up the aisle and receive another one of your blessings! You know, Harold would make a great father-in-law, and his wife Dorothy a real good mother-in-law. Even though she's got a wicked tongue on her, she's a fine Christian lady. Well, according to Harold, that is. What more could you ask for, Anna? See, God's got it all covered."

Francine snickered.

John chuckled, peering over his book. "You must have got a great crash course up there on family genetics." Francine threw John a glance.

"Hey, Anna, if that's not enough to lure you, their son Ernest is a prize wrass'ler and has egzastr'bations of becoming an otturnie." Francine could barely contain herself. "Yeah, I bet you could even have the privilege of leveling out the mud used to take down a feisty bore! Your cherry dress and sparkly cross would add a special touch, don't you think?"

Anna burst into laughter. "Well, if you assume I would look good in a cowboy hat, rubber boots, and helping with who-knows-what, I'm afraid we certainly have very different tastes! Then again, on second thought, I do have other dresses!"

Francine tried to picture it. "Other dresses, Anna? You mean there's more where that came from?" Francine worked her gum.

John couldn't hold his laughter either.

"Yes, Miss Funny Lady, there's more!" Anna blurted.

John snickered. "Mm-hmm, yes, God is good!"

Francine looked at him, then reached for her necklace as her eyes became heavy. She tried to keep them open but finally gave in to the battle.

Chapter Thirty

The shuffling of people on the bus awoke her. She quickly realized she had no pillow and that her head was resting on John's shoulder.

"Crap," she whispered to herself.

Looking up at John, she wished she had stayed in the seat beside Harold.

"I'm so sorry," she said, pulling a ball of sticky goop from his wet shirt. Embarrassed, Francine tried to avoid John's expression. She shoved the ball into her bag.

John grinned. "It's really all right. You were resting peacefully, so who was I to disturb you?"

"Well, that still doesn't make it all right for me to ruin your shirt, does it?" Francine said, dismayed. "Looks like someone took a lot of time to get it just perfect. I feel like a dweeb. I'm so embarrassed."

Turning to Anna for comfort, Francine realized she was on her own. Anna was enthralled with her paperwork.

"Francine," John said gently, "it's for God to judge, not I. So it's all right. God's got this one, honestly."

Francine felt her heart race. She tried to appear inconspicuous, turning to Anna again and stretching her torso toward the woman, across the aisle.

"Pssssssssssst. Anna, Anna. You've got to help me," she implored. "I just drooled all over John's shoulder and now he's talking crazy. Could you trade seats? Please."

"What do you mean, talking crazy?" Anna asked, confused.

Francine cupped her hand over her mouth. "All that God stuff. You know. You need to sit here, Anna, not me!"

"What I need is for you to calm down," Anne hissed back. "He's not going to hurt you. God won't let him! Trust me." She reached for Francine's hand. "Do you hear me, Francine? Get yourself together. Nothing is going to happen, understand?"

"Is everything all right?" John's gentle voice drifted toward Francine.

She took a deep breath. "It's been a real long day, that's all."

"I can't help but ask you," John continued, "but have you been kind of on your own?"

Francine looked dumbfounded.

"That has to be a lonely place to be." John cleared his throat. "You against this big old world."

Francine knew she didn't want to answer the question. What business was it of his if she was on her own? She wasn't sure what he was getting at, and now she was starting to wonder how long he had been studying her. She wasn't sure now if he had followed her all the way from Santa Montrose.

With two murders in her shadow, anyone could be following her, pretending they were someone they weren't. But still she felt it would be rude to sit somewhere else, especially after her sleeping mishap.

"As a matter of fact, yes, I've been pretty much on my own since I was born, I'd say," Francine answered. She looked down at her necklace. "Well, except for my Aunt Julie and my sister, that is. They're both dead now."

She reached into her bag and pulled out a silver wrapper.

"Sorry to hear that," John replied.

"Yeah, thanks. No big deal." Francine rolled the gum into her mouth.

"I was admiring your butterfly earlier. And that's quite the chain. I've always been intrigued by the Lord's creatures who represent freedom while still appearing bound. Suppose your necklace is a perfect symbol of an oxymoron. Interesting, to say the least."

Francine looked puzzled as she twirled the thick chain. "Yeah, I guess."

"Well, Francine, may I tell you something?"

Francine sat motionless. "What would that be?"

"I'm so glad to be the bearer of good news," John said excitedly. "Did you know that before you were born, until this very moment, and then the next and the next, you have never been alone? Nor will you ever be." He grasped the black book. "You see this Bible? The whole truth is right here."

He smiled as he squeezed the book.

"Do you know anything about this book, Francine?" He smiled as he ran his fingers across the bold inscription on the bottom of its cover: J.C.

"No, can't say I do," Francine said. "Heard things about it when I was a kid, but it was all jibber-jabber to me."

John laughed. "God's word isn't supposed to be complicated. See, that's what Satan wants us to believe, but he will never hold a candle to God's word. He is only a master of deceit. If he can plant his seed of trickery in God's children, especially when they're very young, he thinks he's taking God's power away. But the truth is, God's power can never be taken away. It's still much bigger than his. He's all show, Francine. Satan's only job is to steal, kill, and destroy. That's it."

Francine nodded and chewed on her gum.

"Just out of curiosity, do you have a favorite Bible verse?" John asked with anticipation. He shuffled through the pages.

"Not really. But I remember we'd sing a song in church a couple times when I was a kid. I always thought it was called Jesus Sloves Me. Anyway, that's what I thought." Francine sighed. "I thought that dude, Jesus, wanted to hit me. I believed that for years. Even after I figured out what the actual words were, and that was a lot of years later, it never really changed my mind about him."

John chuckled. "Really."

"Yeah, really. Guess it's kind of like when you learn chocolate milk never did come from brown cows."

John was trying to understand her analogy as their eyes met.

"What I'm getting at is it's all the same crapola, only different," Francine said, looking away. "None of it really matters, if you never liked chocolate milk anyway. Get my drift?"

John's face broke into a huge grin. "Yes, I believe I do get your drift." As he flipped through the pages of his Bible, he knew he had a lot of work ahead of him. "Well, there's something else I'd like to share with you. None of us likes to endure hardship—it hurts, Francine. There are a lot of people who believe happiness comes from their circumstances. They either go through their lives chasing happiness or trying to mold their circumstance to how they think it should be. Really, they're only attempting to fill a bottomless pit, over and over again. Trying to keep up that facade will wear you down faster than anything in this life. That's why I fill myself from God's well. Girl, it never runs dry."

John smiled and looked at the book that lay open on his lap.

"Tell me something, Francine. Don't you ever just run out of steam?"

Silence filled the air as John waited for a response.

"Yeah, sometimes when I was working long hours, I found myself dragging, I suppose," Francine muttered. John's words stoked the fire inside her. If she could find the nerve, she would politely ask him to shut up. But remembering the sleeping accident, she thought the least she could do was suck it up and listen for a while. "So, John, getting back to your question about the verse thing, it would be 'no'."

Francine worked on her gum.

Anna had been trying to listen to their conversation. Though she didn't want to appear nosey, she couldn't contain her smile. She also knew John had met his match.

Francine turned to Anna. At times like this she missed Max's happy cabinet.

One more second and she would have missed the plastic bowl. The butterfly swayed back and forth as Francine ran her hand across her mouth and turned toward the sink. The cool water felt good on her face. Embracing the necklace, she felt her throat tighten as it unleashed her sadness and anger. The sobs were uncontrollable.

"Anybody in here?" a man's voice yelled.

She saw the metal handle move.

Francine wiped her eyes, then unlocked the door and saw a handlebar mustache.

"What part of a locked door don't you understand? Can't you tell this room is in use?" Francine raged.

"Sorry, my mistake."

"You betcha!"

Francine attempted to shut the door, but he held it open. "Please, Francine, I just want to give you a head's up. The detective has been going seat to seat asking about you."

"Just what makes you think my name is Francine anyway?"

"Put it this way: most of the passengers out there have learned what your name is by now. I'm just trying to help, that's all."

"Well, I don't need your stupid help!" She slammed the door shut, then pounded the wall. "Where are you now, you so-called God? Where are you, you coward? We both know where you've been. That's nowhere!"

Francine tried to stop crying. She feared that she had finally come undone. She had always believed that one day she would unravel, though she'd never imagined it would happen on a bus.

Wiping her eyes, she quietly opened the door. There were no uniforms in sight.

Cautiously, she made her way down the aisle, sitting in the first vacant seat. She could feel her skin tremble. Trying to come to terms with her latest plight, she turned to the passenger beside her and saw a familiar face.

"Everything okay?" John asked.

"Yeah."

"I hope you weren't offended. You left so quickly."

"Nope, I just have lots on my mind."

"Well, I'm sorry if our conversation bothered you." Before Francine had a chance to reply, he continued, "Though if it isn't too forward of me, may I ask what you do for a living?"

Francine knew she had carelessly let her guard down. "I'm in human relations," she said wearily.

"That sounds interesting. You certainly must have your work cut out for you these days."

"You have no idea." Francine sighed.

"Are you employed with a company?"

"Pretty much. I've worked my way to the top, so to speak. And the money's good."

"Well," John said, adjusting his fedora, "have you ever thought about using your knowledge to help the less fortunate? For instance, maybe getting yourself acquainted with some type of outreach program? You could share your experiences with others. There are a lot of centers crying out for help. And just from the short time I've come to know you, I think you may be able to share quite a lot. The training is ongoing, of course. Besides, it pleases God when he can use us. Yes sirree, that makes him happy with his children. After all, we are all God's children, you know."

"It's never crossed my mind. Thanks anyway."

She glared at John as she realized this trip to Mexico had the potential to taint a life that had been working for her—at least for the most part.

John turned to Anna and grinned. Anna smiled back.

Francine closed her eyes, trying to escape her present circumstances. Although she had been convinced John was just a nice guy, now she wasn't so sure. Hearing the pages flip, she couldn't help but feel sympathy over John's need for his God.

She closed her eyes.

"Francine Moonie?"

Francine looked up to see the same detective she had spoken with earlier. "Yeah."

"Miss Moonie, could you come with me? I have a few questions for you."

Francine flung her bag over her shoulder and stepped into the aisle. She glanced back at John. He lowered his head and, Bible in hand, turned a page slowly.

She followed the detective to the front of the bus. He motioned for her to sit by an empty window seat, then sat beside her. She was trapped.

"Miss Moonie," he said as he opened his notebook. "Did you know the deceased, Mr. Bagly, before your excursion here?"

Francine pulled a silver wrapper from her bag. "No, never seen him before. First time I saw him was at the bus depot back in Santa Montrose."

The detective studied her face as she spoke. "Apparently there was an altercation between you and the deceased at the Santa Montrose depot. Miss Moonie, witnesses claim you threatened Mr. Bagley. Is that true?"

Francine shoved the grey stick into her mouth. "Well, to be honest with you, Mr... what was your name again?"

"Detective Taylor."

"Well, Mr. Taylor, if one of you guys had been there to see him, you would have thrown him in the slammer. As far as I can figure, he'd probably still be alive then. I feel sorry for his family and everything, but a guy like him makes his own problems. Other than that, I can't tell much else."

The detective glared at Francine. "So what transpired between you and Mr. Bagly before your stop at the Greasy Spoon? Would you call it a friendly encounter, Miss Moonie?"

"Not really. The guy was getting under my skin. He threatened me, too. He was a psycho. If you don't believe me, you can ask Anna back there. She'll tell you."

The detective looked at her, expressionless, careful not to reveal what he was thinking.

"I've got most of the statements from the other passengers," Taylor said. "But I'm going to have to ask you to come with me to the LAPD at the next layover for more questioning. I'm only doing my job. We just need to clarify a few things. Again, where did you say you're heading?"

With hesitancy, Francine answered, "Tijuana."

"Well, if it's any consolation, Miss Moonie, the department's not far from the bus terminal. After we talk in Los Angeles, as far I can tell, you should be all right to continue on your trip. That is, if the interview goes well. Are you travelling alone?"

"Yep."

"Where did you say home was?"

"Indiana and around."

"Well, if I didn't know better, I'd swear I've seen you somewhere before, but I've never been to Indiana."

The detective rose from his seat and Francine followed. Feeling his eyes on her, she tried to squeeze past him. But he wasn't giving up any space. She felt his body press hard against hers as she struggled to get by.

"You sure we haven't met somewhere before, Miss Moonie?" he whispered. She felt his warm breath.

"I'm sure."

"Thanks for your cooperation." He grinned. "I'll see you when the bus stops."

Francine felt nauseous. She wasn't surprised by the detective's actions. After all, she was used to scumbags. But the incongruity of a uniformed man acting that way made her uncomfortable and reminded her just how much she had come to hate the law. Somehow the police always managed to show up at the wrong time—or never show up at all.

Whatever was about to transpire, Francine knew in her heart she could never have a satisfying relationship with power-tripping cop, let alone get swindled by some vagabond Bible-thumper.

Through the dimly lit aisle, she nervously made her way back to the seat beside John. She pulled the bag from her shoulder. Her hair got caught on the handle. Francine tried frantically to clench the wig, but not before all her personal things were strewn into the aisle. Adjusting her hair, she looked over at Anna. Anna smiled as she attempted to help Francine retrieve her belongings.

"Things usually have a way of appearing worse than they actually are," Anna said.

"Sure," Francine replied somberly.

"Everything all right?" John asked as he watched Francine toss the remainder of her items back into her bag.

"Far as I can tell," Francine said. "Though I have to go to the police department with Detective Taylor and answer some questions at our next layover. It's no big deal."

"Really? Now that doesn't sound so good," John said, closing his Bible.

"It's all right. They just want any information they can get about the guy who died. Anyway, can't blame them for not wanting a killer on the streets."

"Well, if you feel comfortable, I'll gladly go with you," John said eagerly. "I could use a good stretch. Besides, I've never really seen much of Los Angeles. But no pressure, Francine. It's up to you."

Her mind raced as she crafted a response. "No thanks. I'll handle this on my own."

"I get it. But if you change your mind, let me know."

Trying to calm herself, Francine reached for her butterfly. "If only you could talk," she said to herself, sighing. Francine knew if the butterfly could speak, with everything it had endured, it would be either a sought-after storyteller or seeking the help of a shrink. Her head spun. At times like this, she missed Abby. Max was going to be her new life soon, and she had to hand it to Wendy for trying to fill her sister's place. But not even Wendy could replace Abby.

"Well, we're here," John said. "L.A. at last. Only a few more stops from our destination. It's never by our watch, though. God's plan can be a little unpredictable, to say the least." He smirked as he hovered over Francine.

Francine grabbed her bag and looked at him.

"It's all right. Laugh, Francine. You should see how tall my little sister is, and she doesn't even wear a fedora!"

Stepping from the bus, Francine heard the buzz of traffic and saw the horizon aglow with neon lights. Above her, the moon appeared asleep, graciously resting behind a jagged cloud tinted orange and red.

Most of the passengers were headed to a restaurant across the street, except the man with the handlebar mustache. He stood alone.

Francine tried to take it all in. She shifted her hair and loosened the straps on her stiletto.

"Miss Moonie?" Detective Taylor said, offering to take her arm. "Could you come with me?" He pointed to a parked car. "If you're cooperative, this shouldn't take long."

"I guess, but, uh... could I have someone come with me?" Francine asked.

"And who would that be? I thought you were travelling alone."

"I was until I met John. Isn't that right, John?" Francine bellowed, trying to get John's attention from across the parking lot.

John had been talking to Anna when he heard Francine's call.

"Excuse me, Anna, but if I'm not mistaken I believe that young lady needs me." John made his way calmly to the detective. He tipped his fedora. "Hi, I'm John. I think my friend here would feel more comfortable if I came along. Also, I'm just curious, do you have a warrant for this young lady?"

"Uh, matter of fact, no. However, we do have some routine questions for Miss Moonie regarding our investigation." The officer glanced at Francine. "As you know, a bus is not exactly conducive to meeting those needs. It's not as good as an office."

"Well then, I believe my presence is appropriate, Mr... Mr.... what did you say your name was?" John held out his hand.

"The name is Taylor, Detective Taylor."

John shook his hand. "Yes, I do believe this is going to be a grand night, Detective Taylor," he said with a smile, confident all would be well with Francine's soul.

Detective Taylor opened the car door. Francine froze as she felt a hand slide across her thigh. She turned quickly and found the detective grinning at her.

"Oh, yes, Miss Moonie, everything is going to be just fine," Taylor whispered out of John's earshot. "Trust me. Well, as long as you comply, that is. Remember, gorgeous, I've got your number."

Not saying a word, Francine slid in beside John.

The ride to the police department was solemn. John sat motionless, cradling his Bible.

Francine hoped a nightmare wasn't about to unfold, but the pit in her stomach suggested differently. She looked at John and realized that she'd had little choice in dragging him along, even though she'd always thought she was capable of handling herself. But she was learning the hard way that it was important to have a witness when you really needed one.

Although Francine was certain this would turn out to be yet another messed-up chapter in her life, she wished she could shred it. Then she could move on to her next trainwreck. It was just her luck to be interrogated by a detective with ulterior motives, and be dogged by a Bible-carrying holy roller.

She didn't know who to trust. As far as she was concerned, Max had it right: no one. She found herself missing Max and the confidence he exuded. Now she had all the proof she needed that he had been right on target, at least regarding the law. Trusting most cops was wrong, no matter what disguise they presented to the rest of the world. A number of them were just perverted old bloodhounds. They all seemed to be looking for some slice of egotistical recognition at the expense of their victims.

She also believed nothing could be done to make order out of the chaos she had left behind. Even the Shelbytown horror wasn't about to leave anytime soon. The writing was everywhere.

She wrapped her fingers around her silver chain and glanced at the moon. Tonight she hoped Abigail would come through for her—and have her back.

Chapter Thirty-One

In a brightly lit room, John motioned for Francine to take the seat beside him. He pulled two chairs out.

"Oh, before we go any further, Miss Moonie, we need to confiscate your bag," Taylor said. "Temporarily."

"Excuse me, Detective?" John asked. "I don't believe there are any laws saying you can leave this room with someone's personal belongings, not without just cause."

"Well, that's the way it's done here. I'll be back shortly."

John put the worn Bible in front of Francine.

Remembering the knife at the bottom of her purse, Francine felt a chill run through her body. She had never imagined the detective would take her bag. Silence sliced through the air.

"Okay, Miss Moonie, ready to get serious?" Detective Taylor asked harshly as he reentered the room. He threw her bag on the table.

"Sure, fire away." Francine hesitated as she looked down at her purse.

"Now, you don't mind if we tape this conversation, do you? You are not under arrest, at least not yet, so it's still your prerogative."

Francine looked at John. "What do you think?"

John adjusted his fedora and cleared his throat. "Well, I'm just here for support. The decision should really be up to you."

Francine looked at the black recorder, then nodded. "Whatever you want. I've got nothing to hide anyway."

"Really, Miss Moonie?" Detective Taylor sounded snarky. He pressed the start button. "Can you please state your full name for the record?"

"Francine Agnes Moonie. Pretty sure that's my name. At least that's what I've been told."

Detective Taylor stopped the recorder. "Uh, Miss Moonie, can you please get rid of the attitude until you're on the other side of this door? And do you think you could remove your gum until the questions are over? And please just answer the question asked."

John handed her a Kleenex as she took the wad out of her mouth.

"Did you know the deceased before yesterday?" the detective asked.

"Nope. Never seen him before."

"Did you threaten him at the Santa Montrose bus depot?"

"Nope, not really." Glancing at the Bible, Francine looked at John. He was about to hear something he probably didn't want to be reminded of. She made eye contact with the detective. "Oh, I almost forgot. I think I said something about a bamboo tree and his cowardly butt."

"Miss Moonie, I'm going to cut to the chase. Did you threaten Mr. Bagly while holding a weapon?"

"Uh, not that I remember." Francine thought for a moment. "Wait a minute. I think I had my shoe in my hand, if that's what you mean."

Francine heard John clearing his throat, and the tick of the clock.

"Miss Moonie, can you tell me the real reason why you left Santa Montrose?" the detective asked, tapping his pen on the table. "You see, your story isn't cut-and-dry. I'd hate to have to keep you here for hours, but I will if I have to. It's in your best interest to tell me what's really going on. You see, I found this in your bag. Could you explain the connection here?"

He set a slip of paper onto the table. Francine took it and examined it. Someone had drawn an outline of a snake. Below, a few words had been sketched: *Need Help, Call Rattler.*

"Rattler? Um, I really don't know who that is."

A phone number was also scrawled across the bottom.

"For your information, Miss Moonie, I tried calling the number. No one picked up. I made the call, because me and the other detective in the back room vaguely remember that there was a nationwide bounty on a thug who went by the name Rattler some time ago. He was bad news. From the information we received, he was apprehended and did some time in the pen." He looked at Francine. "Now, Miss Moonie, you seem to be in a jam here. Are you ready to tell me the real story?"

As Detective Taylor leaned forward, Francine felt his leg rub against hers under the table. She knew it wasn't an accident.

Unaware of this, John pushed the Bible forward on the table.

Undeniable

The detective raised his eyebrows. "Miss Moonie, I'm waiting. You don't want to miss that bus, do you?"

Francine nervously tried to formulate her response. She knew things were turning bad quickly. The facts weren't in her favor, and besides, the detective still hadn't mentioned the weapon she had been carrying. She had nowhere to run. She glanced at John, then abruptly moved her leg away. Her body trembled.

"Okay, here it is... all of it, if you really need to know. I don't know any dude called Rattler, so let's get that cleared up. And I'm not into fashion, and I hate riding buses. I packed a knife in my bag to protect myself from scumbags—and I'm going to Tijuana because apparently I'm having a baby that I didn't want in the first place!" Francine glanced at the tape recorder. "Oh, and for the world bulletin, yes, I did swipe my mother's lousy bingo chips. And here's something else for your stupid record! If you ever were to come out from under your rock long enough, Detective Taylor, you'd know medical care in Mexico is half the damn price and the scenery is beautiful this time of year. As a matter of fact, the doctors are probably waiting for me right now, so I really don't have any more time to waste."

Francine caught her breath.

"Is there anything else I can help you with before you decide to keep me here for months?" she asked. "You know, I'd hate to have to deliver a kid right here in this friggin' office."

She felt her body shake as she lowered her head. Knowing she was on a runaway train, her skin crawled with anxiety. With no way off, she prepared for impact.

Her mouth shot open.

"I thought he was a respectable guy. But with all that was happening around Santa Montrose, he scared the hell out of me. And I didn't mean to, but he was going to kill me—"

Stopping abruptly, she looked up at the detective.

"You 'didn't mean to' do what, Miss Moonie?" Taylor asked. "And what knife are you talking about? Who scared you? I'm confused."

Francine suddenly realized it was too late to turn back.

"Pardon me, Miss Moonie? You did what?" the detective pressed.

"You know, you know. That lunatic psycho who was beating up on all us girls up in Santa Montrose. Him. He was going to kill me, so I shot him. I shot him dead," Francine ranted. "You might as well know it all. Been on that damn bus for hours, running from there, running to here, like I'm the star of some Hitchcock movie! A movie I never even intended to audition for."

She slammed her hands on the table.

"Woah, wait a minute, Miss Moonie." Deputy Taylor shook his head. "You mean that case that's been plastered all over the news about the serial killer upstate, Todd Clancy, with the fancy car? Or do you mean the other fellow who was shot at Lake Montrose? You're losing me."

"Who's Todd Clancy?" Francine asked in a hollow voice.

"My, my. Well, I guess you didn't hear. They arrested a guy called Todd Clancy a few days ago. He had been targeting prostitutes, leaving a trail of violence and murder across the damn countryside. He was heading for Nevada when they pretty much caught him red-handed. It's all been all over the news. The other deceased guy, who some suspected was the lunatic psycho, well... it turned out to be far from the truth. I believe his name was, uh, Russell, or, uh, Rosco DeFranco. Anyway, doesn't matter. His killer came forward yesterday. Surprisingly enough, his death had nothing to do with the other crimes taking place. Not a lot information on that one yet, but you can bet it will all come out. Always does." He paused. "And it will also come out with this Bagley case. I'm sure we'll be learning that Mr. Bagley had many enemies. Still, you have to admit, your interactions with him haven't helped you any. Have they, Miss Moonie?"

Detective Taylor studied Francine's face. The room spun as she closed her eyes.

"Are you all right, Miss Moonie? You don't look well. Miss Moonie, can you hear me?"

Francine sat motionless, waiting for the room to stop turning.

"I'm afraid this young lady has had a few long days," John said. "Are your done with your questions, detective?"

"Yeah."

John helped Francine to her feet.

"Oh, there's just one more thing, Miss Moonie," Taylor said as they stood. "If I wanted to, I could arrest you for providing false information, admitting to a crime you didn't commit. But the remark about a knife in your bag proves that your state of mind is impaired. Courts would not consider your testimony creditable. I'm certain of that. So, you think you've had a bad day? Really? Good thing you aren't in my shoes. If there's anything else you can think of regarding the Bagley case, call this number." He tossed her a card and peered down at her shoes. "Those things don't help your image much, Moonie. You may want to get rid of them."

Francine glanced at John. "I guess I'm done here," she muttered.

"Detective, since you asked, yes, there is just one more thing," John interjected. He hovered over the table, pushing his Bible closer to the black recorder. "We all know there's a whole lot of useless information on this tape here. And for your information, Detective, my name is Pastor John Connors. Yes, that's Pastor Connors. I believe your recorder has an erase button, does it not?"

John and Francine exchanged glances as the detective reluctantly reached down and pushed the erase button.

"Thanks, Detective," John said. "I'm sure you have a daughter. Or a sister maybe? Look, you and I both know there are some people in this world who just need an honest break." He glanced at Francine. "Yes, I believe we were all placed in this room together for a reason?"

Detective Taylor shot a glance at Francine.

"Well, that should just about wind things down here." John smiled. "So if there's nothing else, no warrant or anything of that nature, I guess Miss Moonie and I will be on our way." Tipping his fedora, John reached for his Bible and turned to leave. "Oh, Detective, I almost forgot. Who's going to take us back to the bus station?"

John opened the car door and slid in beside Francine.

"Thank you, John," she said, clasping her necklace. "I didn't know you were a pastor, and I sure don't know who, what, or where a 'Rattler' is." She sighed. "I'm not even sure where you came from, Pastor, but thanks."

"It's all going to be fine, Francine. Now I clearly understand why we've met."

John chuckled as he held his Bible.

Chapter Thirty-Two

"We still have time for a bite before the bus departs," John said as the police car dropped them off. "It's been a long night, Francine. We'll all feel better after some food, don't you think? It's on me."

Francine was contemplating his offer when she caught him glancing at her baby pouch on their way into the depot's cafeteria.

"I'll be right back. The ladies' room is calling," Francine said. Her stomach rolled. "Just a burger. Thanks."

Placing the order, John felt enthusiasm race through his veins. He believed that God never failed, and this was his opportunity to talk about Jesus's goodness and forgiveness toward all of his children. That included Francine. Even as Mexico got closer, it all came down to God's watch.

"Okay, Lord, it's all up to you," he prayed. "Let's show this lovely young lady what you're really made of. Show her your plan, Jesus. Thank you." John rubbed his hands together, then noticed the waitress glaring at him. He smiled. "Guess I should get us some seats now."

"Here you go: two burgers." The waitress placed them on the table.

"Thanks, I'm starved," Francine said, tearing into one.

John removed his fedora and bowed his head. She wondered how long it had been since she had even heard someone say grace. She put her burger down, hoping the embarrassment she felt didn't show.

"Thank you for this day, Jesus, and all your blessings that have come with it. Also, thank you for this new friendship, and for shining your light on these

Undeniable

trying times of your precious child, Francine. We will do our best to honor you as we continue receiving your gift of life." He peeked at Francine. "Amen."

Francine scanned the room. She noticed the man with a handlebar mustache staring at her. He turned away quickly.

Cautiously, she picked up her burger again. "So that's it, John? Nothing about 'Thy bounty in your grace?'"

"No, but if you like, I'll gladly add a little more." John smiled. "It doesn't matter how or where you choose to thank God. The most important thing is that you do. Lord, I'm hungry!"

John grinned as he bit into his burger, weighing Francine's expression. She tried to smile.

He waited until he finished swallowing. "All right, I really don't know where to start, so I'm just going to let my heart lead the way," John said, wiping his mouth. He reached for her hand. "Francine, I get it. Your life has been in upheaval for a very long time. You do believe God has a plan for all of us, don't you?"

"Uh, no. Not really." Her heart pounded.

"Francine, do you believe me when I say there are no coincidences in this life? Every step you've taken has been planned by God to bring you here to this very moment." He placed his other hand on the Bible. "I say this because no one could ever make these words up. No one can make this stuff up. No one except for God. Do you believe that?"

"To be totally honest, not really. For one thing, if it's true, why has he always tried to ruin my life?" Francine groaned, lowering her head. "Ever since I was a kid, he's been out to get me, and now here I'm in my twenties and I still don't know what he's had against me."

"Francine, please look at me." John leaned toward her. "You need to hear this. Think of it this way. Picture yourself sitting on your heavenly father's knee, and he has his arms wrapped around you. Your heart is breaking, but you still don't want to tell him things because you think he doesn't even exist, and even if he did, why would he care about you? Well, he certainly does care about you. Our God is full of grace and forgiveness. Second and third chances are always permitted in his equations. The fact is that you'll do better when you know better. All you have to do is take that first small leap of faith and confide in him a little at a time. Now, isn't that the best news you've heard in a very long time?" He smiled. "The more he hears, the tighter he embraces you. This is your God, Francine, and mine too. His love is bigger than any love you could ever imagine. Even the plan he has for your life is far greater than you could ever dream of.

All you have to do is give him a chance." He smiled again. "We sure do serve a mighty, faithful God. He will always fight Satan on your behalf. You're his child, not Satan's. But the bad news is even when we honor God to the fullest, Satan will still mess with us because he wants us to stop believing in God's goodness. Satan never disappears forever. That's a given. You can pretty much guarantee that when you're doing something that pleases God, the enemy will rear his ugly head." John laughed. "That's always an indicator you're doing something right! Isn't it reassuring to know you have the biggest army behind you, fighting your battles for you? Psalms 91 is the reassurance we all have. Now, it doesn't get much better than that!"

John looked into Francine's glossy eyes. Uncomfortable, Francine fidgeted, wishing she could disappear. She slid lower and lower in her seat.

"Here's something." John flipped through his Bible and began to read enthusiastically. "'Trust in the Lord with all your heart and lean not on your own understanding; in all your ways submit to him, and he will make your paths straight.'[5] See, Francine, you have to love it! It's not complicated at all. Don't you think it's time to let go of the wheel? God will be the best navigator you'll ever have." John smiled. "The guidelines printed across these pages help protect the purpose of our lives. And it's all right here at our finger tips."

John was enthused as he closed the book and took one last bite.

"I think we better split before we miss our bus," Francine said anxiously. She put down the remainder of her burger.

"Yes, God's watch is always perfect timing." John grinned and adjusted his fedora. "Check, please."

"Would you look at that! The bus is still right where God left it." John laughed.

"And look, there's Anna," Francine said with excitement. She hurried toward her new friend as they lined up to enter the bus.

"Well, it's about time you two got back," Anna said, smiling. "So how did it go?"

"I'll tell you on the bus. Are you coming, John?" Francine bellowed as she heard the engine start.

John nodded as he walked alongside the man with the handlebar mustache. Why did he keep showing up? Moonlight caught the stranger's dark mustache,

---

5 Proverbs 3:5–6, NIV.

and when his head turned a dirty blonde ponytail could be seen dangling down the back of his neck. Francine wondered where he'd come from and noticed that John seemed to be in conversation with him.

"Here we are," Anna said when they got to their row, seeing paperwork spread across the seats.

"It's been a long night. Would you like a chew, Anna?" Francine asked, pulling out the yellow package from her bag.

Anna glanced out the window. "No, I've still quit."

"You know, there's a method to my madness, Anna. Sitting here, I have you on one side, and John across the aisle. It's the best of both worlds for the remainder of the trip. Unfortunately, my backup seat is taken." Francine saw the man with the cowboy hat sitting next to John now. "I can't imagine what those two are going to talk about."

"Well, it's apparent they have a common interest."

"What's that?" Francine asked, puzzled.

"Hats, Francine. Hats."

Francine's laugh was followed by a snort. "Well, if that's the case, I'm sure glad I'm not wearing a dress with fruit on it."

"So what happened with the detective?"

"A whole lot of nothing, I suppose. But I'm glad I went, or I wouldn't have found out."

"Found out what?"

Francine smirked. "Uh, that I'm in need of a new pair of shoes."

"Shoes?" Anna asked in disbelief.

"Yeah, shoes."

Francine sighed. Looking up the aisle, she could see the mustached stranger as he took a seat. Relieved that he was distant from her, she tried to get comfortable.

She wanted to decipher everything that had happened to her since Wendy had dropped her off at the depot, but she knew that would require more energy than she could summon at the moment.

"Wendy. Oh, I forgot to call Wendy," Francine blurted out.

"What's wrong?" Anna asked.

"I promised I would keep in touch with her."

"Well, if we stop again I'll remind you. Don't worry. I'm sure she'll understand. Good friends always do."

"Sure."

Across the aisle, John's overhead light was streaming down on some papers.

"Hey, Francine," he whispered. "You know, everyone can learn to fly. It doesn't matter where they've been or where they think they're headed. The same God who gave me wings gave you wings, too. You just got to believe they're there. That's all."

Francine smiled and closed her eyes.

―

The screeching pierced Francine's ears. People screamed as the hideous sound of brakes seemed to go on forever. Jolted from her sleep, Francine was violently rocked from side to side, like someone shaking a ragdoll. Then, as if being launched from a cannon, she slammed into the seat in front of her. The sound of exploding glass multiplied like gunfire. The lights went out and suddenly there was twisted metal all around her.

The bus halted with a wrenching bang. Dazed, Francine tried to focus through the dim light. She hoped she was just dreaming, until she noticed red on her hand after she rubbed her forehead.

Anna was perfectly still, sitting ramrod straight in a tangled web of metal. Her eyes were closed and parts of her cherry dress had turned a darker shade of red.

"Anna, Anna. Are you okay? Anna!" Francine yelled. "Wake up, Anna!"

Francine nudged her, but she didn't answer. She trembled as she noticed a jagged piece of metal embedded in Anna's chest.

Frantic, she called out again, "Anna! Anna!"

After holding her wrist and searching for a pulse, she realized Anna was gone.

Francine screamed, then threw herself toward John, slouched in his seat and covered with broken glass and debris.

"John! It's me, Francine! Just tell me you hear me, John!" Through the sparse light, she could see his lips move, slightly. His Bible had disappeared. "You're going to be all right, John. Help is coming!"

Francine cried as she tried to console him. His eyes were heavy, his voice faint. She lowered her ear to his mouth.

"Time for you to fly, Francine... just trust in..."

"No, you aren't leaving, John. You need to stay here." Francine sobbed. "I know your family needs you here."

She thought she saw a slight grin as she wiped the dark liquid from his lips.

"Trust in him." He sighed.

Then, with a deep breath, his eyes closed.

Francine looked at the man beside John. The cowboy. Harold. Horrified, her mind raced as she realized his hat was gone, his lifeless head tilted to the side, his eyes wide open, unblinking.

A huge hole had been ripped in the side of the bus near his seat, letting a stream of cool night air rush in across his body.

Francine rubbed the blood from her forehead. Gasping, she looked up the aisle. Pieces of clothing hung haphazardly from the overhead compartments. The aisle was clogged with litter from the impact of the crash. People frantically struggled to push their way off the bus.

Francine sobbed as she shuffled through the carnage amidst screams.

"Ma'am," a highway patrolman said to her. "Are you all right?"

Dazed, Francine wasn't sure how much time had passed. "Uh, I don't know. My friends are on that bus. I... I need to help them."

The officer grabbed her arm. "Sorry, ma'am, you have to stay back."

"No, you don't understand. They need me."

"I'm sorry, ma'am, but the people who are left on the bus no longer require help. Please, do yourself a favor and stay back."

Francine shivered as she watched the patrolman clutch the bus driver's bloodied forage cap.

"Ma'am, we'll be getting you medical attention soon, but for now we're assisting the most critically injured."

Francine looked at the devastation. There was little left of the crumpled hindquarters of the bus. It looked like a plastic playtoy that had been stepped on, its end hideously deformed. A lone tire sat off to the side. The hood of the semi-truck that had ploughed into the bus was tented. It resembled a massive sheet of foil that had been erected to protect the windshield and hide the horrors of the scene.

Francine sensed the terror in the air. The scent of death seeped its way into the crowd.

An array of stars shining brightly. She breathed rapidly, looking for just one familiar face among the huddled survivors. The mother of the twins was on her knees.

"God, no!" she screamed. "Not my girls! No!"

Francine felt sorrow pierce her heart. Looking elsewhere, Margareet and her daughter had their arms wrapped around each other. Francine began to cry.

"Hey, Francine, you all right?" a voice asked.

Francine turned and found herself face to face with the familiar handlebar mustache. She stood motionless. "Are you alright?" he asked.

"Yeah, I think so, but my friends are on that bus." With all the energy she could muster, she pointed to the wreckage.

"It's okay, Francine. You're gonna be okay, understand?" He draped his jacket across her shoulders and handed over her purse. "I take it this is yours?"

"Who are you?" she asked, shivering.

"Michael." He reached out his hand, holding a book. "I'm not sure whose this is, but I found it in the aisle. Your bag was sitting on top of it. It looked like they were just waiting for you to come back and pick them up."

Francine studied the initials on its worn cover. "It's John's Bible! Give that to me!"

She yanked it from Michael's hand and began racing through the unsettled crowd toward the wreckage.

"Stop, ma'am!" a voice bellowed. In front of her stood a uniformed man, his arms outstretched. "You cannot enter, ma'am."

"But this is John's and I need to get it back to him!" Francine shrieked as she waved the worn book in the night air. Speechless, she listened to the commotion behind her and turned around. Cradling the Bible, she slowly she made her way back to Michael.

Minutes felt like hours as the gurneys came and went from the wreckage.

"All right, everyone," someone instructed. "Another bus has just arrived, and we would like all of you to board it. We're taking you to the nearest hospital."

Francine entered the vehicle slowly. Michael hobbled as he attempted to guide her.

She dropped the Bible into her bag and took a seat. He sat beside her.

"My name is Michael, but if you want you can call me Rattler," he said.

Francine gasped. "Wait a minute! You're Rattler? I don't get it! You know, you almost got me busted with that stupid note you left in my bag! And now all this!"

She sobbed as she looked around.

"I'll explain everything later," Michael said. "You have to trust me, Francine. First, we need to get you taken care of."

He calmly wiped her forehead.

Chapter Thirty-Three

The waiting room was buzzing with nurses as they one by one assessed the condition of the survivors.

Francine and Michael sat together, waiting their turn.

"So where were you heading?" Francine asked, exhausted.

"Well, uh, it depends on where *you* were heading, if you really want to know."

Francine glared at him, shivering. "What the hell does that mean?"

"I'm not sure how to tell you this, but Mr. Cardosa hired me to follow you."

"He did what? What are you talking about?" Francine gasped, then threw the jacket from her shoulders.

"Well, he was so afraid someone would harm you that he hired me to make sure that wouldn't happen. The deal was that I would keep an eye on your safety until you at least got to Mexico. You sure had me on my toes a few times, I must admit."

"Okay, whoever you are… Michael?"

"Like I said, most of my friends call me Rattler."

"Well, I'm not your friend, and whoever you are, I'm having a hard time believing anything you say, in case you haven't noticed. Look, you tell me all this stupid crapola, like you're supposed to have my back. You left me with a perverted detective to answer his crazy questions! It doesn't add up. And it sure was a lucky thing that John offered to go with me to the police department. If what you're saying is true, where were you?"

"Settle down, Francine. There are a still a few things I need to tell you. For starters, let's just say I knew you were in good hands. I'd talked to that John fellow earlier. He sounded decent. We talked about the Dodgers. Turned out we were both huge fans of Valenzuela a couple years ago when he was drafted." Michael smiled. "Man, did that lefty ever have a screwball. So I knew right then

John was a good guy—and then he handed me a card. Seeing as he was a pastor, I was even more relieved."

"What else do you know about me?" Francine snapped.

"Not much. Max and I go a long way back, though. I took a huge rap for him years ago. I think I finally forgave him. Well, sort of, I guess. The real problem is that I've never forgotten. Although I still help him out when he's in a jam, it'll never be the same between us. But I kind of got my retribution, because he now has to pay through the nose for my services. And I draw a line with what I will and won't do. Francine, do you remember when you had that standoff with the guy at the bus depot?"

"Yeah, why?"

"Well, I knew time was scarce, so I hurried and put my name in your bag, in case you ever needed me. I knew you'd find it sooner or later. I tried jamming it into your purse because you were hopping back quickly, with only one high-heel on. You almost caught me, but I think you were more concerned about the gum package I left on the floor." He laughed. "Well, if you thought you were being watched, trust me, you were. To make a long story short, I spoke with Max before the accident to let him know you're okay. He says he needs you to call him as soon as you can. And if you really want my opinion, that guy has it bad for you."

Francine hung her head. "Oh, crap. I forgot to call Wendy. Anna was supposed to... supposed to remind me."

"Let me make a suggestion, Francine. Call Max first. Okay?"

"What the hell is going on up there?" she demanded. "Is everything all right?"

"That's for Max to tell you, and that's all I can say."

"Well, I'm not calling until you tell me something!" Francine yelled with the little energy she could muster. "Anything!"

"Okay, okay, settle down." Michael looked at the faces around the room. "This is probably the last thing you need to hear right now, but it's Wendy."

"What do you mean? What's wrong with Wendy?"

He reached into his pocket. "First of all, I don't mind hanging onto this for you." Rattler pulled the black knife from his pocket. "I saw you accidentally dump your bag on the bus. Max sensed you thought the blade was illegal, and he decided to keep it that way because he wanted you to be careful with it. When you missed picking it up by your seat, I couldn't believe it. So I grabbed it." He held the knife loosely, running his thumb over the blade. "So I'm giving it back to you. It's yours."

"You keep it. You were—are—protecting me. Weren't you? Aren't you?" Francine said snottily. "Tell me about Wendy, now!"

Michael shoved the knife back into his pocket. "Okay, take a breath and listen to me, Francine. And you need to hear every word I say. After I tell you this, I want you to know that I'm still going to have your back, whatever you decide to do. Understand?"

Francine glared back at him. "Just tell me. What's going on back in Santa Montrose?"

"Wendy was arrested for the murder of Rosco DeFranco."

Francine could feel her heart pound through every vein. "What are you talking about? There's no way in hell. Is this some sick joke? It was me who pulled the trigger, not her. Wendy wasn't even there."

"Well, apparently she was there. And she even handed over the gun when she turned herself in."

"What do you mean, she turned herself in?"

"Look, Francine, I don't know if she freaked out or just decided to do the right thing and go to the cops. Suppose we'll never know. It don't matter now how they got her, but they got her. Guess the cops asked her why she shot him, twice, and she said it was because that was all the bullets she had. Apparently she told them she would lay down her life for you, and she would do it all again if she had to. Anyway, they matched up the ballistics and, sure enough, she was their guy."

Clasping her head, Francine felt numb as she made her way to the phone. "Operator, I need to make a collect call," she said, then waited for the call to connect. She quivered. "Hello. Max? It's Francine here."

❀

"I'm afraid nothing good has ever come out of those reckless truck drivers barrelling their way onto the busy freeways. Still, it looks like you got off better than most tonight, young lady" the doctor said as he slid Francine's necklace back into place. "Someone must have been watching over you. It's understandable that you're shaken up, but your injuries could have been far worse. After these stitches heal, don't be alarmed if you still find small slivers of glass for a while. And if it's any consolation, remember that you were one of the lucky ones tonight. Besides, I doubt you'll even have a scar to remind you of the accident." He peeled off his gloves. "Get lots of rest the next few days, and plenty of nutrition for that baby you're carrying."

Leaving the room, Francine felt like a zombie as she walked down the hall.

Michael joined her. Together they passed the waiting room and headed for the door.

She looked over at Michael, and stopped.

"I'll be right back," she said, then walked to the nearest payphone. "Operator, I need to make a collect call."

Once again, she waited nervously as the phone rang.

"Hello?" a familiar voice answered.

"Hello. Dad, is that you?" There was a long pause. The phone shook as she tried to speak. "It's Francine. Can I come home?"

Chapter Thirty-Four

"Do you remember how we say our prayers?" Francine asked as she closed the picture book. On her knees beside her son, she folded her hands. "Okay, it's all yours, handsome. Take it away."

She grinned at his pudgy fingers.

"Dear God, thank you for everything. And thank you for the moon tonight. Uh, but could you please turn it down, God? I know you made it, but sometimes when you make it really big, it shines on my face and wakes me up. And could you keep Mommy safe and let her make some more macaroni and cheese? Yeah, a little more cheese too. Thank you, God. Please watch all my friends. I know you can, because you are bigger than the whole wide world." He spread his arms open. "Mommy and I love you, Jesus. Amen."

"Good night, little man." Francine smiled as she tucked him into bed.

"Mommy," Matthew said, hesitating. "Why does that butterfly with the funny looking wings just sit inside your window, Mommy?"

Francine thought for a moment. "Well, I think it's safe to say it was passed down from your great-great Grandma Agnes all the way to me. Guess you could call it a good luck charm now. Who knows, Matthew, it may even decide to fly one day."

"But Mommy, why is there a chain tangled around those funny shoes in your closet then?" Matthew asked as he rubbed his eyes.

"Matthew James, sometimes you ask Mommy too many questions. One day you'll understand."

Matthew yawned. "Kay. Night, Mommy."

"Oh, before you totally conk out, remember that Michael is picking you up from Grandpa Randy's tomorrow. I have to work late at the center. Make sure you have lots of kisses for Grandma Jane when you see her, okay? And you know what happens Sunday, don't you?"

Francine laughed as she tickled him.

"Stop, Mommy! I know! I know!"

"Okay, mister, you've got one chance to tell me, or I'm bringing the tickle monster back!"

"I get to take my new picture Bible to Sunday school and show all the kids," he said, laughing. "And then we're going on a picnic with them."

"That's exactly right, Mister Matthew."

"Hey, Mommy, when Michael comes back, is he gonna stay here forever?" Matthew yawned again.

"We'll see, Matthew."

Francine kissed his forehead.

"Good night."

※

"And this is a picture of the Garden of Eden. Nope. God told Eve she wasn't supposed to eat that apple over there, but she didn't listen," Matthew said, pointing to a picture of an apple tree. "But I guess she was hungry. And Adam over here... well, that was her boyfriend in funny underwear."

Matthew giggled along with the other kids.

"My mommy said she didn't think there was underwear then," he said, "so God made sure there was lots of leaves."

"Very well said." The teacher smiled. "Don't you think so, children? I think we need to give Matthew a big clap. Thanks for sharing, Matthew. Now, let's bow our heads and thank Jesus." She lowered her head. "Thank you, Jesus, for this day and for all your blessings. Amen."

All the kids looked up.

"All right, everyone. Now let's go and have some fun at the picnic."

※

"It's a perfect day, isn't it, Michael?" Francine asked.

Listening to the laughter of the children, Michael wrapped his arm around Francine.

"What more could anyone possibly want?" Francine said as she leaned on his shoulder.

"Well, I know one thing I would like," he answered softly.

"Like what? Like for my father to be a little less leery of you, and help erase your history with the cops?" Francine laughed.

"Come on, Francine, that's not fair. Even God has given me a break. Sure, I was hell-on-wheels way back when. And good for your father to help get people like me off the streets. I thank God for blessings in disguise, because here I am, a changed man." Michael frowned. "You know, I really liked my handlebar mustache. Sometimes I regret that I ever shaved it off, but on the other hand, that doesn't compare to what I would really like."

Francine gazed at the perfectly blue sky above. "Now what on earth would that be, Michael?"

"Oh, you'll find out one day soon." Michael grinned and kissed her cheek. He looked skyward. "Wow! Would you look at that!"

"Isn't that awesome?"

A red-tailed hawk had extended its long graceful wings as it swooped and soared through the sky. Gliding majestically, it rose and dipped overhead.

Francine couldn't contain her laughter.

"What's so funny about that?" Michael asked, watching the bird pirouette high above.

"Oh, it's nothing really."

Francine's heart fluttered as she stared into the sky.

Epilogue

Pastor Matthew stood and looked out into the audience. People were applauding. He acknowledged their excitement. Clapping along, he waited for their emotions to simmer down.

"Now, wasn't that a story?" He grinned as the smiling faces looked back at him. "I'm so grateful, just standing at the podium, because it seems to me you are all good-looking people. You know, it would be a little difficult for any pastor, let alone a new one, to stand here week after week if that wasn't the case!" He laughed. "You are all such a blessing."

Smiles lit up every face.

"All right, everyone, now that I have your attention again, can you please take your seats for a few more minutes?" he asked.

The congregation settled in.

"So, do you think you're ready for me, week after week, here in the house of the Lord?"

Pastor Matthew raised his arms as the people cheered, "Yep, bring it on! We need the truth."

Matthew chuckled. "Well, believe me, you haven't heard anything yet! We're going to rock the house every week in the name of our Lord, the maker of all things! If you aren't ready, you better hold on, because there is a monster wind coming. It's called the Holy Spirit and it's going to sweep you off your feet!"

"That's what we need, Pastor!" a man shouted. "Some old scripture from some new blood that's going to make us jump right out of our skin! Right?"

The crowd cheered.

"All right, folks! I need it quiet for a minute," Pastor Matthew said, waving his hands in midair. "Next week, God has placed it in my heart to speak about forgiveness, kindness, and the greatest of them all: love. Our focus is going to be on the New Testament. Thank you, Jesus! And may I add, if you believe you've never needed or owed anyone forgiveness, including your wife or mother-in-law, your presence is definitely required here next Sunday."

Pastor Matthew smirked, then looked down at the weathered Bible. Even after all these years, the tarnished cover still told its story. He opened it slowly. Its silver pages were left unscathed, but their corners had curled.

He raised his arm. "Yes, we're going to rock this house with a fire you haven't felt before!"

The congregation hollered joyfully.

"Shhhhhhh, please! Yes, Jesus is the only way and the life. Yes, folks, we may have quite an agenda of sermons ahead of us, but keep in mind that we serve a mighty big God. And everything is possible with him. Amen!"

The congregation applauded and whistled.

"Settle down now. Just a couple more things. You know, I really love to tell the story you just heard, because it inspires my faith in Jesus each time I have the privilege of sharing it." Pastor Matthew pointed to the lady in the third row with the floppy hat. He wiped his eyes. "However, this lovely lady, Mrs. Murphy, unfortunately knows it better than me. In fact, she has lived it."

All eyes locked on the smile from under Mrs. Murphy's pink hat.

"May I please introduce you to my mother, Francine Moonie Murphy!"

Francine stood and smiled. Timidly, she glanced around the room.

Cheers erupted, and people shouted out, "Thank you, Francine! That was some story!"

After a while, the pastor motioned for everyone to be calm. Tears rolled down Francine's cheeks as she unwrapped a grey stick of gum and brought it to her mouth. She smiled back at Matthew.

"All right, folks, just when you thought that was all, I have a couple more introductions," he said. "We will be seeing most of these amazing people here every Sunday. Daddy Michael, could you please stand?"

More applause.

"Please, he prefers being called Michael Murphy, although he was once known as Rattler. And Grandpa Randy Moonie, could you please stand, too?"

More applause.

"Shhhhhhhhhh, congregation. I have one more small surprise." Pastor Matthew wiped his tears, then withdrew a small object from his pocket. "We had a family meeting, and to be on the safe side we all agreed to borrow this for a few hours, just in case."

He held out a small plastic device with a wire dangling from it. Pastor Matthew laughed and then motioned for an elderly lady to stand. Sitting a few rows back, the woman smiled and nodded. Randy helped her to her feet.

"This is my dear, amazing grandmother, Mrs. Jane Moonie," the pastor proudly announced. "I know she doesn't hear you or me very well, because I have this right here. You see, she never does like to wear it anyway. She thinks it makes her look old!"

Realizing it was a hearing aid, the crowd stood and applauded.

"Thank you, Jane! You're all the proof we need!" someone yelled.

Jane humbly looked across the room.

"There is one more revelation for the congregation today, in case you haven't guessed," Pastor Matthew exclaimed. "Yes, I was the reason my mother was on that Greyhound bus."

He laughed as he wiped another tear.

"Amen, Pastor," a voice cried out. "You're the real deal!"

"God bless you, Pastor!" someone else shouted.

The pastor studied the cover of his Bible for a moment and then ran his hand over its faded stitched initials: J.C. He remembered everything his mother had told him about the book through the years. Its journey of survival not only continually amazed him, but it confirmed that it had ended up where it was meant to be, at least for now. He felt his heart skip as he thought of his own expectant wife home on bed rest.

Catching his breath, he looked out at the congregation. Picking up the old worn Bible, he swung it in midair and looked upward.

"Yes!" he said, beaming. "God is good all the time!"

How often we look upon God as our last and feeblest resource. We go to him because we have nowhere else to go. And then we learn that the storms of life have driven us, not upon the rocks but into the desired haven.

—Author George MacDonald

I tell you the truth, if you had faith even as small as a mustard seed, you could say to the mountain, move from here to there; and it would move, nothing would be impossible.

—Matthew 17:20

About the Author

Raised on the Great Lakes, I come from a very humble beginning and have a mother with a gift to write. My passion for writing started in public school with poetry. Later, I discovered that I also enjoyed telling a story through songwriting. I wrote the lyrics and collaborated with musician Josh Smulders, which led to winning contests.

I then set my pen down for a time. After years of struggling with a relentless disease, I decided to pick writing back up, this time in the form of a book. While writing this novel, many days I wrote solely by the grace of God, nothing else. Writing this book was a constant reminder of how God's hands are always near, no matter what challenges we may face.

I love my late grandmas: Grandma Gertie, who believed that a sip on spirits and a mustard patch could cure anything, and Grandma Nellie, who knew that a prayer would cure everything!

Carmen would love to hear from you!
Connect via:
www.carmenthomasnovel.com
@fb.me/UndeniableNovel

CPSIA information can be obtained
at www.ICGtesting.com
Printed in the USA
LVHW04*0550260418
574918LV00004B/54/P